$\mathcal{E}$mily pulled out a card, and scrawled a phone number on it. She slid the card forward.

It was a plain business card. No fancy gold, no script. Just her name, her position, a cell phone number, a fax number, and an e-mail address. No street address. No town listed. Just the numbers. Like every other manager he had ever known.

She stood up and slid on her coat.

"How do you plan to get home?" he asked.

"I live just a block from here. I think it's safe to walk these streets at night."

Probably. In comparison to the big cities. But he didn't like it. "I drove you here. I can take you home."

"No need, Josh." It was the first time she'd used his given name. It sounded good coming from her. Warm and intimate, whether she had meant it that way or not. "I want you to think about what we've been talking about."

"I probably won't do anything else." And that was true. She had just opened a door on a world for him. A world where he could sing as Josh Candless.

A world where he could be a musician, not a superstar.

A world where Davy Moss was still dead.

KRISTINE KATHRYN RUSCH

*wmg*PUBLISHING

The Death of Davy Moss

Published 2015 by WMG Publishing
www.wmgpublishing.com
Cover and Layout copyright © 2015 by WMG Publishing
Cover design by Allyson Longueira/WMG Publishing
Cover art copyright © Blazeofglory/Dreamstime
ISBN-13: 978-0-615-86201-9
ISBN-10: 0-615-86201-2

the Death
Davy Moss

This book is set in 1997. Since then, the music industry has changed so much that we can legitimately start this story with that lovely phrase:

Once Upon a Time...

Part One

...A new biography of legendary pop star **Davy Moss** appeared this week, this one by music critic and historian **Riley Platt**. Platt's thesis? Moss would have been one of the country's best musicians if he had survived the single-car collision that took his life fifteen years ago. Platt bases his theory on Moss's background as a childhood classical music prodigy and a few surviving compositions. Add this one to the collection of strange Moss cultish material that has arisen after his death... and cross it off your Christmas list.

—*Rolling Stone*

one

Emily Lukovich stopped in the foyer of the Sea Grotto Restaurant and took a deep breath. It calmed her a little. She had taken the job, she reminded herself, for good or bad. A consultant consulted. Even if the people she was advising didn't want to hear what she had to say.

She slid off her raincoat, adjusted the sleeves on her silk blouse, and touched her hair lightly. She had been in Oceanlake a week, and she still wasn't used to the informality of the town. No one dressed up here. Not even for business. She had shown up to her first appointment with the board of the Rolling Waves Casino in a Donna Karan suit and found herself so overdressed that it felt as if she had worn a bridal gown to a barn.

The hostess behind the desk smiled at her. Emily smiled back. At least this place was friendly. She needed friendly after her years in Vegas and Los Angeles. Even the casino was friendly.

She liked that.

"May I help you?" the hostess asked.

"I'm meeting someone," she said.

"Are you with the rehearsal dinner or the casino?"

"The casino," Emily said, glancing over her shoulder. Near the dance floor, a long table had been set up. A young couple sat at the head, with older people—obviously parents—in the seats beside them, and couples around the age of twenty filling the rest of the seats. No one had dressed up for that, either.

Emily would have. In fact, Emily had. She'd been a bridesmaid three times in the past year—never, as the cliché went, a bride. Not that she wanted to be. Once upon a time, she'd thought herself too avant-garde for marriage. Then she became too busy. And later, too hurt.

"This way please," the hostess said. She led Emily down three stairs, not pausing like Emily wanted to when she saw the view. The windows at the Sea Grotto overlooked the Pacific Ocean. It was steel gray and frothy, a winter ocean in twilight. Yet the stark beauty grabbed her, as it had every day since she had arrived. She almost wished she could give up everything and stay in this tiny Oregon town with its provincial casino and stunning scenery.

Almost.

She did like her job. It provided a way to stay in the music business without all the hassles of artist management. She had rebuilt her reputation and she got to hear all the up-and-coming bands, satisfying the hidden music geek inside her while keeping a hold on the business.

She had been hired by Rolling Waves as a consultant and promoter to get their concert series up and running. Rolling Waves, owned by a consolidated tribe of local Native Americans, had been profitable from the beginning. The casino board, tired of the local and regional acts it could draw, decided it wanted to compete on the Vegas level. It wanted big names to perform in its new concert hall, but didn't know how to get them.

Emily was supposed to set up the system, hire the first year's lineup, and then leave. She estimated she could do the job in six months. Normally she did it in three, but Rolling Waves was a difficult case. It was more remote than the other casinos she had dealt with, and the casino board wanted to learn how to do the promotion themselves.

The problem was—and had been since Emily arrived a few days after Christmas—that the board had no idea what "national level" meant. Tonight was a case in point. They had called her to the Sea Grotto to hear a local band and see if it was worth hiring for the casino bar.

She had expressly told them when she was hired that she did not work with local bands. She did not work regionally. She only worked nationally, hiring top acts for top venues. The key was to make Rolling Waves a top venue.

A local band would not do.

The hostess led Emily to a large booth. Only three of the board members were there: Tom Running Bear, Joe Escobal, and Paul Perdy. They were the important three. Tom Running Bear, a heavyset man with thick dark hair, was the casino's chief executive officer and the only board member who actually worked in the casino. Joe Escobal, the nominal head of the board, was a young man from one of the tribe's most important families. And Paul Perdy was a small elderly man who disappeared into the booth's back corner. Emily had learned immediately to pay attention to Paul. He was the real power in both the tribe and the casino, and with the flick of a hand could change a decision.

Bear slid over to make room for her. She hung her raincoat on the peg beside the booth and sat down. Her seat faced the dance floor and the rehearsal dinner table. She must have looked disgruntled because Joe Escobal smiled at her.

"We thought you should hear this band."

"I know." No band had set up yet. She was early. "You realize this isn't part of my contract."

"That's right," Bear said. "But we thought that if you liked them, it might save the casino some money—"

"We need to make a decision now, gentlemen," she said, her voice deliberately harsh. She had to take control of this group quickly or she had to resign and let them find someone else. She might be too high-powered for them. "Either you hire a consultant to help you bring in first-rate talent, or you hire a consultant to bring in the best of the local musicians. I don't work locally, and I don't manage musicians."

The words stung her as she spoke them. Managing musicians had been her first love. But she hadn't done it in years. Not since the Ricky Fink Band.

Bear put his hand on hers. "We know. And we're sorry if this is the wrong direction. But we don't just need musicians for the main hall. We need them for the bar and gaming areas as well."

She took a deep breath. So this was the area that their confusion stemmed from. She hadn't realized it.

"You've been doing a tremendous job hiring musicians for those slots," she said. "I'll bet you and I will have the same opinion of this band. I don't think you need help in that area. In fact, I don't think you need any help if you continue with the local acts in all the arenas, including the concert hall. You only need me to go national."

"People come here to game," Paul said softly, and when she looked at him, his brown eyes moved away from hers. Ah, so there was her opposition. It was becoming clear to her now.

"Yes, they do," she said, "but let me be honest with you, Paul. Rolling Waves is two-and-a-half hours from Portland by car. You cannot fly here. The tourists come for the beach. While they're here, they might go to the casino. Business is wonderful in the summer. It's the off-season that I can help you with."

She slid her hand from Bear's and leaned forward so that she could see Paul's face more clearly.

"Let's say, for the sake of argument, that we hold a Faith Hill/Tim McGraw concert here on Valentine's Day, and then do a sweetheart package, offering concert tickets, a discounted hotel room at the Grotto here, and a nice dinner in the casino restaurant. We advertise this all through the Pacific Northwest. We become a destination. The people who use the tickets, the hotel room, and the meal, will spend the rest of their weekend in the casino, pulling slots, playing bingo, or losing on the blackjack tables."

"On Valentine's?" Joe asked somewhat skeptically.

"You can't be romantic all the time," Emily said, and felt a heat rise in her cheeks as she spoke. As if she knew. She hadn't had a relationship in years. She had been too busy, and the consulting work she did hadn't allowed her to meet people in the new communities. Three months in Kansas City, followed by three months in Tennessee, followed by three months in Illinois did not allow her time to herself at all. The six months she had planned here in Oceanlake felt like a luxury.

"You think you can get Faith Hill?" Paul asked.

"Not this year," Emily said. "Maybe not even next. But if we work hard enough to make this the most exciting venue in the Northwest, I think we could get her three years from now—and pick our weekend."

Paul snorted slightly, but said nothing. Joe shot Emily an apologetic smile.

"We've had this argument before, Paul," he said. "Let's give Emily a chance."

"She's costing a lot of money for a chance."

"I really don't want a chance," she said. "You hired me. If you don't need my services, there are plenty of others who do."

Harsh. So harsh. She heard herself, and marveled. She had learned that harshness in the last few years. Maybe if she had learned it earlier, she wouldn't have lost her reputation. Maybe she could have found a new job, managing a new band. Maybe she wouldn't have lost everything when her relationship with Ricky Fink ended.

"We need you," Joe said, without looking at Paul. "Right now, Rolling Waves is a novelty, but that will wear off. Two other casinos are being built on the coast, and they'll be competition for the tourist crowd. We'll need to be a draw then. And we have to prepare now."

Bear nodded. "It was our mix-up. We didn't know what to do about our lounge acts."

"Keep them," she said. "You're very good at choosing them."

"Since you're already here," he said, "will you listen to the band?"

She smiled. "You sound like you have a stake in them."

"No stake," Joe said. "They called us. None of us has ever heard them."

"But we wouldn't mind a fourth opinion."

She leaned back in the booth. "I wouldn't mind staying if we don't talk about business. It's been a long week."

"That it has," Bear said.

He was the nicest man she'd ever worked with. She could tell that already. And she liked both him and his wife. They had made her supper on her first night in town. Maybe, after six months in Oceanlake, she would have a few nights like this—friendly nights that would help her relax.

She ordered a drink and settled back in the booth, letting the conversation flow around her. The people in the Sea Grotto at this time of year were mostly locals out for a special night. That rehearsal dinner looked like fun. There was one empty chair at the table. She wondered who it belonged to, and why that person hadn't come.

A movement near the door caught her eye. A tall man entered and shook the rain off his dark hair. He looked familiar, and she felt as if she had seen him before a long, long time ago. He had an angular face and electric blue eyes. Like the other locals, he wore a flannel shirt and faded jeans.

He was scanning the room, looking for someone. Probably a woman.

A lucky woman.

She smiled to herself and looked away, not wanting to be caught staring at a stranger. The men at the table were arguing about how good a local musician had to be, and she sat back to listen. Outside the window, the ocean glistened. It had whispered to her since she arrived that something was going to change.

Something had to change.

And she suspected that something was her.

two

*J*oshua Candless walked into the Sea Grotto's bar, feeling decidedly out of place. He rarely went out anymore. At twilight, when he finished whatever construction project the crew had been on, he returned home, cooked himself a meal, and spent the evening alone.

He preferred it that way.

He had an aversion to crowded bars. And the Grotto was crowded on a weekend. It was next to the Sea Grotto hotel, one of the nicest in Oceanlake. The hotel shared a parking lot with the new casino he had helped build. Ever since Rolling Waves had opened, Oceanlake had become crowded even in the winter.

Initially, he had chosen to live in Oceanlake because it was secluded. Oregon beach towns had small populations, and the influx of tourists had been confined to the summer. But now, he and the other locals had to contend with tourists year-round.

He didn't like the change.

He stopped at the top of the stairs and looked for the wedding party. Kevin and Lucy had chosen to have their rehearsal dinner a week before the wedding—Kevin had jokingly said he wanted lots of time for his bachelor party—and in a moment of weakness, Josh had agreed to come. He had changed from his work clothes into a clean flannel shirt, a pair of jeans, and tennis shoes. He really didn't have dress-up clothes. Not anymore, anyway.

His hair was wet from the shower, and it sent a chill through him. Or maybe the chill came from something else. He still froze when he went into crowded places, half expecting someone to recognize him. On occasion, people did find his face familiar, but in a comforting way, telling him that he looked like an old friend or a cousin or a long lost relative.

It had been nearly ten years since someone told him he looked like Davy Moss. As he got older, his face had changed. It had grown leaner and more angular. He wore his hair differently. People would always find his face familiar, but they didn't know why anymore. That should have relieved him. It didn't.

He still moved on whenever he felt that he had been recognized, or that someone had come too close. Initially, he'd stayed in large cities, thinking that would be best. But after a sojourn in Portland, he discovered the Oregon Coast, and found himself wondering if a small town wouldn't be better. After all, once people got to know him, they would think of him as Josh Candless and that would be it.

Which, he had to admit to himself, was the reason he was here. Kevin, one of the guys on the crew, had asked him to be a groomsman in his wedding. Josh had felt oddly touched by the request, and had said yes, not quite knowing what that entailed.

What it entailed was a number of parties, a rented tux that felt uncomfortably familiar, and the rehearsal dinner at the Sea Grotto Restaurant. The restaurant certainly wasn't one of the fanciest in town, but it was the best Kevin's family could afford. That was just as well. Any fancier, and Josh would have had to buy a suit.

Even though it was the fourth day of January, the Grotto still had its holiday decorations up. The restaurant was on the beach side of the hotel, and its view of the ocean was nothing short of magnificent, even at night. The hotel lights reflected off the waves, and the water stretched blackly, mingling with the darkness. Josh walked past the etched glass, down the small flight of stairs, and to the long tables set up behind the dance floor. Kevin and his fiancé, Lucy, sat at the head of the table. The parents, who were not much older than Josh, sat on either side of the engaged pair, and several young people were scattered about the table. Josh was the last to arrive, and the only empty chair sat with its back to the ocean.

He grinned, mumbled an apology for his lateness, and slipped into his seat. Three other guys from the crew were in the wedding party, and one was the best man. They had already started on their drinks, and the conversation was loud. Josh grinned. He wasn't the only one with wet hair, flannel, and jeans.

Nick, one of the other guys on the crew, sat beside him. Nick was Kevin's age—twenty-one—and he wore his blond hair in a crew cut that made Josh wince.

"Gosh, boss," Nick said, "if I'da been this late, you'da docked me."

"I didn't know we were getting paid for this," Josh said.

"Just in beer," Nick said, holding up his glass.

Josh stared at it a moment. He didn't drink in public. That was a rule he had seldom broken. Each time he had, the situation had gotten out of control. He'd had to skip town twice.

But he was a lot older now, and even if he slipped, it wouldn't be that bad. He was among friends, after all. He ordered a local microbrew, and settled into the gathering.

Lucy's bridesmaids were all her age: eighteen. Josh had met the bridesmaid he was supposed to escort at celebrations earlier in the month. He was old enough to be her father, and he felt all of the years. Eighteen didn't seem that long ago, but looking at her, looking at all of them, made him realize just how old thirty-seven really was.

He kept up his end of the conversation, and also kept up with Nick on the beers. Since he couldn't watch the ocean, he watched the bartender, Keith. Keith had been a part-timer on the casino crew, who quit when this bar opened. He was a natural bartender, working the regulars and keeping an eye on the waitresses. Josh felt looser and more relaxed than he had in quite a while. Once he recognized the feeling, he stopped drinking.

A band came in the side door, shaking rain off their coats and putting their instruments beside the dance floor. They left the service door open as they went to get their amps and sound equipment. Josh remembered the feeling, the anticipation, the work involved. Lifting equipment, moving instruments, the hope that someone—anyone—out in the audience was listening. He had played his first club in high school, when he had been too young to drink in the establishment. Liquor laws were different in those days. He could be inside as long as he didn't consume any alcohol.

These guys had to be twenty-one, or at least have ID that showed they were.

God, he missed it. He missed playing his music in public. He missed the audience's reaction.

He missed *sharing*.

Josh pushed away from the table. He had to move, had to get those musicians out of his direct view. He stood just as Nick grabbed his arm.

"Hey, man, you okay?"

"Sure," Josh said, amazed at how calm he sounded. "Just needed to stretch my legs."

"Well, stretch 'em to get me another beer, wouldja? That waitress is slow."

Josh's smile grew. Nick had probably had enough beers. He had just given his boss an order. But it didn't really matter. The kid lived around the block. He had probably walked here, and he could just as easily walk home.

"No problem," Josh said, and slid his way out of the long table.

He headed to the bar, shoved a stool aside, and leaned against the polished wood. Keith grinned at him.

"Hey, Keith," Josh said.

"Never expected to see you in here," Keith said. He was tall, balding, with the beginning of a potbelly. He also had three kids at home, and a fourth on the way.

"What, I don't look like Grotto clientele?"

"You don't look like anybody's clientele," Keith said. "I never known a man who keeps to himself as much as you do."

Josh shrugged. "I decided to get out more."

"Thanks to Kevin," Keith said. "The wedding of the century."

"I doubt that," Josh said, even though he knew the wedding would be big by Lakeside County standards.

"Kids shouldn't get married that young," Keith said.

Josh frowned at him. "I thought you did."

"The first time. Cindy 'n' me got married in our thirties, and it's still tough." Then he grinned. "But worth it."

"Maybe it will be for Kevin," Josh said.

"Maybe." Keith wiped a nonexistent spot on the bar. He didn't sound too convinced. "You come up here for conversation or to get away from the crowd?"

"Neither," Josh said. "Nick needs another beer."

"Okeydokey." Keith grabbed a glass and pulled the tap. A guitar riff came from the dance floor. Josh glanced over there before he could stop himself.

The drummer, a slender boy with nose rings and spiked hair, sat behind a relatively cheap set, tossing his sticks in the air and catching them with one hand. The bass guitarist, a girl wearing ripped jeans and a skintight blouse, was tuning her guitar. The lead guitarist had an older, more expensive model. He was teenage-boy skinny with stringy blond hair pulled back into a ponytail. He had a tattoo on his left cheek, and another on his right hand. The keyboard player was working off a cheap Casio plugged into an amp. Josh winced in spite of himself.

"They any good?" he asked Keith.

Keith shrugged. "Better than most in this town. You want real entertainment, go to the valley."

Josh nodded. Real entertainment was sparse even there. Large acts traveled down the I-5 corridor, playing at venues from the Schnitzer in Portland to the Hult in Eugene. But the local garage bands were still stuck in Seattle grunge, and the days when Oregon had been the center of West Coast jazz were long gone. He'd heard enough local music by accident to know that he didn't want to hear much more.

"Thanks," Josh said, taking the beer and heading back to the table. Then he paused. A woman he didn't recognize sat at a booth with three members of the casino board. She was stunning. She had shoulder-length dark hair, large eyes, and high cheekbones. She didn't look local. Her cut was too stylish, her blouse too expensive. He almost went to the booth for an introduction, and then stopped himself.

All of his relationships ended the same way, with the woman telling him he was too secretive, too closed off, too much of a loner. She would always want to know why he kept one door in the back of his apartment locked, and why he never turned on the radio, why he surfed past MTV, why he refused to listen to her favorite CDs.

At first, such things would be a curiosity. Then they'd become an irritation. And finally, a point of contention.

A point he would never discuss.

He didn't dare.

He sighed and almost drank the beer himself. Regrets were something he tried not to think about. He had too many of them.

He made it back to the table, a bit shakier than when he had left. The loose, relaxed feeling was gone. He handed Nick the beer, then slipped into his chair as the band announced its name.

"Great. Now we can't talk," Nick said.

The drummer hit his sticks together in three-quarter time, a professional move that caught Josh's attention. The band started with a cover of an old Springsteen tune. The beat was right but everything else was off: the bass guitarist was out of tune; the keyboardist was playing too fast; and the lead guitar was being drowned out by all the electronics. The singer, the boy with stringy hair, was trying to do a Springsteen imitation with an Irish tenor's voice.

"God, I hate this." Nick was slurring slightly. "Why can't they ruin their own songs? Why do they have to pick on somebody better than them?"

"The restaurant probably told them the kind of music to play," Josh said.

"Damned shame," Nick said.

Someone shushed him from the other side. Kevin and Lucy got out onto the dance floor and danced. A few other couples followed. Josh's bridesmaid looked at him hopefully. Josh shook his head. Maybe some guys could dance with a girl young enough to be their daughter, but he couldn't.

Without a pause, the band swung into "Rock 'N Roll Music" and more dancers hurried onto the floor. A guaranteed crowd pleaser, no matter how bad—or mediocre—the band was. Even Nick went out, grumbling, as his bridesmaid pulled him with her.

Josh leaned back, arms crossed. He would wait a few more songs, then make a discreet exit. The party was moving into its drunken phase anyway. Good thing Kevin had decided to have the rehearsal dinner a week before the wedding. Everyone would have been too hungover to enjoy the ceremony.

Then the drummer started a familiar beat, and Josh froze. He hadn't gotten out soon enough. The bass guitarist matched the beat—in tune this time—and the keyboardist was covering the electric guitar part. The lead guitarist was tapping the body with his right hand, coming close, but not hitting, the odd, tinny sound the song required.

As the singer leaned toward the mike, Josh winced. He had written this song twenty years ago after a night just like this, when he thought his dreams were impossible, when he thought he couldn't live through another night of drunken, clueless dancers trying harder to get into each other's pants than listen to the music.

The kid didn't have the voice for it, and he didn't have the understanding. He was doing a cold parody of Josh's take on the opening lines when a man roared in anger.

Josh recognized the voice. It was Nick.

"Stop! Just stop! Just! Stop!"

Josh cursed under his breath and slid his chair back, but he couldn't get out quick enough. The drummer kept going, but the singer was staring at Nick as if he were a crazy man. The keyboardist held his hands above the Casio, and the bass guitarist played a few more measures before she too stopped. The dancing trickled to a halt, and the dancers, confused, milled on the tiny floor.

The drummer kept going, shouting at the lead singer, but it didn't help. Finally he put his sticks down.

Nick was advancing on the band, clearly drunk, and clearly angry. The little bridesmaid was trying to grab him, but he shook her off.

Josh stumbled on the pulled-out chairs as he tried to get around the table. Keith came around the bar.

"You aren't good enough to play real music," Nick said. "Make up your own stuff and ruin it!"

"We're plenty good enough!" The lead singer swung his guitar to his back and came forward. The bass guitarist had moved near the wall, and keyboard player had picked up his Casio and joined her. The drummer was still coming forward.

"Hell, *I'm* better than you are," Nick said.

"If you don't like the music, shut up and get out!" the lead singer said.

Josh had made it around the table. He made it to Nick's side about the same time Keith did.

"Come on, Nick, sit down." Josh put his hand on Nick's shoulder. "You've had too much to drink."

Nick looked up at Josh. The sight of his boss's face must have been enough to stop his tirade because Nick leaned into Josh. "He can't play, man."

"That's not your problem," Josh said.

"Yeah, it is," Nick said. "I gotta listen."

"No, you don't," Josh said. "Besides, you don't want to ruin Kevin's party, do you?"

Nick cursed again. "Do you think he'll be mad at me?"

"I don't know," Josh said. "You'd better ask."

Nick stood up, straightened his shirt, and spun around, looking for Kevin. When he saw him, Nick headed in that direction, away from the dance floor.

"Thanks," Keith said to Josh. He had his hand on the lead singer's collar. Keith let go. "You can get back to work."

"Hell, no," the kid said. "We can't play for this crowd. They wouldn't know good music if it bit them."

"Neither would you," Josh said under his breath.

The kid heard him. "Don't you like rock music?"

"I love it," Josh said. "When it's done right."

"We do it right."

"You will," Josh said. "With practice."

He started to move away when the kid grabbed his arm.

Josh looked down at the kid's hand. "You don't win over an audience by arguing with it."

"As if you would know," the kid said.

Josh shook the kid's hand away. He wouldn't get involved. He wouldn't. Just because Nick was right didn't mean that Josh had to continue the argument. Even if he was angry at the way the kid had ruined one of his songs.

"Get back on stage," Keith said.

"That ain't a stage," the kid said.

That was it. Josh whirled. "It's all you got, kid. And it's all you're going to have if you don't learn how to be a performer."

"I don't need lessons from you, old man," the kid said.

Josh studied him for a minute. The kid's arrogance was familiar. But arrogance without talent and a willingness to learn had no place in the music business.

"I think you do need lessons," Josh said, and snapped the kid's guitar off its strap.

"Hey!" the kid said.

Josh ignored him and went to the bass guitarist.

"Three chords," he said to her, "in this progression."

He pulled the guitar in place and showed her what he wanted.

"You sit out," he said to the keyboardist. Then he turned to the drummer, who had somehow returned to his seat.

"Here's the beat," he said. "Jump in when I nod to you. Got it?"

The drummer looked young and scared despite the nose rings. He gripped his sticks so hard his knuckles were white.

"And loosen up," Josh said. "We're jamming."

He wasn't going to play anything they knew. It was too obvious. Besides, he would take Nick's advice. He would woo the audience with something they *didn't* know.

At the count of three, he started the bass player. She fumbled the first progression, but caught onto the second. He nodded to the drummer, then started to play himself. He got caught up in the opening: He'd never played this piece in public. He had only played in public five times in the last fifteen years, and each of those times had been an accident, like this. All the songs he'd written since he was twenty-two had gone unperformed.

The music took him—and it wasn't until he stepped up to the microphone that he realized his mistake.

Three

his new guy was good.

Emily leaned back in the booth and stared. Until the new guy got on stage, she had ignored the band. Even Paul had apologized to her, saying that he had heard they were better than they were. Then the fight had broken out, and the new guy took the stage.

The man she had seen coming into the restaurant.

He looked even more familiar with a guitar in his hand. She squinted. Why was it that every musician these days had a little bit of Elvis, a little bit of Lennon, and a little bit of Davy Moss? The singer's style was all his own, but his voice had elements of all three, with Moss being the strongest.

Fortunately his music was different, and his features were sharp. Moss had always been slightly ill-defined, a skinny boy with a half-formed face.

And Moss was dead. This guy clearly wasn't.

"Wow," Bear murmured beside her.

He only echoed her thoughts.

Wow.

KRISTINE KATHRYN RUSCH

The singer was taller than most musicians, taller than the kid he replaced, surely. He'd had to pull the mike up with one hand without, somehow, missing a beat. His shoulders were broad, tapering down to narrow hips. His shirt and jeans were faded, his tennis shoes scuffed with mud. He didn't dress like a musician.

But he played like one.

"Who's that?" she asked.

"Josh Candless," Joe said, and it sounded as if he were surprised.

"Candless." She hadn't heard of him, and with moves like that, she should have. That look. She had seen him perform before, she knew that much. But where and when, she couldn't place. His hunch over the guitar, the way his long bangs fell onto his forehead, all seemed familiar. She squinted. It was as if she wasn't seeing him clearly, as if she were watching through a filtered lens.

She stood, and slowly made her way to the dance floor. The couples that had been milling a moment before were dancing again, and the drunk who had started the whole thing was leaning against a table, looking amused. Only the kid seemed dissatisfied. He had his arms crossed, head bent down in a deep and obvious frown. The bartender held the kid's arm tightly, as if he expected something to happen, and a cocktail waitress worked the bar.

God, the singer's voice was liquid sex. Emily could feel it run down her spine, caress her nerves, soothe her raw edges. She felt as if any man in the room could ask her to go home and she would, even though the singer was the man she wanted. This feeling didn't happen with just any good musician. Only a few held that power, and most of them didn't wear faded flannel and play hotel bars on a whim.

She glanced at the other women. The cocktail waitress had her elbows on the bar, and was staring at the singer. The dancers were frenzied. And the older women sitting at the large table had their mouths open like teenagers suppressing their excitement over meeting John, Paul, George, or Ringo.

Gorgeous. And polished. He'd played professionally. She'd bet her career on it. But where? The music wasn't familiar.

The music. She'd been focusing so hard on him that she hadn't really listened to the music. He was playing what some stations would call hard rock, but it had bits of rockabilly and jazz. The drum carried a rock rhythm, but the bass progression was sweet jazz. And the guitar part that he played had strong country overtones.

Finally the lyrics caught her. He wasn't singing about lost loves or sex. He was singing about faded dreams—the kind of blue-collar blues songs that Billy Joel made popular in the early eighties with hits like "Allentown." Yet it wasn't imitation Joel. It wasn't imitation anyone. This sound was new and rich, and embodied with a pathos that would appeal to anyone from the most hardened CEO to an out-of-work logger.

He backed away from the mike, hit three concluding chords, and suddenly it was done. The revitalizing air that had swept through the bar vanished with the last reverb.

The cocktail waitress and the women at the table burst into applause, followed quickly by the dancers. The drunk whistled, and someone "woo-wooed" as if they had just heard the last set of a really fine concert.

He looked shocked. He took step forward and handed the kid the guitar as if it burned him. The kid took the guitar, said something sharp to the bartender, and stalked out. The rest of the band watched, stunned, as if they didn't quite know what to do.

The dancers swirled around the singer. He shook his head, held up his hands, and seemed absolutely miserable. She almost approached, but then decided against it. She had just told the casino board she wasn't interested in locals. She didn't need to go back on her word immediately.

But she would speak to him.

He was too talented to remain in hotel bars forever.

She returned to the booth. Bear had scooted sideways so that Paul could see. She slid into her place.

"What do you know about that guy?" she asked. She was still trembly. Sex. The best performances were all about sex.

"All I knew about him was that he was one damn fine worker," Bear said.

"Yeah," Joe added. "He was on the construction crew for the casino."

"He was more than that. He did some of the fine work in the casino, master carpenter work," Paul said. "I hired him. He had a valid contractor's license, had worked in Portland, and was looking for honest work. He was so good he was hired on by the biggest contractor in the county, and within a month had become a foreman. He did the fine work for us as a favor when the cabinet maker we contracted for never showed."

A contractor. She would never have suspected it. All the musicians she knew were very protective of their hands.

"But you didn't know he was musical?" she asked.

"Musical? He never even whistled while he worked," Joe said.

"Only guy I know who preferred the radio off," Paul said.

"How odd." She leaned forward. The drummer was apologizing to the bartender. The keyboardist was packing up his Casio, and the bass guitarist was standing in the service entrance, arguing with the kid. That little performance had shredded any sense of unity the band might have had.

The dancers were surrounding the singer, laughing and shouting and slapping him on the back. He wasn't laughing. His smiles were courteous, but they never reached his eyes.

What a powerful mix of emotions in his body language. Tight shoulders, small movements, a darting gaze. Shame, surprise, and a bit of something else.

Fear?

The man who had performed had been fearless. But offstage, he looked lost.

"Excuse me," she said to the board. She grabbed her coat and slung it over her shoulders. Then she made her way to the dance floor.

The conversation around her was strange:

Jesus, man, you're good.

You been holding out on us.

You should have your own band.

And through it all, he said nothing. Merely smiled, nodding once or twice. What she had taken for fear seemed more like sadness and a sense of loss. She wasn't sure why she understood this man, or if she didn't, why she felt like she did.

He didn't see her as she made her way toward him.

His hands were at his side, and clenched. He was inching toward the door, but people kept stopping him. The drunk was hanging on him, repeating, "You showed him, man. You really did."

Loss, fear: Whatever the emotion he felt, it was clearly secondary to his need to leave. And the crowd, thrilled as they were, weren't about to let him.

She'd seen this with performers a hundred times.

She knew how to solve it.

"Mr. Candless," she snapped in her best business voice. "You need to come with me, sir."

Her voice penetrated and stopped the conversation. He raised his head, saw her, and looked startled. Almost as if he'd recognized her. But she'd never spoken to him before. She would have remembered.

"Mr. Candless," she said again, using that same commanding tone that could turn multimillion-dollar performers into whimpering children.

"Ah, sorry, guys," he said to the people around him. He pushed his way past them, and she took his arm, leading him away from the crowd.

His shirt was warm, the flannel soft and well used. She could feel muscles beneath the fabric: real muscles, not gym-created oversized things.

"You looked like you needed to be rescued," she said, softly.

He glanced down at her. His eyes were a radiant blue, what her mother used to call *Paul Newman blue*. Emily hadn't expected that warm feeling to run through her again. At least, not without the music. It almost made her let go of him. The last thing she needed was another musician in her life.

"Thanks," he said, and his voice was as musical as it had been when he was singing. Deep and warm and fine. "I did need rescuing."

Then he slipped out of her grasp, bounded up the stairs, and disappeared out the door. She froze, startled by the suddenness of his escape.

He'd done this before. He knew how to get away.

Well, she'd done it before too. And she didn't want him to disappear. Not yet anyway. Not until she found out why a world-class musician was wasting his time in a small Oregon town.

She shouldn't have followed him, but she did. Part of her job, she reminded herself, was to find talent. A small part, but a part nonetheless.

Besides, he wasn't from Los Angeles. He'd probably never heard of Ricky Fink.

And that thought spurred her to move even faster.

four

Stupid, stupid, stupid. A little beer, some hurt pride, and yes, the phrase *old man*, had goaded him into something he had avoided since he had come to Oregon. Playing in public. At least he'd been smart enough to play something new, something no one had ever heard before.

At least he'd remembered that.

Imagine if he'd played one of his old songs.

He stepped out the door of the Grotto into a light mist. The restaurant's outside light illuminated the rain, making it look white, almost like snow. But it wasn't cold enough. It was never cold enough here, not even in January. He still didn't wear coats. His Minnesota upbringing had stuck with him. Cold to him wasn't really cold until it hit twenty degrees.

He fished in the pocket of his jeans for his truck keys. He had to get out of here. Had to leave before they caught up with him again. No one in Kevin's party had thought him anything more than Josh—a more talented version of Josh, but still Josh. Keith had been watching him with an interested gaze, but even he didn't worry Josh. The locals didn't worry him—much.

It was the woman.

He had nearly stopped singing when he saw her staring at him from the edge of the dance floor, a speculative gleam in her eyes. It was almost as if she were trying to figure him out.

And he didn't like it.

He especially didn't like the way she had known his name, the way she had barked it from across the room. Kahn used to do that to get rid of groupies, and it had always worked.

Always.

She had saved him, and he had run out on her, and he might have to keep running, if he wasn't careful.

His truck was parked beneath a streetlight. The light mist coated the peeling red paint. He had a one-ton, suited for carrying lumber and equipment. Not for instruments. No matter how many he played in the quiet of his own apartment. No matter how many times he longed for an audience, imagined himself on the stage again, being heard again.

That was an unattainable fantasy anyway. There was no way he could return to music without revealing his true identity.

Returning to music meant returning to Davy Moss.

And he was unwilling to do that.

He unlocked the door, and climbed into the cab. The interior was cool and smelled faintly of sawdust. He closed the door, and leaned his head on the steering wheel.

The old frustration knotted his stomach. He could almost picture his parents sitting beside him, controlling his every note. They had adored their only child—not for his personality or his looks, but for his musical talent. A pure soprano at age three. An accomplished violinist at six. A well-known pianist at ten.

The Minneapolis papers had called him a child prodigy. *The New York Times* speculated whether or not he would burn out in his teens. His parents gave interview after interview, taking his music for themselves.

So he took it back. In bars and restaurants just like this one, playing the demon rock and roll before he was old enough to vote.

His career had started in places like this, and it kept ending in places like this. He would grab a guitar, show off for a set or two, and then have to vanish so no one would figure out who he was.

The problem was that he loved this town. He hadn't really admitted it until now. He'd had vague hopes of staying here, of not running anymore.

He closed his eyes. Maybe this had been his way of testing the place. He knew he no longer looked like Davy Moss. He had aged in fifteen years. He had been lucky that his face had narrowed, that he had grown into his bones.

Davy Moss's music still played on the radio, and Davy Moss was a perpetual twenty-two. His haircuts were a bit out of date now, and his clothing certainly was. He still had an unfinished look, the promise of the man to come, but not the man himself. Josh and Davy Moss had similar looks but they were similar in the way that fathers and sons were similar, if that.

Josh's problem wasn't his looks.

It was his voice.

It hadn't changed at all.

His arrogance hadn't changed either. It goaded him onto the stage every single time. Somewhere, deep down, he did believe he was better than all those other musicians—and he would prove it once and for all.

He sighed, raised his head, and rubbed his eyes. So that was what had triggered it. The kid had reminded him too much of himself, of the life he had discarded so casually, and without any regard to the people he left behind.

A knock on the window made him jump. The woman was looking into his cab. The mist coated her hair, made her look ethereal, ghostlike, as if she weren't quite there.

He rolled down the window because he couldn't think of anything else to do.

"Mr. Candless," she said. "Can we talk?"

She didn't sound like a groupie or a lonely woman hoping to warm her bed. She sounded businesslike.

And that bothered him even more.

"Look, Miss—?"

"Lukovich."

"Miss Lukovich. I've had a lot of beer, and I embarrassed the hell out of myself. I would really like to go home."

"It'll only take a minute."

She wasn't going to back off. He wanted to hear what she had to say. He wanted to know what she had figured out.

"Okay," he said. "Talk fast."

He didn't invite her into the cab, even though that was what she was angling for. She seemed to take it in stride.

"You're one talented singer, Mr. Candless."

"I'm an even better carpenter."

Her smile was tight. "Having not seen your work, I have no basis for comparison. But I do know music."

"You do?" He tensed. Here it came. The moment he'd been waiting fifteen years for. The moment he was recognized by someone he couldn't talk his way past.

"And I think you could have quite a career ahead of you, if you're willing to put in the work."

He almost didn't hear her. But when he realized she had said nothing about Davy Moss, had not asked him why he had disappeared or what had happened to the last fifteen years, he shook his head.

"Listen to me, Mr. Candless. I know what I'm talking about."

"I'm listening, darling," he said.

She winced at the familiarity, but it didn't stop her. "I've worked as a promoter, as a manager, and now as a consultant for some of the biggest venues in the country."

"Yeah," he said. "Like the Rolling Waves Casino."

To his surprise, she grinned. "When they hired me, they claimed they wanted to compete on the Vegas level. Since I've arrived, they've struck me as quite parochial. We're having a meeting tomorrow morning that will determine whether or not I continue to work for Rolling Waves."

He was beginning to like her. Even more, he liked her credentials. She had some promotion experience. She looked a bit young to have been on the scene when he was hot, but she would have been familiar with his music. Everyone was.

And she didn't recognize him.

"You're getting drenched," he said. "You want to get in?"

"What I really want is some good Pacific Northwest coffee. Can we get some away from your fans in there?"

"They're not my fans," he said softly. "They're my friends."

"Well," she said, "tonight they were your fans."

That they were. He recognized the look, the slightly glazed eyes, the expressions of surprise, adoration, and envy.

He had known, in the moments after he stepped away from the mike, that his friends might not be so friendly anymore.

"Get in."

She didn't wait for a second invitation. She ran around the cab and yanked open the door, pulling on it to lever herself inside. She settled hard, spraying the interior with rain and the faint rosy scent of her perfume.

"You don't ride in trucks too often," he said.

Again she grinned. He liked the look. It was impish and self-mocking and sly all at once. "Yuppie trucks. They have steps into the cab."

"I'll bet they have shocks too," he said as he put the truck into gear. The headlights came on, cutting a yellow beam through the rain.

"Shocks?" she whispered in mock horror as he drove forward.

"Yep. This baby hasn't had any since about 1960."

The truck bounced along the small ruts in the pavement, and she looked at him sharply as she realized that he wasn't kidding. "How old is this truck?"

"Older than God. Plus ten years." He deliberately drove off a curb on the far side of the parking lot, and watched her bounce.

"You got seatbelts?" she asked, clutching the dash with one hand, and the seat with the other.

"Probably," he said.

He drove up to Highway 101 and turned right. The highway was pretty empty at this time of night. The tourists were safely nestled in their vacation rentals, and the locals rarely went out. Only one coffee shop with the kind of expensive coffees she liked remained open after 8 p.m. It was a new diner right on the highway. Most of the locals thought it too touristy. He considered it just right for the kind of discussion they were going to have.

A discussion he should have avoided.

But he wanted to hear her out, and he didn't really want to go home yet. He was too shaken by his experience, too full of adrenaline from being on stage.

"You sure you don't want a beer?" he asked. There were a lot more bars open this time of night than coffee shops.

"I prefer caffeine to alcohol," she said, somewhat primly. He glanced at her. She was still clutching the dash.

"I promise I won't go faster than thirty."

"This thing doesn't have seatbelts or airbags," she said. "Thirty could kill us."

"You've led a sheltered life."

"And you like stupid risks," she said.

He almost laughed. Usually he didn't like risk at all. Not anymore. But on this night, her comment was far too accurate.

He pulled into the slightly uphill driveway at the Oceanfront Diner. The diner was long and narrow. It was a bright blue with steel trim, and looked, except for the color scheme, as if it had been the model for Edward Hopper's painting, *Boulevard of Broken Dreams*. The interior was brightly lit, and through the long, curved windows, Josh could see one waitress leaning on the counter and two customers arguing over their burgers.

"Nice," she said.

He shut off the truck and it shuddered for a moment before the engine died. Then he opened the door and got out. The mist had stopped—or maybe it hadn't reached this part of town. The interesting thing about coastal weather was that it changed from block to block and from minute to minute. That was one of the reasons he liked it here: the constant variety within an established setting.

He slammed the door, then watched as she opened hers. She clearly wasn't used to trucks. She hovered for a moment, then grabbed the door's side as leverage and jumped. Her heels smacked the pavement, but she had reasonable balance. She shoved the door shut harder than she needed to, but he didn't mind. She hadn't looked toward him once for help, even though, with her heels and her tight clothing, she had probably needed it.

She came around the side of the truck, and smiled at him. "Remind me to wear my boots next time."

He grinned back and offered her his arm. She didn't take it, moving ahead, and opening the diner door herself. And, in typical female fashion, she didn't hold it for him.

The inside of the diner was warm, and smelled of fresh pie and coffee. A row of Italian sodas and the large espresso/cappuccino machine marred the space behind the counter, making the place look too modern. Still, a lot of the details were authentic: the glass straw dispensers, the steel napkin holders, the pie case attached to the wall. He liked it in here. Somehow, it made him feel safe.

He waved at the waitress—Sally—and grabbed two menus from the stack. Then he led Ms. Lukovich to his favorite booth, on the far side of the restaurant.

Once they sat, and she had gone through the ritual of ordering esoteric coffee ("double light mochaccino with sprinkles") and he had ordered his old-fashioned apple pie á là mode, he leaned forward. "What's your first name, Miss Lukovich?"

He had emphasized the "miss" on purpose. He wanted to know if she was married. She hadn't corrected him.

"Emily."

Emily. He liked that. It was sweet, old-fashioned, and somehow tough.

"I'm Josh," he said.

"I know." She took her mochaccino from the waitress and cupped the glass as if it were a godsend. "I asked Tom Running Bear who you were."

"Because I'm so attractive?"

"Because you sing like a dream."

He felt oddly disappointed at her response. He wanted a sign that she was interested in him as more than a voice.

"You obviously performed before," she said.

"Obviously," he said dryly.

"And you gave it up to become a carpenter?"

"You could say that."

She sipped her beverage and sighed. "Two days is too long to go without one of these."

"I'll take your word for it."

The waitress returned with his pie. His coffee steamed in a mug beside his plate. The pie was warm and flaky, the ice cream melting off the top.

She set her coffee down. "You seemed upset about your performance. Didn't it meet your standards?"

He smiled at her over a bite of pie. Correct question, wrong assumption. If he were a relatively new or untested artist, that question would be accurate. He didn't know how many musicians he had watched drop out of the business because they couldn't attain the level of perfection they had aspired to. He had learned long ago that musical perfection was a gift an artist attained once or twice in his lifetime, and yet needed to strive for daily.

"Oh, it met my standards," he said. "I just hate performing."

"Really?" She folded her arms on the tabletop and leaned toward him. Her lashes were long and curled upwards naturally. She wore no makeup on her eyes at all. She didn't need any. "The man I watched didn't hate performing."

"You're a mind reader now?"

"No. But performers who hate performing usually get ill, either before or after the performance. They don't eat apple pie á là mode and they don't volunteer to go onstage."

"Maybe I just don't like the audience."

She nodded. "Now that sounded a bit more truthful. You don't like the word 'fan,' but you don't mind the attention."

"I like it for the right reasons."

A single line appeared between her eyebrows. "What kind of venues have you played?"

"You name it." He marveled at his own honesty. He wondered how far that would go. What would he admit to her? And what would he put in jeopardy by doing so?

"Bars?"

"Sure."

"Casinos?"

"A few."

"Fairs?"

"What do you have in mind?" His heart was starting to pound. She clearly did have something in mind, and he was going to listen to it. The fact that she hadn't recognized him and that she was in the business made him feel good.

It made him feel better than good.

It actually gave him a bit of hope.

She picked up her coffee again, sipped loudly, and set it down. "That was your song you performed, wasn't it?"

"Yeah."

"How many others do you have?"

He shoved his half-finished pie away. "I don't know. Fifty. A hundred. Some people write poetry. I write songs."

"Then what I have in mind is this: If you let me, I can launch you." Her eyes widened as she said that, almost as if she hadn't expected the words to come out of her own mouth.

He certainly hadn't expected it. "Launch me?"

"Launch you." She sounded more confident this time. "This country doesn't have enough singer-songwriters. You have the charisma, the stage presence, and the ability to make those songs live. The song you sang is worth the presentation. If the others are, you have a hell of a career ahead of you. If we play it right, we can make you the next Avril Lavigne."

"Avril Lavigne?" He struggled to keep the laughter out of his voice. "In case you hadn't noticed, I'm not twenty-something, and I'm not female."

"No, but you have a unique voice. So does she." Emily didn't even sound defensive. "And she's had hit singles, Grammy attention, a launch that any artist would be proud of. Not a superstar yet, and maybe she never will be, but she makes a decent living and has a great following. What musician could ask for more?"

"Indeed." He wondered how it would feel, starting all over again: new name, new face, new music. Never quite achieving what had slid into place for him at the age of eighteen. Superstar status. Crowds and limos and no privacy at all.

She leaned back in the booth. His silence seemed to disturb her. "You've done this before, haven't you?"

He clenched a fist. Suddenly the pie churned in his stomach. "I already said I've performed."

"No. You've gone beyond regional things. I've seen you perform. I could swear it. You're very familiar."

Here it was. And this time from someone who knew the business.

He waited.

"Is that why you're so uncomfortable about talking to me?"

He let out a small breath. He had staked a lot, over the years, on assumptions. People might think he looked like Davy Moss, but they assumed Davy Moss was dead. They might have recognized him when he was alive, but assumed that Davy Moss would never have come to their hometown. Once he had walked through Disneyland with only a baseball cap as a disguise, and no one had recognized him because they hadn't expected to see him there.

But when it came to the stage, it was harder to hide. He was always afraid that his secret would disappear on stage.

It seemed, from talking to Emily, that it only partially disappeared. She recognized him, but didn't know from where.

Death, especially a fifteen-year-old death, helped.

She leaned back in the booth. "I don't get you. Most people would be thrilled at this chance."

"Look, Miss Lukovich," he said.

"Emily," she said.

He nodded in acknowledgment. "Emily. I've done enough performing to know it's a succession of impersonal hotel rooms, bad food, and on-the-road loneliness. The attention and the crowds can turn on you as fast as they can be for you. I like working construction. I'm good at it. And I've had enough traveling to last one lifetime."

"But if we can get you to the right level, the money you'd make on your music in a night will be more than you make now in a year."

He shrugged. "I don't need money."

"Right," she said. "Your truck proves that."

"Actually, it does," he said. "I've always wanted a truck like that."

She laughed, not thinking he was serious. Then she pulled out a card, and scrawled a phone number on it. She slid the card forward.

It was a plain business card. No fancy gold, no script. Just her name, her position, a cell phone number, a fax number, and an e-mail address. No street address. No town listed. Just the numbers. Like every other manager he had ever known.

She stood up and slid on her coat.

"How do you plan to get home?" he asked.

"I live just a block from here. I think it's safe to walk these streets at night."

Probably. In comparison to the big cities. But he didn't like it. "I drove you here. I can take you home."

"No need, Josh." It was the first time she'd used his given name. It sounded good coming from her. Warm and intimate, whether she had meant it that way or not. "I want you to think about what we've been talking about."

"I probably won't do anything else." And that was true. She had just opened a door on a world for him. A world where he could sing as Josh Candless.

A world where he could be a musician, not a superstar.

A world where Davy Moss was still dead.

five

Emily's feet hurt by the time she made it home. Her shoes weren't made for walking, especially on a misty winter night on the Oregon Coast.

She couldn't believe what she had just done. She had just offered to jump into the fray. She shook her head slightly, amazed at herself.

For years, she'd told herself she didn't want to manage anymore. She'd thought she was beyond it. The consulting work kept her hand in.

But she had lied to herself. She had followed Josh Candless like the fan girl she had once been, but she'd made him an offer like the businesswoman she was.

The thing was, she could manage him. She just wasn't sure the industry would give her another chance.

She crossed the highway and threaded her way down a windy road toward the beach. The walk was longer than she had let on—five blocks instead of one. But she needed the fresh air.

Still, she was relieved when she saw the two-story beach cottage the casino had rented for her. She climbed the outside stairs and unlocked the door that led directly into the kitchen. Then she flicked on a light and winced. The house had been remodeled in the 1970s and nothing had changed since. The countertops were orange, the cupboards were a brown pressboard, and the blinds were gold wood. It all matched, thank heavens, but it made her feel as if she had walked onto the set of the *Brady Bunch*.

She put her purse on the counter, tossed her raincoat over a chair, and walked through the kitchen into the living room. She turned on the gas fireplace, closed the blinds, and pulled off her wet shoes.

I can launch you.

Her voice came back to her as clearly as if she had spoken aloud.

What had she been thinking? She'd already made this mistake. She had met Ricky Fink in a Seattle bar after a performance, and she had launched him. She'd convinced him to change his name, even, from Chet Rickman to Ricky Fink, and she'd made him go grunge.

It had worked.

For a while.

After he had fired her, his career had spiraled downward, and she had watched with an uncomfortable glee. She didn't like watching someone self-destruct, but he had nearly ruined her life. She was glad to see him ruin his own.

She sat on the brown-and-gold couch and drew the orange afghan over her. The problem was that she wanted to launch Josh. She knew how to launch him. She could picture him on stage, those beautiful eyes drawing a crowd, that sexy voice luring in people who didn't even like music.

She could do this.

If she only believed in herself.

Her mother had told her that years ago. *Your problem, sweetie, is that you're insecure about only one thing—how very talented you are.*

Her mother. Blunt, direct, difficult. She'd been dead two years now. Emily missed her. She'd love to call her and ask what to do, even though she knew.

You've got an opportunity. Take it.

She'd had a lot of opportunities in the last few years. Only she had never found a performer she wanted to represent before now. She had seen a lot of artists with the potential to go all the way, but none had the charisma that Josh Candless had.

Not even Ricky Fink had had that.

She frowned. Candless had confessed to having a career before. She would have to find out about it. She didn't recall the name.

She wrapped the afghan around herself and wandered into the room she had made into a study. Her computer hummed. She left it on much of the time. The screen was dark. She didn't turn on the light. She sat down, and punched a key. Her windows screen came up, filling the room with light. Then she opened her Internet program and went to Yahoo.

Maybe Josh Candless wouldn't even take her up on her offer. That might be best for both of them. Then she could continue as a consultant. She didn't need money. She had enough put away.

Enough put away so that she could work without pay to manage someone whose career might or might not take off.

She closed her eyes. That had been what she was preparing for. She had known it in the back of her mind. She hated so much about the consulting, hated teaching the same things over and over again, answering the same questions, and then moving to another town, another casino, to do it all again.

She had to rebuild and the timing was right. Ricky Fink was no longer a power in the music industry. The last time she had spoken to her best friend Connie in LA, Connie said no one even knew where he was. She'd heard he was playing at some ice rink in Texas. When Emily questioned whether or not there were ice rinks in Texas, Connie had laughed and said, "You get my point."

She did. Ricky was no longer a factor, but she had been gone long enough—and the rumors had gone on long enough—that she had to prove herself again.

She had a lot of questions she had to answer before she made a decision. She had to know what Josh Candless had done before, if he was too well known to start again. Then she had to find out if the one song she had heard was an aberration. And discover the range of his talent. That last didn't really matter, not with his stage presence, but she needed to know so that she could help him plan.

So that she could launch him.

And, most importantly, she had to control herself. He was gorgeous, and he was talented, and he seemed to be alone, but it didn't matter. She would keep this relationship on a professional level.

She had to.

For her own sake.

six

Josh closed the door to his apartment and walked into the small kitchen. He opened the refrigerator, took out a beer, and stopped.

Clouding his mind wouldn't help.

He had performed tonight, listened to a promoter offer to work with him, and considered it.

God help him, he was still considering it.

He put the beer back in the fridge and let the door ease shut. Then he leaned on it.

It had taken him fifteen years to become secure in his anonymity. Fifteen years to make Davy Moss disappear.

But Davy hadn't disappeared. If anything, under Kahn's management, Davy had grown into even more of a superstar. The thing that had disappeared had been Josh's music.

And that had been the very thing Emily Lukovich was offering him—a chance to perform his music again, without resurrecting the ghost of Davy Moss.

He walked through the kitchen to the small dining area on the other side. Slowly he sank into one of the chairs and put his head in his hands.

How naive was he being? Could he perform again without being recognized? Emily Lukovich had had two separate opportunities to figure out his identity, and she hadn't. She knew she had seen him perform before. She thought he looked familiar. But she hadn't figured out who he was.

The change in his appearance had been enough. That, his age, and the fact that Davy Moss was dead.

He had to trust Emily. She was trained in this area. She worked in the business. Her job at the casino seemed small, but such jobs hadn't existed when he was performing. And you had to have a certain level of experience to be a consultant. At least, to be a consultant who made money.

He sighed. He could, he supposed, simply have her represent his music. But he had had that option all along. The problem with selling his songs was listening to someone else perform them. He had written them all with himself in mind. He didn't want to sell them.

He wanted to perform them.

But he didn't want to be Davy Moss anymore.

He looked up. His own reflection stared back at him in the darkened window. He did look different, but his eyes remained the same. That bright, unusual color all the teen magazines used to comment on. If he performed, someone would recognize him. Someone would bring back all the memories of Davy Moss.

Wouldn't they?

Or was that his old fear talking?

He stood and went to the window, closing the blind. Then he leaned against the white undecorated wall.

Performing tonight had been fun. He had forgotten how much fun, and it felt so very good to sing one of his new songs. The look in the audience's eyes, the way they danced, the smiles on their faces reminded him what he should have known all along.

Music was for sharing.

It wasn't meant to be enjoyed night after night in the solace of a back bedroom.

It was enriched only by performance, only by the communion between creator and listener. A man was not a musician without an audience.

He had taken the audience from himself.

Maybe, just maybe, he had an opportunity to gain it back.

seven

I don't understand people who whine about being famous," Bear said.

He was sitting on a folding table in the casino's box office, a stack of files on his lap. Emily was standing beside the computer, trying to find the on switch. Someone had rigged the thing to turn on only when some other component did. So far she had pressed three likely targets, and hadn't had any luck.

"Gimme some of that fame thing," he said, "add a bit of cash, and see how much I whine."

"You already have enough cash," Emily said absently, pressing a button on the side of the monitor.

"Yeah, but I don't flaunt it. I mean look at this. 'Guaranteed suite in best hotel in city. Must not be in same location as performance venue. Limousine service at artist's discretion.' That's crap."

"No, it's not." Emily continued to work with the machine, but now she was paying attention. Ever since she had started consulting for the small, new casinos, she had heard this argument a lot. She used to ignore it, thinking the speaker was simply expressing jealousy. Then she realized that most of these people didn't understand what fame was.

She had seen it most of her life, starting during her brief sojourn at Julliard. She'd been a talented enough musician, but she hadn't loved playing like most people there. The love was what kept them performing, despite the glassy-eyed groupies, the bitchiness from less successful musicians, and the horrible business practices.

She'd burst into tears after too many performances, had grown to despise her flute because it represented so many failures, and finally her adviser had pulled her aside, asking her if she'd thought of teaching.

She hadn't, but the conversation helped her realize there were other careers in music that didn't include performance. Her main love was being around musicians, helping them, organizing them. She saw things so much more clearly than most artists. She understood contracts and business-speak, and she loved negotiation.

Her niche wasn't performing. It was managing. It always had been.

And part of managing—a large part of it—was about protecting the performer.

"Have you ever been mobbed by two thousand people who claim they love you?" she asked.

"People in Oceanlake aren't that way," Bear said.

"They are if they see their favorite rock star for the first time."

Bear looked at the list. "This is a lot of added expense."

"The expense is worth it to save Rolling Waves from a lawsuit. Imagine if Bono got trampled and injured here. What then?"

Bear squinted at her over the files. "You have a lousy imagination, lady."

"It's my job. Or part of it at least." She gave up on the computer. "Look, Bear, the tribe has to decide what they want from me. You can book local acts, you can even book artists with some name value but little draw. But you can't get headliners without me, especially in this little town. Do you even have a first-rate hotel or is the Sea Grotto it?"

"The Sea Grotto's nice," Bear said.

"The Sea Grotto's not the Four Seasons," she said, "and that's what these folks prefer."

"And then they say, 'Poor, pitiful me. I'm so famous that everyone picks on me.'"

She frowned at him. "I thought I took Michael Jackson's file away from you."

"You did," Bear said. "But I'm not over it yet."

She traced the computer's cord down to a surge protector bar hidden beside the file cabinet. "Not every artist's that way. Most of them are nice people and many of them are overwhelmed by what's happened to them. A lot of these expenses are as necessary as microphones."

"We'll spend the money to book the right artist," Bear said.

"Sure you will." Emily flicked the red button on the side of the surge protector. The computer beeped and whirred as it came on. "But will you build a proper sound stage? Will you build a new hotel to cater to a better clientele? Will you hire a decent chef?"

"What's wrong with our chef?"

"Bear—"

The glass doors opened, and a woman peeked in.

"We're in a meeting," Bear said.

"I know," the woman said, "but Josh Candless is here. He's looking a bit put out."

Bear set the files on the table beside him. "What does Josh want?"

Emily stepped out from behind the computer. "I have a hunch that he wants me."

Bear watched as she went past him, looking a bit confused. "I thought you didn't know anyone here."

"I met him last night," she said over her shoulder, then pushed the door open. Bear must not have seen her rescue Candless. And then he had bolted so fast. Apparently no one had realized it was her doing, getting him away from that crowd.

The box office was next to the information booth, which was next to the bingo room. The bingo room doubled as a stage. All three places opened onto the large atrium which was, she had to admit, one of the most impressive entrances she had ever seen in a casino.

The entrance showed a startling lack of desire to get people gambling. Most casinos had slots up front, the first thing that the customers saw. Not Rolling Waves. The first thing gamblers saw there were four pine trees, "growing" beside an escalator that rose toward the glass ceiling. Light streamed down, illuminating the entry and giving gamblers a moment to pause, look, and choose before they committed their time and money.

The word "pause" never occurred to Vegas architects.

Josh Candless was standing in front of the up escalator, examining one of the trees as if he'd never seen it before. To his left, stairs led into the casino's main room. Even at nine in the morning, gamblers dotted the area. Some were pulling slots, some were playing video poker, and some crowded around one small blackjack table.

She studied him for a moment. It was rare that a man in Levi's and a flannel shirt made her heart stop. But he did. And she couldn't quite figure out why. She'd met a number of charismatic performers, though, and they could be wearing dirty towels and ripped underwear and they'd still be attractive to the eye.

It was a good sign for his career.

A bad sign for her.

She hadn't expected him. Not after she had done the research, and combined the information she didn't find with his reaction. She had stayed up half the night and she had found nothing. Not for Josh Candless, not for Joshua Candless, not for a thousand different variations of the name.

If he had done concert work, it had been on the local or regional level, and then he had quit.

Or his work had been so old that no one referred to it online. That was possible, too. If he'd only had a performing career, he wouldn't have had any CDs, and so she wouldn't have been able to find them.

She had finally torn herself away from the computer at 2 a.m. Even then, she hadn't scanned for backup musicians or studio musicians. There was a lot of work he could have done without headlining.

But it still didn't ease her. He had been defensive and difficult— and talented.

So very talented.

She crossed the atrium.

"Mr. Candless," she said.

He turned, and smiled when he saw her, the smile not quite touching the worry lines on his face. "Josh, remember?"

"Josh," she said, and waited. Waiting was an old trick, one she had learned in her first industry job as a secretary for a small recording studio. Waiting intimidated everyone from CEOs to janitors.

"You—ah—had said to contact you if I thought about trying and—" He shook his head like a man waking from a long nap. "Ah, hell. This is just nuts."

He started to leave.

She took his arm. "I don't have an office yet, but no one's playing bingo this early in the morning. Why don't you come with me?"

She led him to the bingo room, and he let her, even though he probably knew the casino better than she did. She had picked the bingo room on purpose. The stage was the most dominant thing about it, recessed in the back, the tables stair-stepped down so everyone had a view. She picked a seat with her back to the sound area, so that he would have to look at it if he didn't want to look at the stage.

"What did you decide?" she asked softly.

"I don't know." His grin was sheepish, making him look boyish and somehow familiar again. That odd feeling as if they'd met, as if they'd seen each other before, felt stronger this time. "Last night I thought that I might like to—you know—see what I can do, and now, after a few hours work, and seeing this place, I realize I'm just crazy."

"Why don't you let me decide that?"

His gaze fell on her. It was warm and sad at the same time. "You can't. I have to make my own decisions. Informed decisions."

Her eyes widened slightly. No beginning artist had ever said that to her. Each one had moved blithely forward, as if superstardom were the only goal, no matter what the cost. They always seemed to worry about cost later, when it was too late.

"I don't have a band, and I'm not sure about performing," he said. "What about selling songs?"

His question surprised her. She hadn't expected that kind of pull back. She had expected him to be an all-or-nothing sort of man.

"You'd need an agent for that," she said.

"Ultimately, I'd need an agent anyway," he said.

"You sound pretty informed already." She leaned back, suddenly uncertain of him. The cues were all wrong. No excitement, too much caution, a willingness to hide. She frowned. "What happened to you? What makes you so frightened of performing?"

"I'm not frightened," he said.

"Yes, you are. I watched you last night. You loved it up there. And then, when you were done, it was as if—"

"As if I were a recovering alcoholic who took a drink." He pushed away from the table. "I can't do this."

She stood. "Why not?"

He turned, looked down at her. They were so close she could smell the soap he'd used, the soap and something indefinable. Something that was uniquely him.

"Because the last time I let it destroy me."

"Drugs?" she asked.

He wasn't looking at her anymore. He was looking at the stage. "It went to my head, turned me inside out, left me arrogant, and stupid, and lonely. And empty. By the end of it, I couldn't write any more. I was angry all the time, and all I wanted was out."

"Then why do it again?" she asked.

He swallowed, his Adam's apple bobbing slightly. "Because I did it wrong before. I want to know if I can do it right."

"That's not reason enough," she said. "Not at the level I think you can go."

He looked down at her. He took a strand of her hair and tucked it behind her ear. The gesture was startlingly intimate, and yet she didn't back away as she would have with almost any other man.

"At some point," he said, "music has to be shared."

Ricky's face flashed in front of her eyes, and she stepped back slightly away from Josh's reach. The attraction was good; it meant he would have appeal. She just didn't need to be the one he appealed to most.

"That's the right answer." She forced herself to meet his gaze. She could still feel the warmth of his fingertips beside her ear. "How long ago did your performing disaster happen?"

"Fifteen years," he said.

"Times have changed," she said. "You don't have stage fright, do you?"

"God, no."

"Then we should be fine."

"I was pretty well known fifteen years ago," he said. "That might create a problem."

"No offense," she said, "but I don't remember you and I can't find any references to you online. If I don't remember—and I've been a music buff since I was eight—no one else will."

The words, harsh as they were, seemed to lighten his mood. He gave the stage one more glance, then said, "Problems just don't go away, you know."

"I know," she said, "and I'll be the first to tell you if a therapist is required. But before that, I need to hear your other songs. I need to know if you're going to be a one-shot wonder and if all of this is moot."

He smiled. "I don't think you have to worry about me being a one-shot wonder."

He was right about the arrogance—and wrong that it had gone away. She wasn't all that worried about it, though. Arrogance carried a lot of performers through the difficult times.

"I'm afraid I do have to worry about you being a one-shot wonder," Emily said. "Tonight, let's go where your music is. You'll play for me."

"It's in my apartment." His head tilted just a little, as if seeing if she minded.

"Fine." She touched her ear. "As long as you keep your hands to yourself."

"Strictly business," he promised.

"Good," she said, and proceeded to make all the arrangements.

eight

He was nervous. For the first time since he was a child, he was nervous about performing. And, for the first time since he was sixteen, he was nervous about seeing a woman.

What was wrong with him?

Josh hid the last dish in the old dishwasher, and wished that he had used some of his money to rent a nicer place. But location hadn't mattered to him in years, and besides, he always felt as if he would be conspicuous if he owned a nice place on his salary.

This apartment was anything but conspicuous. It was located behind a shopping outlet and had no view of the ocean. He would rectify that when his year's lease was up—if he lasted in Oceanlake that long.

At the age of twenty-two, he had thought wandering was the ideal life. Of course, wandering protected him—allowed him to ignore the devastation his death had caused. He didn't listen to the news, didn't read the fan magazines, kept his face averted every time he saw a gossip rag.

Freedom, in those heady days after he disappeared, meant traveling on his motorcycle, cash in his pocket, no destination and no dreams. He had lived that way for five years before settling down and finding a home. That was when he realized he was tired of hotels, tired of camping, tired of eating in restaurants. He learned to cook, he learned the value of real work, and he finally became what he had always wanted to be: an anonymous face in a familiar crowd.

He sat on his battered sofa, put his feet on the coffee table, and leaned his head back.

What was he doing? Throwing it all away, and for what? A midlife crisis? A dream long forgotten? He enjoyed this life. He had found a place where he liked to live. He liked the predictable nature of his routine.

He still remembered the days as a star. He had felt so trapped at the height of his fame, almost as if he were drowning. He never knew—not even as a child—if people liked him only because he was talented or because he was well known. It got worse when he became a rock star. He couldn't go anywhere without being recognized, and the only place he could truly be alone was on the road, in the car, driving himself from one place to the next.

Ironic, then, that he used a car to murder his own dreams.

He didn't want to go back there. But he was tired of hiding his music. He never carried his guitar in public. He smuggled his instruments into the apartment, and played quietly, usually when no one else was around.

And he hated that. He was a musician at heart. He wanted to perform again. He wanted people to hear his music.

To hear it his way.

He let his hands fall. The apartment was two-bedroom, the living room a rectangle with the dining room and kitchen completing the space. The bedrooms ran down a small corridor. A bathroom was at the end. The building had been built in the early 1970s and had never been fully rented. His apartment was the only one in its small section. No one above him, no one below him, and no one sharing the wall to what he called his music room.

He had money, he had privacy, and he loved the town.

Therein lay the problem. He was relaxing. Writing more. Playing more. When he had shown that kid how to perform, he hadn't done it for the kid. He hadn't done it because he'd had too many beers. Emily was right. He had done it because he missed it, because a part of him needed to have an audience.

That part had been silent too long.

But how to have an audience without being crushed by it?

He stood and went to the window. No new car in the lot. She hadn't arrived yet.

A bit of perspective helped. He often thought as he got older that the audience hadn't crushed him. He had *let* the audience crush him. He had forgotten—or perhaps he hadn't known at twenty-two—that life went through cycles, popularity went through cycles, and this year's hot flavor was next year's bad taste. The good artists learned how to be creative while hot and how to survive the downturns.

The good artists.

The ones who stayed.

He had never stayed. He had never given himself the chance to. He might have a chance now. If he was careful.

And if Emily didn't recognize him, no one would.

He hoped.

A car door slammed below. He glanced down again. She drove an MGB, cherried out and shiny. Not a coastal car by any stretch. The rainy winters would make the canvas roof leak, and rust would ruin the delicate interior. She'd be lucky to survive the next few months.

The woman might know music, but she didn't know cars.

She opened the main door and disappeared into the hallway. He held his breath, listening to her heels rap on tile. He had checked up on her. He had called a few Vegas casinos pretending to be a casino owner in Eastern Oregon, verifying her credentials. Her references were impeccable, her abilities as a promoter superb. He'd heard of several of the bands she had supposedly "discovered," and he'd realized then what she was.

She was a scout as well as a promoter. He was so out of touch with his former profession that he didn't think people like her existed anymore.

But he supposed it made sense. He supposed that scouts still scrounged the ratty nightclubs and seedy bars searching for the next Hoobastank. It also made sense that these scouts were also promoters because in today's music world, an act had to have some good-sized regional support behind them before the large studios would ever consider signing them on.

He did know that much. He had kept that current.

He'd also heard some things in the silences that he wondered about. Once, a contact told him, she had been an excellent manager. Another said that it was a shame she no longer managed acts. And a third asked first if she was going to manage, promote, or consult. He had sounded relieved when Josh had said consult.

She knocked on the door, and even though Josh had been expecting it, he jumped. Nerves.

He pulled open the door.

She had changed into a pink silk blouse and snug designer jeans. She wore heels and too much makeup for this town, but on her it looked good. It looked appropriate. Her hair was slicked back, as if she had just gotten out of the shower, and he wondered what she had looked like, naked, under the spray—

"Come on in," he said, to rid himself of the thought. The attraction was stronger than he liked. It had been years since he'd been involved with anyone seriously. Even longer since he shared his music.

"Nice place," she said without conviction. He knew what it looked like to her. A dump. It had Goodwill furniture and poster art. The television and VCR were the only expensive items in the room. The stereo, where he had spent most of his money, was in his bedroom, hidden away from view.

"It works for me," he said. "Want a beer?"

"I'm on duty." She said that as seriously as a cop would. Only the twinkle in her eye let him know it was meant as a joke.

He liked her sense of humor. So dry that the average person might think she was serious. "Okay. Would you like something else? Coffee—although I have Folgers, not that expensive crap."

She pushed the door closed with one hand and joined him in the narrow kitchen. "How about plain, old-fashioned water?"

"From the tap," he said, knowing no true Californian would drink that. "Fine."

He got her a glass, added ice, and filled it. Then he handed it to her. His heart was pounding rapidly and his breathing was shallow. He had felt like this the first time he had played Madison Square Garden, not because of the crowd size, but because of the dream.

He had always dreamed of playing the Garden.

Had he always dreamed of playing for her?

No, but he had dreamed, over the last ten years, of playing for someone, anyone, who was really interested in him.

"My equipment is in the back room," he said.

"Lead the way."

She clutched the glass, but didn't seem at all nervous being alone in a strange man's apartment. He liked that. She was gutsy and she was confident, and she wasn't interested in capturing a husband, like most of the single women he had met around town.

He turned on the hall light, revealing dingy white walls undecorated with anything except scuff marks and nails from previous residents. The door to his bedroom was closed, and he was thankful he'd had enough foresight to do that, for his own sake, not hers. Considering the way he'd been thinking lately, he didn't need any more distractions.

The music room was closest to the bathroom. It was jammed with equipment—his guitar, an expensive Casio on a stand, and a piano. He had other instruments in their cases against the wall—his violin, his sax, and his French horn. The remaining instruments were in the closet, door shut. Two folding chairs were open beneath the window, and sheet music covered them. In fact, sheet music covered everything—the floor, the Casio, the piano—everything. He had planned to clean up this room last, and he had forgotten.

He had forgotten.

On purpose?

He didn't question anymore. He wasn't sure he would like the answers.

"Sorry about the mess," he said, going in and picking sheet music off the floor. He stacked it on the top of the piano, and then cleared off the chairs.

She hadn't moved from the door. She was leaning against the frame, arms crossed, her gaze moving over everything, catching every detail. He felt as if his entire life was open to her, as if she could see into his very soul. He swallowed hard, trying to choke back the nerves that were rising to a fever pitch.

"You're quite serious about this." She raised her eyes to his. They were a delicate brown, almost gold. He hadn't realized how they suited her, gave her the look of a tamed lion. An expensive tamed lion.

"That surprises you?"

She didn't answer him. She stepped onto the clear patch on the hardwood floor, running her hand along the Casio, plunking a note on his piano. "This equipment isn't cheap. If you weren't planning a career, what were you doing with it?"

Good question. He wasn't sure he had an answer that would satisfy either of them. "Dabbling?"

"There are people on tour who don't dabble like this. How many songs do you have here?" She picked up a piece of sheet music, and studied his scribblings while she waited for his answer. Then she looked over her shoulder at him. "Honestly."

He shrugged. "A couple hundred, maybe more. I don't keep count."

"And don't catalog them, either, I suppose."

He shook his head.

"It doesn't really matter yet. But it might." She set the sheet music down. "Do you play all these instruments?"

"Yeah," he said. "I was a prodigy in school, and my folks indulged me."

A bit of Davy Moss history. He'd almost quoted the official biography exactly. Davy Moss had been a childhood prodigy whose parents could afford the best instructors. He'd made his music debut at the age of three. His interest in rock and roll had horrified his parents, and that had given him even more impetus to pursue it. And, he thought, a freedom from the expectations. They had expected the next Mozart. Instead, they had gotten the next Paul McCartney. No that wasn't right. He wasn't anything like McCartney. McCartney defended his silly love songs. Davy Moss was ashamed of his.

"Really?" she said, and he had to focus on her words. Every time he said something about his real past, he expected her to say, "You're Davy Moss!" When she didn't, he was unsettled, as if she didn't see as clearly as he thought she did. "That's unusual. Your parents had some money, then."

"Some," he said.

"Fascinating." She picked up another piece of sheet music, sang the bar to herself, and repeated, "Fascinating," under her breath.

"Fascinating?" he asked, not sure if she was referring to the music or his history.

"Yeah," she said. "Most kids who are pushed like that do what their folks want, for a while. Then they branch off into something else. But rarely do they abandon the pursuit altogether."

"I had cause," he said.

"I figured." She kept the music in her hand as she sat in the folding chair. "We'll discuss your cause someday."

"And see if it was valid?" he asked, more sharply than he intended.

She smiled, ever so slightly. "To see if you're over it."

A chill ran down his back. Over it. That was the question, wasn't it? If he wasn't over it, he could get to the same point and back away again. What would a second try—and a second failure—do to him? Because he had failed that first time. Not professionally, but personally. He hadn't had the stamina to survive in the strange world of celebrity.

"Josh?" she asked.

"Sorry," he said and sighed. "What kind of stuff do you want to hear?"

"I want to hear the whole range," she said. "I want to know what you can do."

"It might take some time," he said. "I experiment a lot."

"Good," she said. "Play me your best."

"I have no choice," he murmured, and picked up his guitar.

nine

He held the guitar like a lover. His long, slender fingers caressed the neck, worked their way slowly down the frets, until they reached the instrument's belly. Emily could almost feel his gentleness, the light brush of his calluses as they touched the wood. She made herself concentrate on business, not liking the way he moved her, not liking her own thoughts.

With his foot, he hooked the other folding chair and slid it toward him. More sheet music fell off it, sweeping across the floor. She bent over to pick it up. His music astonished her, too. It was lyrical—or so it seemed from the few bars she'd read—and he did all the work by hand. She suspected the pages she held were the only copies in existence. He didn't use a computer like most modern composers. He worked in pen on lined paper, like the masters used to, a bit of tradition, a bit of the past. He was old enough to have learned to write music before computers. And his job probably didn't allow him to afford one.

Even though he could afford several thousand dollars for his Casio, and even more for his piano.

Contradictions. They intrigued her.

"We'll start with a little rhythm and blues." He sounded slightly nervous, even though he didn't look it. His long body was wrapped around his guitar; his blue eyes had lost their electric intensity. They were dark, hooded, focused. He leaned back, switched on the Casio, and hit a rhythm program that sounded as if it were specially designed. Finger snapping, light drums and cymbals, and a heavy one-two beat, emphasis on the off-beat.

Then he started a triple chord progression with the guitar. Even though it was an acoustic guitar, not an electric one, it somehow caught the R&B sound, the punchy, angry rhythms of the inner city. When he started to sing, his voice, which had been so warm in the bar, was rough and raw, as angry as the guitar.

She was holding her breath. The music, in the small space, was alive, filling her. The same experience as she had before, only this type of music was different, his voice was different, his style was different. She had never, in all her years, come across an artist who was as much a chameleon as he was.

The song was about being trapped. About surviving in a work-a-day world with no way of getting out, no hope for advancement, only the same thing, day in and day out. Yet in it, he had captured the rhythm of that world, made it sing, made it live.

When he finished, he didn't give her time to respond. He said, "Now a little country."

He switched the rhythm control on the Casio, a simpler drum beat in basic four/four time. The beat was soft, almost invisible. Then he started with the guitar again, and picked it, his double-jointed thumb giving him an extra dexterity that brought out the sound of the steel. He used the same tools and made it sound completely different.

Then he started to sing.

This time he had a slight Texas accent, and he sounded like an untrained tenor, even though she had initially thought his real voice was baritone. The song had a lackadaisical sound, but with that out-on-the-range rhythm, about as far from the inner city as music could get.

Squarely within the form.

And well done.

But the song wasn't the standard mother/truck/lost-love country combo. It was, instead, a plaintive lament about lost time, the inability to enjoy life. Lost futures, mourned as deeply as a lover gone astray.

It was the perfect country song, and yet it was different, unlike anything she had ever heard.

She had stumbled on a gold mine.

If she handled it right.

She closed her eyes, and as she did, the song wound its way to the close.

When he finished, the last chords of the song reverberated in the small room. She let the feeling of it work through her, and finally pass. As it did, she realized that he was silent.

She opened her eyes. He was staring at her, his face naked, open. Young, like there was a boy trapped within his mid-thirties frame.

Then he smiled. "And now, a little bit of rock and roll."

This time, he started with a classic guitar riff, all finger-picked, his fingers moving swiftly over the strings while he held the pick in his teeth. The riff for some players would have been all flare and sound, but he made it sound simple, natural, not difficult at all. Then he grabbed the pick and flipped on the Casio in the same motion. The beat was four/four just like the country song, the emphasis on the off beat just like the R&B, but the sound was different again. Rock and roll, just as it was billed.

He started to sing, and again his voice was different. The accent had the long vowels and the punch of the Midwest, closer to his speaking voice than anything else he had used. It still wasn't warm. It was conversational. With the song and the style, he proved himself to be an heir to Harry Chapin, a man who could tell a story in song and make you glad you listened.

When he finished that song, he didn't announce styles anymore. He simply moved from one song to the next, one style to the next. His range ran from jazz to rockabilly, from bluegrass to blues. He reminded her of artists from Clint Black to Davy Moss, from Jimmy Rogers to Elton

John. He sang first-kiss songs and street anthems, tales of lost opportunity and great pain mixed with spirited tunes of joy. He played for two hours, stopping only to change instruments, using the piano for a bit of ragtime, the sax for a jazz number with no vocals, the trumpet for a glissando that added the right bit of frill to a big band number. He was a one-man orchestra, so much talent bundled up in one body she wondered why no one had heard him before.

And she was worried that no one would hear him in the future.

She was the wrong person to handle his career. She hadn't scouted for a long time, and it had been even longer since she managed.

She was a good promoter and an even better consultant. She'd made a lot of money helping new casinos set up their entertainment programs, and she stayed on retainer for them, clearing up any problems that turned up after she had left. She didn't need to manage someone again.

Especially someone as good-looking, talented, and high maintenance as Josh Candless promised to be.

He ended with a piano piece—no vocals. It took her a moment to realize it was a sonata in the 18th-century tradition: a bit of Bach, a bit of Handel, a bit of Candless all mixed in. It was proficient, and heart-breaking.

She took a deep breath. Talent was no guarantee of success. She knew that. Drive was. Josh had talent—buckets of it—more than she had ever heard in one body.

But he lacked drive.

And that would be his downfall, his failing. No matter how hard she pushed him, she couldn't make him do something he wasn't willing to do on his own, and that was face an audience. How did a man of these immense abilities manage to stay hidden in a small Oregon town?

Then he stopped. He took a deep breath and turned to her. His features were cloaked, the nervous boy she had seen earlier covered in a mask that looked ancient.

"I could keep going," he said, "but that's the range."

She wasn't ready for him to be done yet, even though he had gone on longer than any other artist she had put in this position.

"That's impressive," she said, her voice rusty from two hours of silence. "You'll be hell to package."

He blinked, and brought his head back as if he'd been struck.

She brought a hand to her face. "Sorry. Thinking out loud. I had already skipped a step in my brain."

His eyes were wide. He hadn't moved since she started speaking.

She had to explain, to cover her own error and the inadequacy she had been feeling since he started to play. The fear. This was the opportunity she had been looking for, and she wasn't sure she was up to it.

Managing Josh Candless would take every bit of creativity she had.

"I skipped a step," she said again. "Usually, at this point, I should tell the artist if his career is worth my time. Yours definitely is. You're probably the most talented musician I've ever encountered. You've mastered all the forms. Except pop. You didn't play any pop for me."

His mouth worked as if he were going to say something, but he didn't.

"And that's odd, because pop sells well. When country went a little bit pop, it grew to the industry it is today." She was babbling. Being faced with this kind of ability made her nervous. "What I'm trying to say is, you are definitely worth my time. You may be beyond me already. So I was thinking about how to sell you."

"What kind of label to put on me," he said, his oh-so-expressive voice wooden.

"Exactly," she said. "We could—"

"What if I don't want a label?" He still hadn't moved. His expression was still flat, his body rigid. She was beginning to get a hint of where the problems were.

"You can't record without one," she said. "They need to know how to market you."

"I don't want a label," he said. "I can do a whole range of music. I want to be able to perform my range."

"You need to be a very big name in order to do that," she said slowly, "and big names don't happen overnight."

"I know that," Josh said. "But how you come in determines how you'll stay. Most artists can't switch to a different type of music mid-career without becoming a laughingstock, like Pat Boone doing metal. So if you come in all over the map—"

"No one will know what they're getting, and they won't buy you."

"Not true," he said. "What about Lyle Lovett? He has a great career."

"In country music," she said slowly. "His CDs are labeled 'country.'"

Josh pushed away from the piano. The lid fell over the keyboard, sending an echo of sound through the wires. "Look, we can't do this if I can't play what I want."

This was the problem. She had finally found it. She remained seated, determined to be reasonable, and to talk him through it.

"You can't play what you want and expect to have an audience. I can only think of two performers who did that—Sinatra and Presley—and they mostly stuck to their roots."

"They weren't composers."

"No, but they were damn fine businessmen."

"Elvis was a lousy businessman."

"But Colonel Tom Parker wasn't."

Josh glared at her. "Is that what this is going to be about? Business?"

"Yes." She stood slowly. He was finally beginning to make her mad. "If you want to do art, then don't change a thing. You've committed a lot of art in this little room. But if you want an audience, then you better think of business, buddy."

"I don't like business," he said.

She studied him for a moment. Handsome, charming—most of the time—and oh-so-talented. And she had finally discovered why no one made him a star. If she ever heard the word "artist" again from a nobody with a lot of talent, she'd puke.

She knew better than to argue with him. Arguing would only waste his time and hers. And it wouldn't change anything. People who spent thirty years making music in their back rooms didn't have a concept of what the real world of music was like. They didn't understand that it had been a business for hundreds of years. Bach was one of the best businessmen of his time, never without a patron, never at a loss for a commission.

And he had been an artist.

"You don't like business," she said, keeping her voice as flat as his had been. "Well, you don't have to. You can stay in this shabby little apartment with its expensive equipment and play to the silence. You can spend your days hammering nails and your nights alone with your music. No one will care, and the world won't mourn its loss. I'm only sorry that I spent the last two hours with a talented man who stands so firmly in his own way."

She set his sheet music down and went to the door. "Goodbye, Josh," she said. "I'll remember your music forever."

ten

Josh sat perfectly still long after she'd left, her words echoing in his head. *I'll remember your music forever.*

That's what they had done, all of them, his fans and those who became his fans later. They remembered his music—and might, forever.

He had walked this road before, and it had backfired on him. The night he had killed Davy Moss was the night that the entire world turned him into an icon. Davy Moss had been a very successful pop singer before his death. Afterwards, he was mentioned with Elvis and Lennon as one of the great lost musical talents of the age. College kids bought posters of him for their dorm room walls, and his young, puppy-dog face still graced the cover of a magazine every few months. Articles about pop music always discussed the loss of Davy Moss, and what would have happened to pop music if he'd survived.

Every summer, in Vegas, they held a Davy Moss impersonators contest, and every summer, the winner got a contract with one of the big casinos for a month-long run. His death had launched a thousand careers.

And destroyed a dozen others. People who'd believed in him. People who'd been a part of the Davy Moss Band.

Josh willed that thought away. His stomach twisted every time he thought about his old friends.

They were the only ones Kahn hadn't been able to save. Kahn, who'd become executor of Davy's music after Davy died. The Davy Moss estate, like the Elvis Presley estate, had grown to gigantic proportions in the fifteen years since his death.

It was so ironic. He was a bigger superstar in death than he had been in life. He was the kind of superstar Emily had been talking about, the kind with clout, the kind who could make the execs listen.

Only they wouldn't. If Davy Moss came back from the grave, his fans would force him to wear his hair long, be clean-cut, and sing about puppy love. They would want the round-faced boy, not the lean man whose hair had shown early strands of gray. They wanted a twenty-two-year-old boy who tested the limits of pop music, not a thirty-seven-year-old man who hadn't a pop song in his entire repertoire.

The return of Davy Moss would kill any chance Josh Candless had of making the kind of music he wanted.

Josh Candless had to make his own career. And he had to avoid Davy Moss's mistakes. Including the mistake of letting the music trap him. He didn't need to be a superstar. He could be happy with some studio contracts and a few performances. After all, he could always return to carpentry.

He had to establish Josh Candless the musician as someone other than Davy Moss—in his own mind. Emily hadn't recognized him. Neither had anyone in the bar. The days when anyone would look at him and think of Davy Moss were long gone. If he avoided pop, he'd be fine.

If he avoided pop, he might be able to have the kind of career he'd always wanted.

This was his last chance.

And he knew it.

***

*H*e hunched over his guitar, palms sweating, his heart beating in his throat. The bar was hot, and smelled of a mixture of cigarette and wood smoke. The fire in the corner burned brightly, illuminating a group of tourists, all male, all wearing Hawaiian shirts. A hooker sat at the bar, her profession obvious only in the cold, calculating stare she gave the men when they weren't looking. The bartender was leaning against the back bar, arms crossed, watching Josh.

If he did this, there was no turning back.

He licked his lips, knew there was no hesitating. It was now or never, like the song said. And he preferred now.

He had drive. She was wrong about that. He had just let it be overcome by fear.

Fear wouldn't stop him any longer.

He grabbed the mike stand, flicked the side switch, and brought the mike down to voice level. The microphone itself had frozen him when he arrived. It was old, a mid-eighties model that had been on the professional stages when he disappeared. It gave him a momentary flash to his own past.

A past he would have to accept if he were willing to do this.

Accept and overcome.

He decided not to introduce himself. The audience wasn't really an audience, anyway. It was just a bar crowd. He had picked this place—the Ocean Oasis—because it had an open mike every night after 10 p.m. It was frequented by tourists, and very few locals attended. He had come here once, in the summer, to satisfy his own curiosity. Then the place had been full, and drunk after drunk got up before the mike, followed by a fairly good, extremely young comedienne who left the stage in tears after being heckled by the crowd.

Maybe he'd been checking the place out that long ago.

He played several chords on the guitar, warming himself up, getting the audience used to music to accompany their party. The men didn't even look at him. The hooker did, with a bit of surprise. He wondered if he knew her, if he'd seen her around town. Probably. Oceanlake was small enough that everyone saw each other eventually.

Then he launched into a ballad, singing softly, letting the mike take his words. The ballad was one he'd written a few years ago after he'd heard a Davy Moss song on the radio and he'd gotten nostalgic for the boy he'd been. The song was about lost and broken dreams, about how they left, replaced by cold reality. The words were general, but the emotion was specific, and appropriate to his mood now.

He sang to the front window, not really looking at the men, at the hooker, or the rest of the room. He avoided the bartender completely. He had left his fate in the man's hands, probably not something he should have done. When he arrived, he had given the bartender a quarter and a piece of paper with Emily's home phone number on it.

"If you like what you hear," he had said, "please call this number and ask her to come to the bar."

"I don't do that sorta thing, buddy," the bartender said.

"Please," Josh said. "She won't come if I call her myself."

The bartender took the quarter and the number. "I'm a harsh critic."

"That's fine," Josh had said. "In fact, I prefer that."

He didn't want to know what the bartender was doing. If the man never called Emily, Josh would call her himself tomorrow. He wouldn't let this chance pass him by because of an old, useless attitude.

The men had stopped talking. They turned their chairs, and watched him. He nodded to them, then wrapped up the song and immediately segued into another one. This song was similar in theme, but it wasn't a ballad. It had a strong back beat, which he managed with the guitar it-self. This song, one of his favorites, was about putting the past aside and driving into the future—what he had felt he had done that night when he had driven Davy Moss to his death.

Only, the song felt a little hollow tonight. Because he had never really put Davy Moss behind him. He had, in fact, run away from Davy. Suc-cessfully abandoned his old self—everywhere except in his own mind.

By the third song, one of the men had asked the hooker to dance. The request startled her, but she accepted. The door opened and two other women came in. They were in their fifties, dressed in expensive slacks and silk blouses, obviously visitors to the coast, obviously slumming. They hovered in the door, looked at the dancing couple, then looked at Josh. After a moment, they walked to a table as far from the men as possible. It was also right beside the small stage. The bartender came over and took their orders, and Josh continued to play.

He went through song after song, building theme upon theme, letting one set of lyrics move him to another. He hadn't built a concert in over a decade, yet it felt natural to him, like writing a song. More patrons came in, couples this time, and soon the hooker and the tourist weren't the only ones dancing. Even the fifty-year-old women consented to dancing with a couple of the tourists.

He hadn't seen anything like this since he drove his car off the road in Central Idaho all those years ago. People losing themselves to his music.

It was a gift.

He had just segued into a fairly bluesy number about having no money and how that should lead to no cares, even though it really didn't, when the door opened again. He didn't see who entered, but he could feel it, like a cool breeze on a hot summer night.

Emily was here.

The bartender had called her.

Josh resisted the urge to lean over so that he could see past the dancers. But he didn't. He kept playing as if nothing changed, even though the muscles in his back and shoulders were suddenly stiff, and he could feel aches in his fingers that hadn't been there before.

Tension, mixed with fatigue. God, he remembered that, too.

Night after night on the road, when the exhaustion finally hit, when he knew, no matter how much the audience wanted it, he couldn't go on.

Actually, he learned, even then, that he could go on, but he would pay for it the following night—and so would the following night's audience.

This time, he didn't have another audience waiting, so he decided to use up everything for this one.

He let the music get even rowdier. He liked the guitar. It could be soft and gentle, or it could have the power of an entire rock-and-roll band. He let it have its power, worked the dancers into a greater frenzy. He played until the bar no longer smelled of smoke, but instead smelled of alcohol, sweat, and perfume.

He played until the bartender yelled, "Last call!"

Then Josh leaned forward and spoke into the mike for the first time since he'd started, almost three hours before.

"Thanks," he said. "You've been a great audience."

The crowd cheered and applauded him. Someone whistled in the back, and a woman yelled out, "More! More!"

"Sorry. It's last call. Time for all of us to go home." Josh leaned over and put his guitar in its case, and got off the small stage before the applause died down.

Emily was waiting for him near the bar. She was still wearing her pink silk shirt and designer jeans, only her hair was uncombed and she had removed her makeup. There were deep circles under her eyes. She looked exhausted and vulnerable and angry all at the same time.

"What was this?" she said before he could even say hello. "Proof that you have drive?"

He flushed. That was exactly what it was, and it was also a new beginning.

"Because I know you can play, and I know you can wow an audience. None of that matters if I have to babysit you, if you want to bitch about art for the rest of your life."

He took her arm, and as he did, a woman came up to him. She had long blond hair and she was clearly drunk.

"Nishe music. Nishe." She smiled at Emily, swayed a little, then looked at him. "If she's not interested, I am. Anyone whose fingers move like that—"

"Thanks," he said. "Maybe some other time."

"You gonna be back here, man?"

"I don't know," he said. "But I'll let you know if I will."

"Good." She wandered off. A few other people were hovering nearby, watching him, watching Emily.

"You handled that like a pro," she said.

"I am a pro," he said quietly.

"You *were* a pro," she snapped, "and you clearly self-destructed. I'm not going to babysit you until you self-destruct again."

She tried to shake her arm from him, but he wouldn't let go. "I was wrong earlier. That's why I came here. To show you I can do this. To show you I want to do this. Let's plan my career. Let's work it out. I can always write whatever music I want. I'll play only those songs that fit into whatever category the industry wants to stuff me into."

"You mean that?" she asked. "Or are you just saying that?"

He looked into her very tired eyes. "I mean it."

"Then you'll do exactly what I say," she said. "You'll jump when I say *jump*, you'll show up when I say *show up*, you'll work where I say *work*. Is that agreed?"

"Do I get an opinion?" he asked, not sure if he was willing to let someone have that much control over his life again.

"You get an opinion, but that's all you get. If we spend the next few months arguing and going nowhere, I'm gone."

"All right," he said.

"For my time and advice, you'll pay me ten percent plus a salary to be negotiated later."

He'd had the same agreement with Kahn, way back when. "Fine. Do we shake on it?"

"I don't believe in handshakes," she said. "I'll have my assistant draft an agreement first thing in the morning. I suggest you get an attorney to look at it."

"I will," he said.

"Good." She wrenched her arm from his grasp. This time, he let her go. "Now, I'm going home, and I'm staying home. And if you get any more harebrained schemes in the next forty-eight hours, don't bother to call me. I'm going to spend one evening at home if it kills me. Is that understood?"

"Yes," he said.

She nodded, once, curtly. "I'll call you," she said, and pushed her way through the throng.

As she left, Josh felt obscurely pleased. Her reaction had been better than he expected. After the way she had left his apartment, he had worried that she wouldn't come at all.

A man who'd been standing beside Josh watched her go. "That's one tough babe," the guy said.

"That's what I'm paying her for," Josh said, then leaned across the bar to see if he could get a celebratory beer.

Part Two

…And in the Blast from the Past Department, **Angela Caputo,** former fiancée of the late **Davy Moss**, appeared at the Grammy Awards on the arm of 25-year-old pop singer **Phil Flynn. Jeremiah Kahn**, head of Davy Moss Enterprises and acting manager for Caputo, claims Flynn and the World's Most Famous Fiancée are just friends.…

—*Gloria Stenly's "About Town" column,*
King Features Syndicate

eleven

$\mathcal{E}$mily pulled into the parking lot of the Eagles Lodge. She felt, every time she parked here, as if she were the teenybopper girlfriend of the leader of a popular garage band, not a nationally known promoter who was getting her feet wet again in music management. Part of the problem was the MGB. Spending January and February in Oregon's winter weather had left the car smelling of mold.

Unlike the desert, the Oregon Coast had four seasons, but they were subtle seasons: rain and storms in the winter, the arrival of flowers and greenery in the spring, warmth and clear skies in the summer, and the beginnings of rain in the fall. The temperature didn't vary much—the locals said it wouldn't because the ocean was a moderating influence—but she could feel the promise of warmth ahead, and it was only March. Summer seemed to be just over the horizon, and she had a feeling it would be even more spectacular than the winter and spring had been.

Summer. The idea of it put a little flutter in her stomach. She hadn't told Josh yet, but summer was when she planned to give his band their debut concert. On the Fourth of July, she was planning a big promotion for the casino, with some of the bigger bands in the country. She also planned to have one debut band—Josh's. She would invite studio execs, music critics, and other concert promoters, give them a vacation package to encourage their families to attend, put them up in the hotel, and hope that they would notice the exceptional talent she had on her hands.

They would also get a chance to see the facility, and that, in turn, might lead to better acts, better promotion, and a better entertainment program for the casino. Right now, some of the main acts considered Oceanlake, Oregon, too far off the beaten path.

"It's the has-been circuit," one manager told her disdainfully in early January, and she realized then that she had an uphill climb ahead of her. If they all considered Oceanlake to be the end of nowhere, she had to convince them it was the *happening* end of nowhere, a place where tourists all along the I-5 corridor would come to hear good music—and to gamble.

Her first step had been to get the casino to upgrade the facility. To her dismay, they had hired Josh's company, and that had taken a lot of his time. Even though he claimed he had money, he still insisted on working. So she had been the one who had to drive to Portland, Seattle, and San Francisco to audition some of the band members; she was the one who looked over résumés, who saw the hopes of young artists dashed, and who listened to the sometimes excruciating performances. Her problem, as she discovered, was that the more experienced artists didn't want to move to the Oregon Coast, not even for a few months, and Josh, damn him, didn't want to be anywhere else.

Still, in those auditions, she'd found him a keyboardist, a bass player, another guitar player—a man who could also play violin (or fiddle, as he called it)—and a talented woman who could play most winds and brass. But the greatest stroke of luck she'd had, had been purely accidental. She had found a professional drummer, one who'd been on the national tour circuit in the eighties and early nineties, and who'd earned enough to "retire" to his favorite place in the world: the Oregon Coast.

Her meeting with Luther Tigoro, the drummer, had been odd. She had heard about him from one of the local disc jockeys, and had gone to Tigoro's house, armed with Josh's music and prepared to beg. Tigoro had taken one look at the music, flushed, and then excused himself. When he returned, he asked if he could join the band.

She got out of her damp, smelly car, wondering how, with her two jobs, she would ever find time to get it detailed, and then she closed the door with her hip. It had taken her almost a month to find rehearsal space. Most rentals, when they discovered that she wanted a band to practice, had turned her away. Only the Eagles helped, although they had insisted on setting the hours and demanded a "donation" that was higher than any rent she had been initially quoted.

By then, she'd paid it gladly, only to find a check from Josh in the mail a few days later.

I pay for the band, he'd written. *If it fails, I'll be out of pocket, not you.*

She'd admired his willingness to pay, although she doubted he knew how much money it would run into. She figured, when they had their first I'm-short-of-cash discussion, that he'd let her pay the way from then on.

She stood for a moment in the gravel parking lot, unable to believe her nerves. Why was this so important to her? She'd helped other bands start up, and she'd never felt this way.

Although she had never put them together before, and she had never met a man like Josh Candless before.

In the last two months, he'd been busy, both with his own practicing and with rebuilding the casino's entertainment area. The casino had pressured the construction crew to move fast so that the place wouldn't lose a lot of bingo revenue. The casino had moved bingo to the conference center, but with summer coming, that conference center would be busy.

He was almost done with his work on the casino project. But as that time wound down, he seemed to fill it writing music. Judging from the circles beneath his eyes and the general look of fatigue in the way he held himself, Emily bet he wasn't getting more than four hours of sleep a night. She'd also heard reports that he would show up occasionally at the open mike and test new material.

After today, she would put a stop to that. She wanted to control when and where the band appeared. There would be a few practice venues, but none locally. When Josh's band made its debut at Rolling Waves, it would be a true debut.

"You going to stand here all afternoon?" Josh spoke softly in her ear. She jumped and turned in the same movement. He was so close to her that she could feel his warmth against her shoulder.

"I didn't hear you come up," she said.

"Obviously." He had a mischievous smile that warmed his face. "I didn't try to hide anything. I brought my truck, crunched my boots on gravel. I thought of calling hello, but you looked so worried standing there that I was afraid I'd give you heart failure."

"I'm not worried," she lied. "I'm just trying to remember if I brought everything."

"If you didn't, this town is small. It'll only take you a few minutes to get it."

"How come you're not inside?" she asked, worried that no one was there to greet the new band members.

"Oh, I've been inside five times," he said. "I brought some instruments and a whole raft of sheet music. No one else had shown up when I left twenty minutes ago."

"Good." She was unusually relieved. She took a deep breath. "You know, if this band doesn't work out, we can always hire other musicians."

"I know," he said. "You've told me that about five hundred times. I figure that if we can't get a band to work out, I'll go solo."

"We could do that too, but your music cries out for the full treatment." Actually, she would have liked to get him a full orchestra, but that would have to wait. She had to see how this worked first.

She had decided to push him as a country artist, even though his best stuff was leaning toward rock and roll. But traditional rock wasn't selling as well as country, and, since the early nineties, country had proven itself capable of handling bubblegum music, rock and roll, blues, and bluegrass all under the same label. Josh had been surprisingly tolerant of the decision.

"Shall we go in?" he asked.

"You go," she said. "I'll—"

"Stand out here and brood? I don't think so." He took her arm, sending a jolt of warmth through her. They hadn't touched since that first week, hadn't even really stood close to each other, and that had been his decision as much as hers.

He led her to the door. The Eagles Lodge was an old wooden structure, painted a faded red. One side of the building was lined with newspaper boxes for the lodge's recycling drive. The back had a huge concrete surface that was used for Christmas trees in December. The main door was a blond wood with the lodge's meeting hours painted on the front.

They went in. The lodge was empty—as promised—never used on weekday afternoons. It smelled of cigarette smoke and dust, even though the place seemed spotless. Josh had placed signs on the post with the word "Band" on them, and an arrow pointing in the correct direction. From there, she could hear voices and the strum of guitar strings.

"Guess the others got here before us." He kept his grip on her arm, and she wondered if that were purposeful. His touch was light, gentle, and she could feel his calluses through the thin material of her shirt. If they went in together like this, the band would know, for good or ill, that Josh and Emily shared power.

She supposed that couldn't hurt.

The back room was a pseudo-gymnasium with a wooden floor and a stage on one end. Folding chairs had been stacked against the wall, and equipment from basketballs to hockey sticks stood in boxes near the chairs. Four of the band members were milling around the middle of the room. They had taken chairs and set them down, placing instrument cases on them. Other instruments were on the stage, and Emily recognized Josh's Casio and his guitar among them.

"Hey, everyone!" she said, pulling slightly away from Josh as they entered the room. "This is Josh Candless, the man I'd told you about."

The four musicians stopped their conversation and looked up. She followed their gaze. In the moment she'd left him, Josh transformed from a construction worker to a man with presence. His smile was dazzling, his body somehow taller, his eyes bright.

"Hey." He snagged his thumbs in his back pockets. The gesture did nothing to detract from his presence, but it did make him seem more relaxed.

She made herself look away from him. One band member missing. The drummer. She would accommodate that next time by telling him an earlier rehearsal time than she told the others.

"Okay, Josh," she said, "let me introduce you to the band."

She decided to do it in order of hire. She set her papers down on one of the chairs, then grinned up at the bass guitarist. He smiled back at her. He was young—barely twenty—but he handled the bass like a pro. She figured Josh could teach him a few moves in the next few months, and the boy's obvious desire, and his clear drive, would make up for his lack of experience.

"This is Bobby Agar. He's from Portland, and he'll be playing bass."

"Hi," Bobby said, his voice breaking. He flushed.

Josh smiled at him, nodded, but did nothing else to put the boy at ease. That unsettled Emily. She had expected Josh to be warmer to these people. After all, they would be taking on some of the risk along with him.

She moved to the next person over, a pudgy, balding man in his mid-forties. He wore flannel, granny glasses, and Birkenstocks, the traditional costume of Eugene, Oregon. He was the other guitarist.

"This is Peter Sphinx," she said. "He's our second guitarist. He's done some touring, and used to get in jamming sessions with Jerry Garcia when the Grateful Dead came to Eugene. He's also worked with Mason Williams on a few projects."

Peter, no dummy, caught the seriousness of the moment, and only nodded at Josh. Josh nodded back.

Emily was growing more and more uncomfortable. She hadn't expected Josh's coolness. She had gone to a lot of trouble to pick out this group; he should have some faith in her abilities.

She stopped beside one of the two women. This woman had long blond hair wrapped in a bun on the back of her neck. She wore Capri pants and an oversized sweater that dwarfed her thin frame.

"This is Debbie Daily," Emily said. "She'll be our keyboardist. She was a finalist in the Van Cliburn competition about fifteen years ago, and has performed with some of the best symphonies in the world. She's presently on sabbatical from her teaching position at the University of Oregon."

"Married, Debbie?" Josh asked, and Emily felt a flare of shock run through her.

Debbie clearly felt it too. "What of it?"

"What's your maiden name?"

"Anelli," she said.

He smiled. "Like the librettist?"

"Yeah," she said, sounding stunned. "Not many people make that connection."

"Josh isn't many people." Emily tried to swallow her own irritation. She hadn't heard of this Anelli either.

"Your maiden name will have to be your stage name," Josh said. "Debbie Dailey is too alliterative."

"Sure, okay," Debbie said. "I was thinking of going back to it anyway."

Josh didn't comment on that. Emily took a deep breath. His sudden professionalism stunned her. She hadn't expected him to be thinking ahead on what the band should do, and she hadn't expected him to be right. But he was. Names were an important thing in the entertainment industry, and that was something some artists never learned.

"Emily?" he said, a bit of a prompt in his voice.

"Oh, sorry." She stood next to the fourth band member—another woman, barely five feet tall, with glossy black hair that hung loose and ran to her knees. Her eyes were bright blue, her features slightly exotic, and her skin was the color of porcelain. She had the petite beauty of the china dolls Emily's grandmother had had.

"This is Lisa Fujimori," Emily said. "She is a music major at the University of Idaho, specializing in jazz. She's taking the next year off to earn some money for tuition—"

"This may not be the way to do it," Josh said.

"—and," Emily said, not allowing him to continue, "to gain some experience. Frankly, she caught me by surprise. I was only going to hire four band members, but she brings something your music needs."

"A drummer?" he asked.

"The drummer's late," Emily said. "Lisa can play any brass and any woodwind instrument. She's proficient in all of them, although she specializes in the saxophone."

"All of them?" Josh asked her, his tone light. His gaze was on Lisa. "Tin whistle? Recorder? Pan flute?"

"I hate the pan flute," Lisa said softly.

Josh grinned. "Good. So do I. Besides, Zamfir has the market cornered."

"I didn't know there was a market," Peter said.

"There has to be," Debbie said. "They advertise his music on CNN."

"A well-known music network," Bobby said dryly, and then he bit his lip, as if he felt that he should have remained quiet.

Emily smiled as a bit of relief ran through her. They were gaining the beginnings of a rapport. That was good. And that was important.

"Em," Josh said. She froze. No one had called her "Em" in years. Not since Ricky. "Where is that drummer?"

"He'll be here," she said. "You can start without him. And next time, I'll make sure he's on time."

"Sure," Josh said.

"Josh, he's a professional. He has twenty years' touring experience, and then he retired to Newport. He's good."

"It doesn't matter how good he is," Josh said, "if he never shows up."

"He'll be here," she said. She picked up her papers and slung her purse over her shoulder.

"Where are you going?" Josh asked.

She sighed. "I have to go talk to the casino board. Seemed they hired an opening act for next week's show without consulting me."

"Is that a problem?"

"It is when it's one of the board's relatives. God only knows how bad this will be."

"Can't you stay for at least the first set?" Bobby asked. His voice broke again, and she felt a bit of compassion for him. He was nervous, and she was his lifeline because she was the one who hired him.

"I'll be back before you're done." She started for the door. As she crossed the wooden floor, the fifth and last member of the band she'd hired came in.

He was tall and slender with a bit of a pot belly. His graying hair was big and curly. His sweater and jeans were new, and he wore dark brown deck shoes.

"Hey," he said, "my set's in the van. Can I get some help carrying it in?"

"You're late, Luther," Emily said.

"Traffic jam near the Aquarium," he said. "I forgot it's spring break and there are tourists everywhere."

She didn't answer him. Instead, she said, "Folks, this is Luther Tigoro. He's played drums on tour with everyone from Billy Joel to Harry Connick, Jr. He sees us as a hobby. Let's prove him wrong, all right?"

She looked at Josh, expecting his smile, his warmth, or at the very least, a nod like he had done before. Instead, he had gone a ghostly white.

"We don't need to be anyone's hobby," he said, his voice sounding oddly strained. "We can rehearse without a drummer today."

Luther studied him for a moment, as if sizing him up. To Emily's surprise, the flush she had seen days earlier had returned to Luther's cheeks.

"I'm sorry about being late," Luther said. There was an edge to his voice, as if Josh's comment had angered him. "I seriously didn't think about the traffic."

Emily went to Josh, and put a hand on his arm. "I'm sorry about the *hobby* comment, but he's a bit out of our league. I thought you should know why he's here."

"We don't need him," Josh said.

"I think we do," Emily said.

His hands were shaking. Emily wasn't quite sure what was wrong. He licked his lips, took a deep breath, and turned slightly.

"All right," he said to Luther, "but if you're gonna stay, the afro has got to go."

"Hey, man, it's my trademark."

"I don't care," Josh said. "I don't like it. Dump it."

"You seem to think you're hot shit. Are you?" Luther's voice was deep and angry.

"Josh," Emily said, appalled. She'd never imagined that the man she'd known all these months, the man whose music she'd respected, had this side to him.

Josh closed his eyes, swallowed hard, then brought a shaking hand to his face. "I can't have him here," he said softly, to Emily.

But apparently Luther overheard him. "Why? You afraid of me, *Josh*?"

The emphasis on Josh's name made him go even paler. Emily's hands fluttered between them. She hadn't thought this was going to be a problem.

"Josh," Emily said. "There are no other drummers of his caliber available. Please."

"He stays, and I go." Josh pushed past her and disappeared out the side door. Luther turned and went out the other door, without saying goodbye.

Emily sank onto one of the folding chairs, wondering how such a promising beginning had turned into such a nightmare.

twelve

His is past had slapped him in the face.

Josh stopped outside the Eagles Lodge and leaned his hand on a moss-covered tree. The moss was damp and cold beneath his fingers. He stood with his back to the lodge, facing down the narrow side street that ended in the ocean.

He was shaking. A few moments ago, he hadn't been standing in an Eagles Lodge. He was backstage on the night of what would become his last concert, staring at the Davy Moss Band.

Staring at Luther Tigoro.

Luther had survived. Josh knew that. Luther and Kyle Breslin and Mike Fischer. They'd been studio musicians before the Davy Moss Band, and they had gone back to it—touring with other groups, filling in for missing players, recording soundtracks whenever they needed work.

They'd been fine.

But Ross Elligen, Ross—he hadn't been fine. He'd tried to go solo, and when that hadn't worked, had begged Kahn for a chance to reunite the Davy Moss Band. And when *that* hadn't worked, he'd tried to revive the band on his own, only to have Kahn sue him.

And that wasn't the worst of it. Ross claimed, in half a dozen interviews, that Kahn prevented him from performing. Not six months later, some hotel maid found Ross in his past-due room, hanging by a sheet from a beam in the ceiling.

Josh shivered. Maybe that was when he'd first realized—really realized—how many lives he'd ruined by just walking away. By disappearing. By ending it all.

Not just Ross's, but the roadies and the managers and the friends—God, how he hated thinking about the friends.

Friends like Luther Tigoro.

They'd been close. They'd written a few songs together. He had even been at the Idaho ranch the night Davy disappeared.

And Luther remembered him. It was clear from the look in his eyes, from the emphasis on his name. Luther knew who Josh was.

Josh hadn't expected it; at least, not so soon. He needed time to prepare, time to give it a run before anyone had a chance of discovering him. Now, it was all before him. The choices, the changes.

The apologies.

So far, Luther had said nothing. With luck, Josh scared Luther off. With luck, he'd be able to go back in there and find the rest of the band waiting for him, Luther gone, and everyone ready to work.

Josh rested his forehead on the back of his palm. God, what did Emily think of him now? She probably thought he was an asshole. And he wasn't quite sure how to change that impression.

"The lady fights for you." Luther's voice. How well Josh remembered it.

"Does she?" Josh said.

"She caught me getting into the truck. Said you were tense about the rehearsal. I think it's b.s. I think I threaten you."

It was an out. If nothing else, it was a graceful out. Josh took a deep breath, but didn't turn around.

"You do," he said softly.

Luther put a hand on his shoulder. Josh remembered the feel of it, large and warm and friendly. They had stood this way before.

"You know," Luther said. "It's odd. You live your life, you have your moments in the sun, and you retire. Then this woman shows up at your door with some new music written by a long-dead friend. I kinda thought I'd come here and rip the face off the guy who stole the music."

Josh swallowed and closed his eyes. "Instead you want to rip the face of the guy who wrote it."

"Naw," Luther said, but his hand left Josh's shoulder. "My face-ripping days are past me."

Josh turned, his heart beating. "You're not mad at me?"

"I didn't say that," Luther said. "And what I feel don't matter at the moment. What does matter is this fresh start. I got me a chance again to play some music that might make a difference. I think I'm gonna take it."

"And that's all?" Josh asked.

"Ain't that enough?" Luther turned and started to walk away. Josh felt odd, as if this moment were both less and more than he expected. Luther had recognized him, and had done nothing. He hadn't revealed him before the group, and he had used the right phrase.

Fresh start.

Luther understood.

"Luther, I'm sorry—"

"Sure you are." Luther's voice was filled with sarcasm.

Josh felt that panic rise again. "No, really, I—"

Luther held up a hand and Josh stopped talking. "Let's not insult each other right off. You got your reasons for doing what you're doing, and I've got mine. I'm not going to interfere with yours, and you're not going to interfere with mine. Am I right?"

"Right," Josh said, feeling as if a measure of control had just left his life. A second person knew now, and it had been simple. The world hadn't shifted like he thought it would.

And besides, he had missed Luther. He had missed him a lot.

"Well, then," Luther said. "It's settled. I'm staying."

"Yes," Josh said, feeling slightly dizzy.

"Good," Luther said. "Then you can come to van with me and help me get my drums. Or do them newly acquired muscles only work in the gym?"

"No, they work out here just fine." Josh caught up with Luther. Luther glanced at him.

"Different look," he said quietly. "You aged lucky."

"Yeah," Josh said.

"Quite a risk," Luther said.

"I know," Josh said. "Are you ready for the ride?"

Luther grinned. "I wouldn't miss it for the world."

***

*E*mily and the four new band members were still inside the lodge when Josh and Luther came in, carrying his drum set. They put the equipment down, then Luther turned to Bobby.

"There's still a few things. You can help me."

Bobby didn't seem to know what to say. He followed Luther and Josh sighed. This was his moment.

Emily kept her back to him. He could feel her fury without even looking at her face.

"Luther's staying with us," Josh said, deciding that an apology to the group would start things on the wrong foot. A lot of people join bands expecting it to be a party atmosphere. Let them learn early about personal tensions, about the way living in each other's back pockets could cause outbursts like his earlier. If they couldn't deal with conflict, let them leave now. "I hope the rest of you will stay, too."

"Is this what it's going to be like?" Debbie asked. "I'm in the middle of a divorce. I don't really need tension right now."

"Then this might not be the right place for you." Josh wasn't sure this was the right place for him, either, but he was going to try. "We're going to take this band somewhere, and that'll require a lot of hard work on all of our parts. And sometimes that'll cause tension."

Debbie crossed her arms.

"Your choice," he said.

Lisa smiled at her. "Give it a chance."

Debbie sighed.

"What can it hurt?" Bobby asked.

"Nothing, I guess." Debbie went to the Casio and plugged it in, running her fingers lightly over the keys.

Emily stopped beside Josh. "We need to talk."

"No," he said. "I'm getting ready to rehearse."

"Josh," she said. "I just spent fifteen minutes calming them down."

He gazed at her, making sure he took a deep breath. He had blown the opening with the group, but he wouldn't blow this. He had learned long ago that it was crucial to establish who led the band.

Emily could talk to him, but she couldn't run the music. And she couldn't have control once the band started rehearsing.

"Don't you have a crisis at the casino?" he asked.

"Yes," she said. "That's why I want to settle this."

"It is settled," he said.

At that point, Luther and Bobby came in with the last of the drum set. They were laughing as they came through the door.

They wouldn't have been laughing if Luther told Bobby who Josh was. Josh took a deep breath. He'd have to learn to trust Luther.

Again.

"See?" Josh said to Emily. "We're getting along fine."

"But Debbie—"

"Em," he said, "you did me a favor by hiring the band. Now do me another favor by letting me run it. Go solve your casino crisis."

Two spots of color appeared on her cheeks. "Josh—"

"Go," he said.

She clutched her papers to her chest, suddenly looking like a cheerleader who had just gotten into a very public fight with her boyfriend. "We'll settle this later."

"There's nothing to settle," he said, and picked up his guitar. She hovered near his shoulder for a moment, then disappeared.

He took a deep breath. He had never taken such steps with Kahn, and as a result, the band always went to Kahn, the choices were always made by Kahn, and Kahn always had the final word.

Josh wouldn't allow that to happen.

Not again.

thirteen

Emily was still shaking with anger as she drove back to the Eagles Lodge. Her meeting with the casino board had not gone well. They understood that she was to handle the music, but they insisted that this was a special case. They wanted to hire someone themselves, an opening act, a boy of about sixteen who needed a break.

She had snapped that a lot of artists need breaks, but very few earned them. And that had silenced the board, but hadn't changed their minds. They refused to back off the opening act, leaving it to her to explain to the incoming professionals why they had to cut their concert fifteen minutes short.

All that after her run-in with Josh.

He hadn't been sensible. First his unbelievable reaction to Luther, then his rudeness to the band, and finally his hard-headedness with her. If the band was still together by the time she got back—and she doubted it would be, but if it was—she'd have to establish some ground rules, right from the start.

She wasn't just angry at him, either.

She was angry at herself for leaving, just like he ordered her to.

She was done taking orders from temperamental singers. She'd been done with that a long time ago.

The sun was setting over the ocean as she parked her MGB. She got out and stared for a moment. The sky was an amazing orange and gray, the water itself a steel blue, and calmer than she had ever seen it. The beauty of this place stunned her no matter what was happening in her life. It muted her dark moods and accented her good ones.

But it didn't entirely alleviate this mood.

As she got to the door, she heard the bass line of a piece of music. It startled her. She hadn't expected any sound at all. She pulled the door open and went inside.

Guitars—two, plus a bass—the drums, and a keyboard. Then Josh's lyrics, strong and rough, in his rock-and-roll style. He sang a chorus and two female voices yeah-yeahed him. Then she heard a tambourine playing eighth notes to the drum's half beats, and she wondered where the instrument came from. She didn't remember it on any of the songs they had discussed for that day.

She went into the hallway and stopped near the door. The band was on the stage. Josh was up front; the women were beside the keyboard. Lisa, the talented brass and wind player, was beating a tambourine against her hip, and wriggling like she was part of a sixties girl group. Bobby was frowning at his bass, and Peter was watching Josh, matching him move for move. Josh was playing an electric guitar, and its sound had a slightly seventies feel. Luther's drums were keeping them all together.

If she hadn't introduced them that morning, she would have thought this group had been together for months.

They weren't a unit yet. The experience showed. Luther was the glue for the entire group. Peter knew how to stay with Josh. Lisa was enthusiastic, but her singing was slightly off-key. And Debbie struggled to keep the rock beat on the bass line of her Casio.

The bass was the problem all along. Bobby wasn't keeping up. He was trying, but he was so far behind that instead of playing with the drum's beat, he was almost a full step off.

Finally Josh cut it off, using a classical conductor's motion—circling his right hand, then clenching his fist. Emily winced: She was afraid he was going to tear into Bobby.

"You're all tense," Josh said, his voice echoing through the room, "and you're thinking too hard. I understand that you're learning, but the key to music is to absorb it. Relax with it. Let it become part of you. Don't worry about making a mistake. If you worry about making a mistake, you will make a mistake."

Bobby bit his lower lip.

Josh smiled at him, lowered his voice, so that Emily had to strain to hear. "We all screw up. I flubbed the lines a few minutes ago, and covered it with a bit of scat singing, made it sound intentional. Luther dozed off for an entire measure—"

"Half a measure," Luther said.

Emily swallowed. The response was banter, not anger. How had Josh formed a group after that beginning? What had she missed?

"—and it took one run-through before Lisa managed the tambourine. She just covered it well. Ever heard a jam session? Sometimes all it is are musicians covering for each other."

"I'm not ready for this." Bobby sounded miserable.

Josh put his hand on Bobby's arm. "Sure you are. You're just getting tired. We all are. I think we should call it quits for today."

"Probably a plan, man," Luther said.

Josh grinned at him. Emily frowned. It almost felt as if these two men were old friends. Then Josh turned his attention back to Bobby.

"Look, Bobby," he said. "I want you to do something when you go home tonight."

"I know." Bobby held his head down, clutching his bass guitar to his chest. "Practice."

"No," Josh said. "I want you to go listen to all your live in-concert albums—" then he grinned. "Listen to me. I'm showing my age. Your live in-concert CDs. I want you to pay attention to the flubs, the differences between the recorded versions and the live versions, the false starts, the jokes, all of it. I want you to hear the muffled guitar parts and the mispronounced lyrics. And then when you come back tomorrow, I want you to tell me how folks covered their mistakes and how it affected your listening experience."

"All right." Bobby sounded unconvinced. But Emily watched Debbie, who was staring at Josh with—what? interest?—as though he had given her a revelation.

"Good," Josh said. "Tomorrow then. Same time. Except for Luther, who must come a half hour early, in penance."

"I'll be on time, man," Luther said.

"Sure." Josh grinned at Luther, who grinned back. Then Josh set his guitar in the case and got off the stage. He headed straight for Emily as if he had known she was there all along.

He stopped in front of her, and even though his movements were confident, his expression was wary. "What'd you think?"

She bit back an unprofessional response. She wanted to lash at him, to say, *I thought it didn't matter what I think.* Instead, she said, "It was better than I expected so soon."

"You put a good group together," he said. "They're professional."

"Even Bobby?"

"Even Bobby," Josh said. "He's young, but he's talented. And he wants to learn. Can't beat that."

"I suppose not," she said.

Josh studied her for a moment. A frown creased the space between his brows. "Rough time at the casino?"

"I couldn't change their minds," she said. "They don't care what kind of disaster this kid's going to be."

"How do you know he's going to be a disaster?"

"He needed connections. No one good needs connections."

"Everyone needs connections," Josh said.

"That's not what I mean." She brushed a strand of hair out of her face. "He used his connections to get a gig without an audition. Talented ones use their connections to get an audition."

"Maybe he didn't know," Josh said.

"Maybe," she said. "But I doubt it. He's coming up from Reno. He's probably tried to get work there. I'll bet you money this kid's got an ego the size of the Pacific, and the talent of a peanut."

Josh grinned. His smiles seemed to be coming easier this afternoon. "Aren't you poetic?"

She shrugged, refusing to smile at him yet. She was still angry at him, not matter how well rehearsal went.

The band was picking up. Bobby and Lisa were talking softly as he put his guitar away. Peter was sitting on the edge of the stage, running through chords as he thumbed through the sheet music Josh had brought. Debbie was standing beside Luther. They'd obviously been conferring.

"Hey, Josh!" Luther called. "Can we leave this stuff here?"

Josh looked at Emily. He didn't know the terms of the lease. She nodded. "They'll tell us when they need the room."

"Will it be safe?" Josh asked softly.

She shrugged. "It's Oceanlake. It depends on the tourists."

"No one's going to steal a drum set—at least, not quietly," Luther said.

"Find out if the lodge is insured," Josh said under his breath. "We do need to be covered if something is stolen or damaged."

She nodded.

"Is there any way we can lock this room up?" Debbie asked.

"I have a key," Emily said, "and so does Josh. I'm not sure who else does, but I'll find out."

"Let's put the Casio away anyway," Josh said. "It's easier to walk off with than drums."

"Yeah, right," Luther said. "Leave me to take the risk."

"I'll help you carry stuff back to the van," Bobby said.

"You're a good kid," Luther said, "but you're not old enough to realize that a back can be a lot more expensive than a set of drums. Besides, this set is my second. I didn't bring the good one."

He got up, stuck his sticks in his back pocket, and climbed off the stage. As he passed Josh, he leaned in. "I'll be a half hour early. I expect to see you when I arrive."

"You got it," Josh said.

Then Luther left, followed by Lisa and Bobby carrying his bass. Debbie packed up the Casio. "Josh, this is yours, right?"

"Right," he said. "I'll take it."

She nodded and then trooped out with the others. That left Peter, sitting on the edge of the stage.

"Hey, Pete," Josh said. "Take the music with you. I'm going to lock up."

"This stuff is pretty different," Peter said. "You've got some challenging guitar parts here. They don't all read rock and roll. Or country, either."

"They're not," Josh said. "We'll get to them later."

"I haven't seen some of these progressions," Peter said.

"Well, work on them," Josh said. "I think you'll be surprised."

"All right." Peter tucked the sheet music under his arm and put away his guitar. Then he waved good-bye and left.

Josh let out a sigh and put a hand over his face.

"I hope those weren't your only copies," Emily said.

"I made photocopies last week." He sank into one of the folding chairs. "God, I'd forgotten how tiring this could be."

"More tiring than construction work?"

"It's a different kind of tiring. It's less physical, but more demanding. I'm not used to managing people this way. I'm used to giving them a task and letting them finish it. Here, I'm concentrating on the sound, on the people, on the whole experience." He brought his hand down. "It was kinda fun."

"Kinda?" She said.

He nodded. "I didn't mean to make you angry before."

"Yes, you did," she said.

"But not quite in that way." He grabbed the two folding chairs and brought them closer. "Sit down."

"Why?"

"God, Em, don't fight me on everything. I want to apologize."

"Then apologize," she said.

He sat. The chair groaned beneath his weight. "Well, I can't, really."

She crossed her arms. "That's an interesting way to apologize."

He looked away. "You see, I didn't do anything wrong. Except to Luther. And we patched that up."

"You did?" she asked. "After what you said?"

Josh nodded. "I know I was out of line. We cleared it up."

"That's one easy-going man," Emily said. "I'd have been furious."

Josh smiled. "You were furious."

"Yeah," she said. "I saw all my free work disappearing in the space of an afternoon."

"Still feel that way?" he asked.

She had expected to find the place empty, to find Josh here alone, defeated. She hadn't expected the music.

She hadn't, if she were being truthful with herself, expected him to be so much better at managing people than Ricky had been.

"No," she said softly. "I'm amazed at what you've done. I thought they'd hate you."

His smile grew. "That wouldn't make for a good band, now would it?"

"No," she said.

He put a hand on her arm. It sent warmth all the way through her. "Have a little faith in me, Em."

Em. Why did they all call her Em? And touch her? And why did she like it so much when Josh did?

She stepped back, deciding to be as cold as she could.

"If that's all," she said, "then I really should go."

"The casino?" he asked, seemingly unperturbed by her coolness.

"Home," she said.

"I'm not done."

"Well, you said you weren't going to apologize to me after all, and if you're not going to, then we have nothing to say to each other."

"Yes, we do." He patted the chair beside him. "Sit. Please."

She sat slowly, keeping her arms crossed. She leaned as far away from him as she could.

"You did me a great favor by choosing this band," he said.

"I wasn't doing you a favor," she said. "I'm your manager."

"Yes," he said, "but we agreed the band would be mine. I should have auditioned them, and I didn't have the time. You picked a good group."

"Thanks." His compliment didn't warm her. It didn't even please her. It made her angry again. "So now you're going to fire me, right?"

"Fire you?" He did swivel to look at her, his blue eyes intense. "We're just getting started."

"That's what the pseudo apology is about, though, isn't it? About how I assembled the band and now you're in charge?"

"No!" he said, then frowned. "Well, sort of. But I'm not firing you."

"Then what is it?"

He sighed, folded his fingers together, and put his hands behind his head. The motion made him look curiously relaxed, even though she could feel his tension. "I was in a difficult position today."

"You put yourself there," she said.

He didn't move. "I'm not talking about Luther. I'm talking about the band itself."

She wasn't following. "All right," she said, rather tentatively.

"You hired them. You brought them together, and you introduced them to me. I had to establish, right from the start, that they were working for me and not for you."

"But they are working for me," she said. "You and I work together."

He let his arms drop and he sat forward. "No. You work for me, too."

"Josh—"

"You said it, not me," he said. "Ten percent plus a salary to be determined later. That's not a relationship of equals. You work for me."

She couldn't sit anymore. She pushed off the chair and paced around it. "I'm the one who pushed you to perform. I'm the one who decided how this would work. We're taking risks together. I've been taking time away from my real job—"

"No," he said. "You would have had to go to Portland and Seattle anyway to listen to bands for the casino."

"But not Eugene," she said. "Not Newport."

He was silent.

"I'm taking as much of a risk as you are," she said.

"No." His voice was quiet and full of conviction. "No, you're not."

"Josh, if you're going to give me some crap about how an artist risks everything—"

"I failed at this once before." His voice was low, soft. "I won't fail at it again. And one of the things I did wrong was I let someone else control every aspect of my career. I signed bad contracts, I listened to bad advice, and I let someone protect me from my own mistakes until I had only one big mistake left to make. I'm not doing that again. It's my career. You'll manage it. And if that doesn't work, then I will decide what I do next. It's the only way, Emily. The only way."

She was hooked suddenly by the plaintive edge in his voice. She had failed at this, too, once, only in a different way. And she didn't want to tell him about it anymore than he wanted to tell her.

She didn't want him to find someone else to manage the band.

She didn't want to lose him.

Not yet.

She sat on the edge of her folding chair. "You can't make me pay for someone else's mistakes."

"My previous manager didn't make any mistakes," Josh said.

"But you just said—"

"I said I made a mistake. I let someone take over my life. I won't do it again, Emily. I can't."

"I'm not trying to take over your life," she said. "I just want to make sure you have a career."

"So do I," he said.

She studied him for a moment: the bowed head, the hunched shoulders. It wouldn't work this way, and he didn't know that. He had talents, yes, and so did she, but they had to work those talents together, not separately. Together for the same goal.

She put her hand on his. His skin was warm and sun-roughened. He looked down at her hand in surprise.

"I won't be your employee." She couldn't do that again. She couldn't allow anyone that kind of control over her life.

She couldn't be fired just because she was honest.

And right.

She took a deep breath and said, "I won't be your employee, but I will be your partner."

"Then we have to redraw everything," he said.

"No," she said. "Ten percent, plus a salary to be determined later. There are some areas of your career that I don't belong in. I don't need the copyrights. I don't want them. But I do want to be more than a glorified secretary. I have a lot of experience that you don't have. You need me, Josh."

"I know that." He didn't move his hand away. She could feel it, tense beneath hers. "But you can't control me, Emily. You have to let me do things my way."

"I'm not interested in control," she said. "That's what you don't understand. I want to work *with* you, Josh, not against you. Partners inform each other of everything, and then they decide together what needs to be done."

"I've never worked that way before," Josh said.

"To be honest," she said, wondering if she was revealing too much, "neither have I."

fourteen

*J*osh looked up at her. She was beautiful as she sat there, her sharp features pensive, her hand soft on his. He put his other hand on top of hers, holding it prisoner.

Her gaze met his. "Josh—" she said, and he could hear the warning in her voice.

To silence it, he covered her lips with his. She moaned slightly but didn't pull away. He explored her mouth, tasting each part. She leaned into him, putting her free hand on the back of his neck, holding his head in place. The touch of her fingers against his skin was electric; he deepened the kiss.

She tasted of honey and sunlight and something so very her that he couldn't get enough of it.

So that was why they fought. To keep the distance between them, so that they wouldn't be able to explore this, this compelling tie, this warmth, this attraction between them that ran so deep and fine.

He let go of her hands and put his fingers in her hair. It was silky, her ears small against his palms. He pulled her closer, her breasts against his chest, the scent of her enveloping him—

Suddenly she pulled away. Her lips were kiss-swollen, her cheeks flushed, her eyes a bit too bright.

"No, Josh," she said. "We can't."

He was still getting used to her absence, still reeling from the impact of touching her, the way that she had aroused him. He hadn't felt passion like that since he was young, and maybe not even then.

"What?" he managed.

"We can't." She stood up. Her arms were crossed over her chest.

"We're adults," he said, and was surprised at how calm his voice sounded, considering how shaken he felt. "We can do whatever we want."

"No." She turned her back to him. "I didn't tell you why I don't manage anymore."

He took a deep breath, trying to settle himself. This wouldn't continue, at least not yet, not while she had something to tell him. "No, you didn't."

"Ricky Fink. You remember him?"

"Yeah," Josh said, biting back the inevitable *Whatever happened to him?*, a question Josh vowed he would never ask about any artist at any time.

"I was his manager."

He couldn't picture Emily in the grunge music scene. "You were?" he asked, mostly because he was so startled.

She nodded. Her back was straight, but her shoulders were hunched. This still bothered her. And that thought cleared his head. He wanted to put his arms around her, make the pain go away.

"Ricky and I were lovers," she said.

The phrase caught his heart. He remembered Ricky Fink, the grunge artist with the obviously made-up name. He was an angular man who wore baggy pants and ripped shirts. He had a tattoo on his right cheek and he shaved his head.

"You and Ricky Fink?" Josh couldn't stop the question. Or the surprise in his voice.

She turned then, and smiled when she saw what must have registered as obvious puzzlement. "Ricky Fink. His real name was Chet Rickman.

Not something kids could relate to. And he was older than he looked. The grunge thing was an affectation for the band. And it worked."

"You're not going to make me do that, are you?" he asked.

She laughed. "God, no. You'd look as ridiculous."

"Thanks," he said. "I think."

Then he sighed, because they'd have to get though this moment to get back to the moment they had earlier.

"What happened, Em?" he asked.

"Ricky fired me."

He hadn't expected that. He stood, half ready to defend her. "Why?"

"Because I disagreed with him, I think." She ran a hand through her hair, messing its perfect style. He'd never seen her do that before. "I never got a straight answer. I tried."

"He didn't tell you?"

She shook her head. "He had someone else fire me, and I never saw him again. He wouldn't return my phone calls. Or my lawyer's phone calls."

"You sued?"

"No." Her voice was tight. "They threatened to destroy my name, say I did nothing, say Ricky only let me 'pretend' to be his manager."

"But you could have stopped that."

"It would have been very public." She sighed. "I had enough for a case against him for unlawful dismissal, but I didn't want the publicity. Or the reputation. I know how Los Angeles is when people resort to the courts. They never get work again."

"Emily," he started, but she wouldn't let him finish.

"I know, I should have told you from the beginning. I'm not an incompetent manager. I'm not. I managed several bands before Ricky. He just went the farthest. I brought him out of a lounge and introduced him to grunge, and I brokered all his deals." She took a deep breath. "And I slept with him. Which was my mistake."

Her words hung between them, just like the attraction did. Josh felt heat build in his face. He understood what she was saying. If she acted on the attraction between her and him, she could never face herself again.

She could never really trust him—because of who she was.

He struggled to keep his expression neutral. He didn't want to think how she'd react if she found out that he hadn't told her everything about himself. He'd tried in a roundabout way, but he'd never been completely honest.

He had felt he couldn't.

He still felt that way.

His heart twisted. He liked this woman—maybe more than liked her. He didn't like to think of anyone hurting her.

He didn't like to think how he could now hurt her if he wasn't careful.

"Were you still an item when he fired you?" Josh asked, as tentatively as he could.

"It was ending, and I think that's really why he fired me. That, and the starlet I saw him with. They had their photo in *People* the following week."

"And in ten years, he'll be in their 'What Ever Happened To?' issue," Josh said.

Her smile was childlike. "There's that. But it's petty revenge."

"Naw," Josh said. "It's karma."

Her smile remained. It was like a gift. Then she shook her head. "If I hadn't slept with him—"

"Did you love him?" Josh asked, not sure he wanted to know the answer.

"I thought so," she said. "But it was so unprofessional."

"His behavior was," Josh said. "And he paid for it. Once you were gone, Ricky Fink disappeared. I think that would have made it clear to anyone who the business brain was."

"I compromised my professional position," Emily said, "and I nearly did it again. Just now."

He brought his hand up and stroked her face. She didn't pull away. She had courage.

Or maybe she was as attracted as he was.

"This attraction has been between us from the beginning, Em," he said. "If we ignore it, we fight."

"And if we don't ignore it, we'll ruin this chance."

"Not necessarily. The band is the band. We've always known this probably wouldn't be the group to take us all the way."

"It's not the band," she said. "It's the way they'll see us. They'll see me as your girlfriend, not as the manager."

"No," he said. "A lot of people work together and have a relationship. It depends on how we handle it."

She tilted her head sideways. "Is that what we'll have? A relationship?"

He smiled, making sure his expression was gentle. "Isn't that what you want? I'm getting too old for one-night stands."

It felt risky pursuing this. Risky for both of them.

But it also felt right. He'd spent fifteen years running from risk. He had to take some now.

"It didn't work with Ricky," she said.

"I'm not Ricky." He cupped her face in both hands, smoothed her hair back, felt her.

He could see the desire in her eyes. She leaned her head into his palm.

"Let's see what we have," he said.

"If we do this now, we'll never go back," she said.

"Better now than on tour somewhere. It'll happen eventually," he said.

"You're so sure of yourself," she said.

"No," he said. "I'm sure of us."

At that, she moved her head back. The desire in her eyes mingled with sadness. "You're good. You almost had me."

She grabbed her purse. "I'm attracted, Josh. I'd be lying if I said I wasn't. But I can't do this. Not and work with you. There's too many risks for me."

"There's risks for both of us," he said.

"Not in the same way." She kissed his forehead. His skin burned where her lips touched it.

"I'll see you at rehearsal tomorrow," she said, and walked out.

He sat on the chair for a moment, the coolness of the metal seat as real to him as the sensation of her still in his hands. He could smell her perfume on him, taste her against his lips.

Over the years, he'd become a master at hiding his feelings, even from himself. He hadn't realized how much he missed performing until he'd climbed on that bar stage. And he hadn't realized how much he'd been hiding until he started stepping into the light.

He certainly hadn't realized the depth of his attraction for Emily until he kissed her this afternoon. He wasn't lying when he said he wanted more than a one-night stand. He could get a one-night stand by going to any bar in town and playing until closing.

He wanted more.

He had spent the last fifteen years hiding from the world, telling no one who he was, making only casual friends. Being alone, as alone as a human being could be.

She was the first person in a long time to even see a corner of his soul.

He wanted her to see all of it.

He stood. Maybe she was right. Maybe it was too dangerous.

For both of them.

fifteen

Emily walked into her rented house and flung her keys on the counter. She slammed the door behind her, and the entire building shook. The place was poorly built.

She closed the blinds and turned on lights. The house still didn't feel like home. Over two months there, and she felt as if she were living in someone else's place.

Because she was.

She kicked off her shoes and flopped onto the tacky couch. Who the hell did he think he was? Calling her an employee and then kissing her like that? He'd let her talk about partnership, and then he'd taken that to mean she wanted to sleep with him.

She touched a finger to her lips. They still throbbed slightly. Damn, he could kiss. She hadn't gotten that aroused by a kiss since she went parking in high school.

She'd left things unfinished then, too.

She brushed her hair out of her face. The problem was she did want to sleep with him. He'd excited her from the moment she saw him. Very few performers had that sexual quality, and the few that had it usually became stars. She'd analyzed it clinically from the beginning, but only to distance herself.

Because every time she saw his fingers move along the guitar's neck, she wondered how they'd feel moving along hers. Every time he tilted his head and closed his eyes as he sang, she imagined him in that posture in the height of passion.

She kicked a pillow and closed her eyes. No man had ever affected her like this. Not even Ricky.

Ricky.

He'd had something, too—a lot of drive, a lot of ego, and a small amount of talent. He hadn't had any sexuality on stage, which was why she had suggested grunge to him. He hadn't come naturally to it, like most of the Seattle bands. They'd started out in clubs, wearing the clothes they normally wore. He'd wanted to try the Tom Jones type of performance and she'd steered him away from it. Ricky would have looked terrible in a shirt open to his navel, pants too tight. He would have looked pathetic.

The look would have worked with Josh, though, only Josh didn't have the ego that would have allowed it. Josh, his shirt open to the navel, with those moves—

She sat up suddenly, not liking how she was thinking. She couldn't get involved with him, no matter how much she wanted to. Ricky had proven that. And Josh, no matter how much he denied it, had some similar tendencies. If she crossed him once he had power, he wouldn't think twice of firing her.

But he couldn't. She had drawn up the agreement. He'd signed it. He couldn't summarily fire her. They had to submit to arbitration in any dispute. She learned that one after the Ricky Fink incident.

She got up and made herself a cup of chamomile tea. She microwaved the water, then cupped her hand around the mug as she waited for the tea to steep. The warmth soothed her.

The problem, if she was honest with herself, really wasn't Josh. It was her. If it weren't for the mistakes she had made with Ricky, she would be with Josh right now, his hands on her body, that mouth—

"God!" she said, and shook herself to break the image. She was obsessed. Obsessed with a man who was wrong for her. He'd kissed beautifully, knew how to touch her to get the right effect. He'd been a musician before, and musicians, at all levels, had groupies. Hell, he'd had one that first night at that open mike. A man like that had opportunity after opportunity.

Ricky's opportunities had grown as his popularity grew. It didn't matter what he looked like. It didn't even matter that he lacked stage presence.

Imagine what would happen with a man like Josh. A man who was already so good-looking that women stared at him off-stage, when he wore his flannels and dirty jeans. She would constantly be defending herself, as either the girlfriend, or the manager, or both. She wouldn't be able to keep the roles straight, and if she couldn't, no one else would, either.

And that wasn't the worst of it. The worst of it was that she was thirty-one years old, and she'd had only two lovers in her entire life: one a college boyfriend her senior year. He'd been a musician, too, although that had been hard to avoid at Julliard. He'd been a musician, and so had she, and he dumped her when she decided not to pursue her own music career.

Her boyfriend hadn't understood that her business ability had a place in the music world. He thought she was "betraying everything" they had learned. He thought she was selling out.

She hadn't been. She had simply found her place.

She took the teabag out of the cup and took a tentative sip. Chamomile always soothed her, and this was no different. She opened the window, even though the March air was brisk, and let in the shush of the ocean.

She picked men who were bad for her. That was the bottom line. Men who would treat her poorly. And even though she couldn't see how at the moment, Josh would, too.

That was her nature.

She took the cup over to the dining room table and sat. Her father had died when she was two, and her mother had never remarried. She had worked hard to provide for Emily and had always been proud of her daughter.

But there had never been male role models, not really. Her dead father had qualified for sainthood, according to her mother. And that was no real model for anything. Her mother had been an only child, and Emily's grandparents were dead.

Her friends used to tease that Emily was the man in the family. She had the common sense her mother lacked. She had learned business as survival. By the time she was eight, she was managing the family finances, and did well enough that her mother could retire with a large nest egg at fifty-five.

Which had been good, since neither Emily nor her mother had known she had had only three years left.

Emily put her head on her arm. She missed her mother. And she had no one else to turn to. She couldn't even call friends like normal women. Her friends were as driven as she was, as involved in their own lives. They would listen, but they'd tell her what she already knew.

Stay away from musicians, particularly ones she was managing.

Her friends had told her that in the past, and she hadn't listened. Fortunately, they'd all been kind enough to refrain from saying "I told you so."

She'd never encouraged close friendships. She'd always been too busy with work, and what few friends she did make were inside the business. She didn't want them to know about Josh. Not yet.

Still, she almost picked up the phone and called LaTisha. LaTisha was her closest friend, one of her few remaining single friends, and she was as driven as Emily was. LaTisha was an entertainment lawyer, and she knew the dangers of charismatic clients.

But Emily could hear Tish, too. Tish would say, *Not again, Emily. Didn't you learn the first time?*

Maybe she had learned the first time, just not well enough.

sixteen

Rehearsal was half over, and Emily still hadn't shown up. Josh found himself staring at the door as he sang, hoping she would walk in like she had at the Ocean Oasis. Finally, he had called a break. He had never felt emotions like this before—elated that the music was going well and disappointed that he couldn't share it with Emily.

Bobby went outside to smoke. Lisa had gone outside to talk with Bobby. Josh had sent Peter out for takeout at the nearby American-Chinese restaurant. The food there wasn't bad, but it wasn't great by any standards. It was merely filling.

Debbie sat on the edge of the stage, looking at the sheet music and humming to herself. Luther had hidden behind his drums all day. He had seemed sullen and moody, and Josh had been hesitant approaching him.

They had too much to talk about.

The door opened. Josh looked up, expecting Peter and the food. Instead, Emily stood there.

She was wearing a short skirt and the highest pair of heels he'd ever seen outside of Los Angeles. Her legs were long and slender: She was one of the few who could wear skirts that short and look good. When he managed to move his gaze away from her legs, he saw that she wore a suit jacket and a silk blouse. Her dark hair was pulled into a chignon on the top of her head. Tendrils fell in curls around her face.

She looked business-like and sexy at the same time.

Luther whistled. "Whoa, momma. I hope you're going into heavy-duty negotiations with men who think with their other brain."

Debbie looked up from her place on stage, glancing from Luther to Emily as if she expected a scene.

Emily smiled. "Sort of."

"I thought you were overdressed for a rehearsal," Josh said.

"The casino called this morning. They gave in. I get to audition the kid later today. I thought I'd see how easily distracted he was."

"This lady don't play fair," Luther said, a chuckle in his voice.

"That how she dressed for your audition?" Josh asked.

"I wish she had." Luther put down his sticks and got off his stool. "I wouldn'ta cared how hard you tried to get rid of me. I'd always have hopes of seeing this lady dressed to kill."

She shook her head at him. "Would one of you mind getting me a chair? I'd get it myself but my feet are killing me."

"Take off the shoes," Josh said.

"I take off the shoes and I'll never get them back on," she said.

Josh leapt off the stage and went to the racks of folding chairs. He opened one and brought it to her, bowing with a flourish. "For you, mi-lady fair."

She smiled but didn't quite meet his gaze. "Now I see how easily distracted you are."

"I think I hear Pete." Luther climbed off the stage.

"God, I hope so." Debbie slid off the stage, too, and hurried behind Luther. They disappeared out the main door.

Emily sat. "Did I scare them away?"

"I think we did," Josh said.

She tugged her skirt forward, then clasped her hands in her lap. "Look, Josh, about yesterday…"

He didn't like the sound of this. He grabbed another chair so that he could sit next to her.

She waited until he was seated before continuing. "I'd be a liar if I said I didn't feel the attraction. But we can't act on it. *I* can't act on it, not and respect myself later. Ricky—"

"I'm not Ricky," he said.

"It doesn't matter," she said. "The situation is similar enough."

Josh nodded. He understood that, even though he didn't want to.

"Friends, though, Josh?" she asked, and he thought he heard something plaintive in her voice. "Can we stay friends?"

"And partners." He meant that. And maybe as time progressed, they could move onto something else. When she learned to trust him.

When he learned to trust himself.

"And partners," she agreed.

Then Peter, Bobby, and Luther came in with the food. Debbie and Lisa followed. Bobby grabbed more chairs, and Peter laid the food out on it.

"Can you believe the carrots and celery in this stuff?" he asked. "I've never seen so much bogus food. I had to ask if they put MSG in this, because I wouldn't eat it if they did."

Josh smiled at him. "I warned you. This isn't San Francisco."

"Hell, it's not even Portland," Peter said. "I haven't eaten this kinda crap since I was a kid."

"Yeah, you," Bobby said as he opened the cartons. "A man who hails from Eugene, Oregon, cuisine capitol of the good old US of A."

"At least we have decent Chinese food."

"Did you get plates?" Lisa asked. "Or are we supposed to share the cartons?"

Peter reached into one of the bags and removed paper plates and plastic forks. "I had to stop at 7-11 for those. I figured you guys were too wussy to share cartons."

"You should ask before you assume." Lisa grabbed some chopsticks from another bag, then took a plate and served herself deftly. Josh had never seen anyone use chopsticks so expertly. The others watched in awe.

"No wonder she can play all those instruments," Bobby said.

"They're wind and brass instruments," Luther said. "Embouchure is more important than dexterity."

"Huh?" Bobby said.

Lisa turned, holding a shrimp between two chopsticks as if it were a baton. "He means I'm better with my mouth than my fingers."

Bobby flushed from the base of his neck to the roots of his hair. Josh chuckled in spite of himself.

"Leave the boy alone," Debbie said.

"Why?" Luther asked. "He's so much fun to pick on."

Josh turned to Emily. "You want me to get you anything?"

"I'm not helpless," she said. "I'm just wearing high heels."

"I'm offering," he said.

"Sure," she said. "Anything but the shellfish stuff. I'm allergic."

A fact. He clung to it as if she had just told him her greatest secret. And with that, he realized that while she knew a lot about him, he knew next to nothing about her.

"Sure thing." He used the plastic spoons to dish her some chow mien and egg foo yung. He added some rice and something with a lot of beef and carrots. Then he handed that and a pile of napkins to her.

"We missed you this morning," Luther said as he dished his own food. Josh grabbed another plate and waited until the feeding frenzy started to die down.

"I had a few calls to make and some business to attend to," Emily said.

"Well, I was on time," Luther said.

She grinned at him.

"Actually," Josh said, "he was a half an hour early."

"And Josh was waiting for me."

Josh had been. They hadn't said much to each other—neither were real morning people—but they had set up with a professionalism that felt familiar.

Josh sat down in the folding chair beside her. Emily had eaten most of her food already. He suspected she was so active she hadn't been eating much.

"The casino's keeping you busy, isn't it?" Josh took a bite of food. It was lukewarm.

"Right now, it's the paying work." Her tone made it sound like a fact, not an accusation. "I sure wish I was doing something else, though."

"Hard to work with?" Bobby asked.

She shook her head. "Just stubborn. They tell me what they want, and then they do something else, not realizing how it will effect what they hired me for. Which reminds me…"

Her voice grew in power at that last statement and the entire band faced her as a unit. Josh watched the reaction, realized that Emily hadn't even seen it. She didn't realize the power she wielded just by being herself.

"…I'm going to conduct a bitch of an audition this afternoon. I think you guys should come to see what you might be up against."

"I thought we already auditioned," Bobby said.

"It never ends," Luther said.

"I'll bet the Stones never audition," Peter said.

"The Stones don't have to audition," Josh said. "Everyone knows what their range is. But sometimes, even big groups have to play for promoters or studio execs."

Luther was watching him sideways. Josh wondered if he'd said too much.

"That's right," Luther said. "Those performances might be called concerts, but everyone knows what they are. They're auditions."

"That doesn't seem fair," Bobby said. "I mean, isn't there a point when you've paid your dues?"

"No," Emily said. "If members of the Stones quit, leaving only—" she paused, as if she were thinking, "—oh, for the sake of argument, leaving only Jagger and Richards—"

"The main two," Bobby said.

She held up a finger to silence him. "Then let's say they hire some other musicians to fill the void. I wouldn't be at all surprised if they had to have a few performance auditions for the big promoters—or even for a few execs before cutting the next album."

"*Why?*" Bobby asked. "Jagger and Richards are the Stones."

"Yes, they are," Emily said, "and no, they're not. The others contribute enough to change the basic sound. And if the new sound isn't good enough, then the Stones would slip down a level in draw. It's up to promoters to determine that before the audience does."

"Promoters can be wrong," Peter mumbled.

Josh met Luther's gaze. Potential trouble. Bobby's questions were naive. Peter's comment was spoken with a tone of bitterness.

"Sure they can," Emily said, breezing over it. "We're human. But we also serve as gatekeepers. The last thing a performer wants to do is lose his audience, especially over something that might be temporary, like a new band member."

Josh suppressed a smile. So she hadn't missed Peter's reaction after all, and she had turned it, subtly, used it as a warning to him.

"What do you mean," Debbie asked. "A bitch of an audition?"

Emily set her plate under her chair. She sighed and started to run her hand through her hair, then apparently remembered that she had it up, and stopped.

"The casino wants to hire this kid because he's a relative."

"He might be good," Peter said.

Emily nodded to him. "He might be. He also might be a real dog, and if he is, it'll be my word against his family's. The casino has given me permission to audition him."

"Bet that took some work," Luther said.

"Yeah," Emily said, and there was an unspoken story in that word. Josh resisted the urge to put a hand over hers. "The upshot is that a standard audition wouldn't help."

"Because it comes down to opinion." Lisa had finished eating, too, and had leaned up against the stage.

"Right," Emily said. "So I need to be the worst audience this kid has ever faced. The board will be there, and they'll give him encouragement, but I won't."

"You want to break him?" Peter asked.

She shook her head. "I want to see if he can be broken."

"Some good performers can be broken," Bobby said.

"Good performers have learned how to deal with it," Luther said. "There are tricks to maintaining your cool on stage. If he doesn't know them, it'll be devastating to him, and embarrassing to the casino."

"So it's like a test," Peter said.

"That's right," Emily said.

"But it's nothing like a test a surly drunk audience can give a performer." Josh's hands shook. He remembered many a night where the air smelled of pot, and the audience was in a nasty mood. That time he tried country—

"Better to make the mistakes at the audition," Luther said, "and not be allowed on stage until you're ready."

"What about us?" Bobby said. "Did you give us a bitch of an audition?"

Emily shrugged. "I wasn't easy on any of you, but I wasn't hard, either. None of your credentials included 'related to Joshua Candless.' None of you were expecting something for nothing."

"And that's a warning sign?" Peter asked.

Emily smiled gently at him. "That's the biggest red flag there is."

seventeen

The casino on the middle of a Monday afternoon always startled Emily. It reminded her of the middle of the night. A few players were scattered all over the place, mostly retired people. An elderly woman sat at a slot machine, her casino frequent-player's card shoved in the machine and attached to her hip with a yellow cord. It made her look as if she were part of the machine itself. One table of blackjack was half full. At three others, the dealers stood, palms on the table, cards stacked and ready in the shoe. The poker room was empty, and so was the bingo hall. The first game wasn't until 6 p.m.

Emily ducked her head into the box office, and saw Bear. "Your kid ready to go?"

"He ain't my kid." Bear had been opposed to the audition from the beginning, one of the few members of the board who'd made that clear.

"Is he ready?"

"Yeah," Bear said. "As ready as he's going to be. He's nervous as hell."

Emily raised her eyebrows. "Really?"

"I don't think he's ever passed an audition before."

"You don't 'pass' an audition, Bear," she said. "You get the gig. You win the part. It's not a test."

"Sure it is," he said. "You pass or you don't. You get the job or you go to another audition. I don't care what you call it. Either you pass or you fail."

She tilted her head a little. She hadn't realized Bear was that perceptive.

"Hey," Bear said. "I know you're going to give the kid a real audition, but don't be too hard on him."

"Bear—"

"I mean it," Bear said. "Don't be harsher on him than you would on some other performer who comes in from the street. You've been opposed to him from the beginning—"

"So have you," she said.

"—but that don't mean you have to humiliate him."

Her smile was a bit sad. "It's better for me to humiliate him, Bear, than it is for a crowd to do it later."

"Come on, Emily. He's just a kid."

She nodded. "Sometimes kids become stars."

"And sometimes they give up."

"Sometimes they should give up," she said.

"But not everything."

She closed her eyes, remembering the panic she'd always felt before an audition, the nausea, the palm sweats, the lack of sleep. Sometimes sitting in the chair in the audience as a promoter was as hard for her as actually getting on stage.

"Rejection is part of the business, Bear. I can't be responsible for the way he handles it."

"Why not?" Bear asked.

"Because I've never met him before. We're going to have a business transaction, he and I, and it will remain on that level. What happens to him personally is his responsibility. He is an adult, isn't he?" She hoped. She had heard that he might be younger than that.

"Eighteen at least," Bear said.

She shrugged, acting calmer than she felt. "He has to learn the turf."

"God, that's harsh," Bear said.

"Yeah, that's why so few people succeed in the arts. Because it is harsh." She smiled at him, trying to be as sympathetic as she could after those statements. "He'll survive, Bear, no matter what. If I reject him, and this business is right for him, he'll bounce back stronger. If I reject him, and this business is wrong for him, he'll learn now. The worst thing I could do is encourage him when he doesn't deserve it. Someone else will teach him this lesson down the road."

"Sounds like you think he's going to fail."

"I do," she said.

"You haven't seen him," Bear said. "You don't know anything about him."

"Except that his family wants him to get in without an audition. That's always a bad sign."

"Well, give him a chance," Bear said.

She nodded. "I'll do the best I can. Go get him."

"I gotta let the board know, too. They want to see this."

"Warn them that I'm bringing in a few friends."

"To diss the kid?"

"No," she said. "To give me their opinions, and to form an audience."

Bear shook his head. "Don't ever audition me, okay?"

She grinned. "Deal."

She left the box office. The band was standing in the main entrance, near one of the trees. Josh was leaning on the rock beside the escalator, his hands in his pockets. He was staring through the glass doors into the redesigned stage.

"You guys did good work," she said as she came up beside him.

"Acoustics are still off," he said.

"Can you fix that?"

He shook his head. "First thing you learn is that acoustics are like women. No matter what you do, they'll always do what they want."

"I suppose I deserve that," she said.

"It wasn't meant as a dig." He looked at her sideways; then, almost as if it moved by itself, his hand came up and caressed her face. "I'm interested, Em. I always will be. But I respect your decision. It makes sense to me."

His touch was as sensual as his kiss. She leaned into it. "Thanks."

He let his hand linger for a moment, then took it away. She felt the loss like a personal thing.

"When do they want us?" he asked.

"Now," she said.

"I'll get the band."

She nodded and went inside. The casino's sound man was sitting in the sound booth in the center of the bingo room. The seating was set up for bingo, not for a concert, with tables running perpendicular to the stage, and garbage bags hanging off chairs, ready to collect the assorted bingo papers. But the stage was set up and the curtains closed.

So far so good.

Five of the board members sat in the first row, each at a table, with a piece of paper before them. She hadn't asked for their evaluations, but she would get them.

And she would probably ignore them.

She stood by the entrance, hands on her hips. The board members were spread out to give the semblance of an audience. She would do the opposite.

As the band came in, she said, "I want you to sit together. Fill in the spaces in front row center. Leave me the seat directly in front of the stage."

"You're one tough broad," Luther said as he walked by.

"You could handle it," she said.

"Now," he said. "As a kid, you'd have had me for lunch."

And he kept walking. She squinted at him as he hurried down the steps to the first floor. Something was going on with Luther, something she didn't really understand.

Josh walked down the steps with Debbie, talking animatedly about the audition process. Bobby and Lisa were moving together but not speaking, and Peter brought up the rear. Emily waited until they were most of the way down before she stopped next to the sound equipment.

"The kid has you running sound?" she asked Taz, the casino's sound man. He was a slender man in his mid-fifties with a scraggly white beard and a perpetual red mark on the back of his neck from the headphones that he kept wrapped around him like a scarf. He only had them on his ears when he needed them.

Taz shrugged. "He's doing most of it himself. He says he could set up himself, but this equipment is expensive."

"You don't trust him?"

Taz looked at her. "If an eighteen-year-old roadie told me he knew how to work this thing, I wouldn't trust him either. It's my baby, and if something goes wrong, it's not the eighteen-year-old roadie who'd get in trouble."

"Good point." Emily tapped his headphones. "Can you talk to him back there?"

"I can let him know when you're ready."

"Good," she said. "First, I want you to let him know that I'm here. Go ahead."

Taz slipped the headphones over his head and pressed a button on the soundboard. "Charles? The promoter's arrived. I'll let you know when she's ready."

He took the headphones off.

"Charles?" she said.

Taz shrugged. "He hates Charlie."

"I would, too," she said. "Now I'm going to go take my seat. After I do, I want you to wait a full minute before telling him I'm ready. Don't cut that minute short. If anything, stretch it out a bit. All right?"

"You're the boss." Taz slipped on his headphones, but did not touch the button. She walked down the stairs.

The stage area was large. She'd seen it swallow five hundred bingo players, leaving the room looking empty. The place was built to accommodate over three thousand people comfortably; legally it could handle thirty-five hundred. She was determined to sell this place out for Josh's debut, although he didn't know that yet.

She took the only remaining seat at the first table. Josh had the seat directly across from her. Luther, who was slightly taller, took the seat next to him. Bobby, Lisa, and Debbie had the other three seats. Peter had taken the seat directly behind Emily.

They looked like a group of judges at an Olympic event: serious, focused, and imposing. It was precisely what she wanted.

"When's it going to start?" Bobby asked.

"In about a minute." She took a large legal pad from her purse and wrote the date across the top. Then she sat, pen in hand, tapping it against the pad.

"He's watching, you know," Debbie whispered from across the table. She could see into the wings.

"I'm counting on it," Emily said.

Luther shook his head, a half smile on his face. "Tough," he whispered to her, and she took it as a compliment.

Then the house lights dimmed, the curtains opened, and lights swirled on the stage. Taz's deep voice announced:

"This afternoon, we'd like to welcome to Rolling Winds Casino, Charles Wolrige, Reno's foremost Davy Moss impersonator!"

"Impersonator?" Emily snapped, slamming her pen down. No wonder they hadn't told her what kind of music the kid did. She had already told the casino how opposed she was to impersonation.

But the music was coming up, and the kid slid on stage. He had the walk, the moves;, the right clothes. He wore tight jeans and a white cotton pirate shirt untied to the center of the chest. His body was young and unformed, like Moss's had been, promising the man to come. With his hair combed over his face and a judicious bit of stage makeup, he had the look of Davy Moss.

He was singing as he walked. The song was a gutsy choice. It was the theme of the Davy Moss groupies—a sad, saccharine thing about loss and loneliness, about forever, no matter how young the death.

The choice was gutsy, but poor. The kid's voice didn't have the range of Moss's and because Moss still had such a large following, the range was the most important thing.

Josh had leaned back in his chair, his hands rigid on the table. "This is wrong!"

He started to get out of the chair. She had seen this once before, at the bar the night she met him, and suddenly her attention was taken from the kid to Josh.

"It's wrong," he said again, louder.

"Chill, man," Luther said.

The kid was still singing, but he was watching them, and she could actually see the fear on his face.

"Josh," she whispered. She wanted to be the difficult one, not him. She had not realized that his bad behavior in the bar would ever happen again. Maybe she should have.

"I won't chill," Josh said. "You don't understand—"

"I do," Luther said, and grabbed Josh by the arm, pulling him back in the chair. Luther wasn't speaking very loud, but his voice had authority. It cut through the music. "You sit. Now. Going up there is not worth it."

Josh looked at Luther as if a light had gone on in his head. "I can't stay here."

"You'll stay," Luther whispered. "You'll stay because Emily asked you to."

She shook her head, but neither of them saw it.

The kid segued into another sappy number, this one about the smell of a girl's perfume and how it brought back wonderful memories. The range was smaller on this song, and this time, he sounded like Davy Moss.

A terrified Davy Moss.

He was performing, but his gaze hadn't left her table.

Josh tried to wrench his hand free of Luther's. "I can't."

"You don't stay now, you'd better give this whole thing up," Luther whispered. "Cause you'll hear worse."

Josh closed his eyes, the pain evident on his face. Was this one of the reasons he hadn't performed? Because he couldn't abide bad music? The kid wasn't awful. He wasn't even bad. If he got over his fear, he might move beyond mediocre to kinda good.

Was this Josh's way of getting her to pay attention to the kid? His way of making sure the kid had a good audition? Because if it was, it was working.

The kid hadn't spoken yet. In a typical Davy Moss move, he danced across the stage and started a new song. Emily turned away from Josh, deciding to ignore him for the moment. The third song the kid chose was a logical extension of the set. It was a charming number, one of the few Davy Moss songs she liked, about the first kiss and how it warmed the body, the soul, and told the direction of a romance.

It described her kiss with Josh the day before. The way he melted her with a single touch. The way he gently discovered who she was, who they could be together.

Then the song was over, and the kid seemed, with it, to have gained some confidence.

"Hey-ya." His voice broke in classic Davy Moss style. His Midwestern accent was a bit exaggerated, but it was the only flaw she found. "Thought we'd start in a romantic vein, but now we're going to move to something a little peppier."

God, he even had the lingo down. He must have watched a hundred Davy Moss tapes. She shook her head, her mission to drive the kid crazy in the audition gone. She'd let him perform. He was good enough not to embarrass the casino. But she'd also talk to him afterwards. A kid who was good enough to do a reasonable Davy Moss was more than good enough to have a career of his own.

Because Moss had been an excellent musician whose skills were buried in his music choice. He'd done more for pop music than any other artist of his generation. But before he died, he'd tried a few things that had led her—and other music watchers—to believe he'd branch out. The comparisons to Lennon and McCartney were accurate: He was moving from his "Please Please Me" stage to his "Sergeant Pepper" phase. And the "Sergeant Pepper" had seemed much more interesting.

The next song the kid chose was a falsetto riff that Davy Moss did on "Will You Still Love Me Tomorrow?" When Moss did it, it had a saucy satirical sound—and she had once wagered a colleague that Moss had done a raunchy version. She'd won the wager when another colleague had found a bootleg tape from one of Moss's last concerts. His falsetto version was a complete, nasty, send-up of his own music genre.

The kid was singing that version. With such accuracy that Luther had his mouth open. Josh had his head down on the table, his hands over his skull. And as she stared at Josh, she realized that Josh had a lot more similarities to Davy Moss than she had initially suspected.

No wonder he was worried. He'd tried a career some time ago—and had probably been compared, unfavorably, to Davy Moss.

She had two meetings to hold after this audition. One with the fake Davy Moss.

And one with Josh Candless.

eighteen

Josh had his head on the table, his cheek pressing against the Formica, his hands covering the back of his skull. Luther had been right; he had to listen. He would hear worse once he got out on tour. Some Davy Moss impersonator might open for them someday in Vegas.

Josh couldn't go on stage every time and correct the mistakes.

He let his music skills come back, he started to play again, and his perfectionism reared its ugly head. He used to shove band members aside and show them how their parts should sound. Kahn had warned him more than once that such behavior would lose him musicians—and it did—but Josh hadn't cared. He cared about how the music sounded, that was all. And as he was recovering that part of himself, he cared even more.

The kid was destroying "Will You Still Love Me Tomorrow?" Josh had gone after that song when one of his musicians had described it as the perfect pop tune. Josh had sung it falsetto, accenting the word 'love' and turning it into a sexual pun. The version got laughs. But then his brain started turning it around, and he realized that when sung from a male point of view, expounding on the fears that a woman sings about—will a man still "love" her after a making love?—that he had a great satire on his hands.

It became a concert song, something for the fans.

The kid was doing it as a serious piece. Or, if he wasn't being serious, he was screwing up the satirical element.

It was supposed to sound sincere and insincere at the same time. Sometimes Josh even did the song with one of the female band members as a duet. She would sing the song straight, and he would answer with the bogus male part. The laughs he got were always worth the price of covering someone else's music, something he never normally did.

Slowly he brought his head up. The kid was holding the mike too close, staring down at one of the casino board members. The kid was gyrating his hips, Elvis-fashion, something Josh had only done on his early fifties clone pieces.

The moves were wrong. The voice was wrong. The inflection was wrong.

But the look was right. Josh could remember looking in the mirror and seeing a version of that face looking back at him. The plaintive, slightly sad doe eyes; the unlined face; the peach fuzz on his cheeks. The longish black hair. The clothes.

He'd wanted so badly to grow beyond it, and now that he had, he found himself staring at that old face with longing.

He used to say he would never give up these last few years for anything, but he was beginning to wonder. He had buried most of himself when he left Davy Moss behind, maybe even buried much of it before he killed Davy. And he was discovering, the more he played and the more he composed, that he had missed that part of himself. He had missed it terribly. It felt as if he had cut off a limb, as if he had lost his best friend.

As if he'd finally regained a lost love.

When the kid finished "Will You Still Love Me Tomorrow?" Emily stood up.

"I've seen enough," she said.

The kid pulled the microphone against his chest in surprise. A large thunk! echoed through the theater.

"I'll meet you in your dressing room," she said to him. "Bring up the lights, Taz."

The house lights came up. Josh blinked at the sudden brightness. The background music started for "Sadly, Sweetly, Softly," and it wasn't until then that he realized the kid had been using a modified karaoke machine.

"Someone please shut that thing off," Emily said. She turned to Josh. He felt his cheeks grow warm.

"Stay here," she said. "I want to talk with you when I'm done."

Then she turned and made her way to the stage. Someone opened the stage door for her, and she climbed the steps, showing a lot more leg than he had ever imagined she had. She had never gotten a chance to use the skirt. Or maybe she would backstage, to check the kid's hormones.

Josh shook his head. She sure made his buzz.

He sank back into his chair. It was only a matter of time before she figured it out anyway. Better now than later.

"What should we do now?" Peter was leaning in from his chair behind Josh. "You want us to go back to the Eagles?"

Josh shook his head. "Emily wants me to wait, but you guys don't have to. Let's call it quits today, and meet same time tomorrow."

"When do they use that lodge?" Lisa had both elbows planted on the table, and she was looking at Josh—intensely, he thought. Too intensely.

"Nights, I think," he said. "Emily knows the exact schedule. Whatever it is, it doesn't interfere with us."

"Okay," Lisa said. Then she grinned. He hadn't realized she could look so impish. "What'd you think of the impersonator?"

Luther's elbow connected with Josh's ribcage.

"You mean you couldn't tell?" Bobby asked. "I thought the guy sounded pretty close, but Josh didn't. I've never seen him so bugged. You didn't like it, huh, Josh?"

Luther hadn't removed his elbow.

"I don't understand why a musician would work so hard at imitating another musician instead of developing his own sound," Debbie said.

"Maybe he doesn't know any better," Luther said.

"Musicians cover each other's songs all the time," Lisa said. "What's the difference between that and imitating someone?"

"Musicians try to interpret a song their own way," Josh said, ignoring Luther's elbow. "That's part of what music is. Interpretation. I—"

Luther's elbow dug deeper.

"I'm like Debbie," Josh said. "I don't understand why a person would imitate someone else's interpretation. It's like anti-music to me."

"Harsh," Bobby said.

"True," Debbie said.

"Opinion," Lisa said. "That guy could make a career impersonating Davy Moss."

"That guy could make a career on his own talent," Luther said softly. His elbow had left Josh's ribcage. "Davy Moss was a hell of a talented musician. If the kid can do Davy Moss, he's got a lot of talent on his own."

"Davy Moss sang pop music," Peter said with a decided sneer.

"You ever tried to sing a Davy Moss song?" Luther asked. "Not only does it have range, it has style. His material is hard to do well. That's why very few musicians cover it."

"I thought it was because of his signature style," Bobby said. "Hardly anyone covers Elvis for the same reason."

"A lot of people cover Elvis," Debbie said. "You're just too young to have heard all those lounge lizards."

"I wouldn't go into bars without mosh pits anyway," Bobby said.

"When you're old enough," Luther said rather pointedly.

"Yeah, right," Bobby said. "When I'm old enough."

"You'll probably have to go into some without mosh pits when you're performing with Josh," Peter said.

"We have to rehearse somewhere," Debbie added.

"You've been quiet," Lisa said to Josh. He was hoping no one would notice that. He sighed.

"Just thinking," he said.

She stood. "I'd like to go practice some more. You want to join us after Emily slaps you down?"

He grinned. He liked the girl. She was smart. "No. Go ahead. I'll be back on top of things tomorrow."

"All right," she said as she climbed over the railing. "Anyone else want to run through a few things?"

"I'll come," Bobby said, as if it weren't a foregone conclusion.

"I'll chaperone," Debbie said. "You joining us, Luther?"

"In a minute," he said.

Peter got up. "I'll come too. There's a guitar part on 'Music Notions' that I haven't figured out yet."

They trooped out together, talking and laughing. The board had already left, although Josh hadn't seen them go. He and Luther were alone in the huge room—except for the sound man in the back who was fiddling with the machines.

"You gonna tell her?" Luther asked.

"No," Josh said. "I can't. It's almost too much that you know."

Luther shrugged. "I said I wouldn't say anything."

"I know," Josh said. "And I appreciate it. I do. But I can't do this as Davy Moss. There's too much baggage. I just want to be Josh Candless."

"I don't know if you can be," Luther said.

"No one seems to know," Josh said. "The band hasn't figured it out. Emily didn't. I thought maybe I could perform as Josh Candless."

"You might be able to," Luther said. "You're real different now. But that woman's not dumb. When she came to me, she said she thought you had been a performer and quit. She said you looked familiar. She also said you were too good to be hidden in Ocean-lake. I thought it was all hype until she showed me your music. Then I knew."

Josh raised his head. "How could you know? You hadn't seen me."

"Seeing you is confusing," Luther said. "You don't look like that boy anymore. But the music, well, it's a signature."

"Then how come she didn't see it?"

"Because she didn't write songs with you." Luther slid his chair back. He clipped off each word as he spoke it, as if he were holding back emotion. "A man's writing is like his autograph. You have a way of making sixteenth notes that's completely unique. And your music is another signpost. Only Mozart could compose like Mozart, man. And only Davy Moss can write like Davy Moss."

"You thought I'd stolen the music."

"Yeah," Luther said. "I thought you'd found it, and tried to pass it off on your own. Until I saw you."

"You said I look different. Why would seeing me matter?"

"You're not that different," Luther said. "Besides, it's a relative no-brainer. Davy Moss's body was never found. The cops said that's normal for a guy who runs his car into the Payette River. Some bodies are never recovered. But Kahn didn't believe it. He searched for you, did you know that? He searched for a year, and thought he had leads once or twice."

Josh clenched his other fist.

"He never put it together. That money that Davy gave to the Candless family that Kahn could find no rationale for. And the disappearance of Davy Moss." Luther smiled. "And, to be honest, neither did I, until I saw songs composed by a dead kid. By Josh Candless from Edina, Minnesota, who, records say, died in 1978 of leukemia."

"Davy Moss is dead," Josh said. "He has to be, Luther."

"Maybe," Luther said. "The name died. The boy died. But the man, well, he still composes music, still loves it, and still craves perfection in all things. That's your fatal flaw, Josh. You hear the perfect music in your head, and you expect people to play it that way. No one can. Not even you."

"That kid sounded wrong," Josh said.

"The kid was close. He was better than any other Davy Moss imper-sonator I'd ever heard. And you know it."

"His pitch was off, his inflection was off, he didn't understand the songs—"

"He wasn't supposed to understand the songs. He's supposed to imi-tate Davy Moss's interpretation of the songs. It's a different thing." Luther ran a hand through his hair. "What are you going to do if you play in Vegas and there's a Davy Moss impersonator at the casino? Or worse, if one opens for you? No one will get it right. None of them. Hell, I doubt if you could get it right fifteen years later."

Luther had a point. He had a good point. Josh rubbed a hand over his mouth, then sighed.

"What do you suggest I do?" he asked.

"Josh!" Emily's voice came from the stage. He looked up, guiltily, wondering how much she heard. She smiled at him, then came down the stairs near the side.

"Tell her," Luther whispered. Then he stood. "I gotta go. I'll see you in the morning."

Josh nodded. He was reeling from the afternoon. It was all a bit too strange for him, strange and uncomfortable at the same time. Emily came to the table and sat down. A strand of hair had fallen from her chignon, trailing down her bare neck. Her eyes were bright and her mood was high.

"We hired him," she said. "He was good, don't you think?"

Josh shrugged. "I thought you didn't like impersonators."

"I don't," she said. "But it's not a disaster like I thought it was going to be. It was relatively easy and painless. I gave the kid a lecture on music, though, and told him that I thought he'd be a lot better off doing his own work than imitating a guy who's been dead almost as long as he's been alive."

Josh took a deep breath. He hadn't thought of that. He hadn't realized that a whole new generation had come of age since he drove his car into the river.

"I told him he'd have a better long-term chance at a career if he did his own stuff," she said. "But he won't listen to me. He's just happy to have the job."

"Em—"

"I also told him he used his connections the wrong way. I told him that I expected him to be terrible because of the way he approached me." She smiled. "That shocked him."

"I'll bet it did," Josh said.

"I already told the casino to book him for this weekend. And I made them promise they'd never do this to me again."

"Good," he said.

She tossed her head back and smiled. "I can't tell you how pleased I am about all this."

"It's pretty obvious." He glanced at the back of the room. Luther had left, and the sound guy was gone. They were completely alone. "Sorry I got so upset during the kid's performance."

"Next time warn me," she said. "You were an effective distraction, and you made it clear that he could operate with a hostile crowd, but I was surprised. It would work better if we planned it."

His smile was small. "It wasn't planned."

"Josh, you can be straight with me. It was nice, letting me off the hook like that. The board was pleased that I didn't sabotage the whole thing, but really—"

"It wasn't planned," he said again.

She stopped, frowned at him a little, then tilted her head. "You used to get compared to Davy Moss when you performed in the old days, right? That's why you quit."

"No," he said, his stomach turning over. "I used to be Davy Moss."

She laughed. "Nice try, Josh. You can coach the kid if you want, but I don't want it to take any time from your real rehearsals."

"I'm not lying to you, Em," he said.

The smile left her face. Her eyes opened wide. "Davy Moss died fifteen years ago, Josh."

"No, he didn't," Josh said.

"God," she said, and he heard a flutter of panic in her voice. "You're going nuts on me, aren't you? That's why you're here. Because of some psychological problem—"

"Em." He took her hands. She pulled away. There was a momentary pause in which he realized that she would never believe him. Not without concrete proof. She trusted her own instincts too much, and she saw him not as Davy Moss but as Josh.

He made himself grin. Then he shook his head. "Em, I'm sorry. I carry these things too far sometimes."

"It was a joke?" she asked. "You were kidding with me?"

He shrugged, grinned again. "Bad timing."

She put a hand to her mouth. "God, Josh, you must think I'm a lunatic or something. I mean, the way I reacted—"

"It made you forget how I behaved, didn't it?" he said.

She smiled, with, it seemed, relief.

"Em, one of the many things that drove me away from music was my own perfectionism. It came out today, when the kid was performing, and it came out the night you met me. It's a destructive thing. I get into a mode where I feel I'm the only one who knows how things should sound, what they should be. I thought it had gone away, but I had buried it. Not the same thing at all."

"No," she said, "it's not."

"I've got to learn some moderation somehow, or I'll embarrass all of us."

She nodded, serious now. "Maybe some counseling?"

He laughed in spite of himself.

"Wouldn't that be interesting?" Then he shook his head. "I just wanted to apologize. I'll keep an eye on myself."

"If you think that will work," she said, a bit skeptically. She stared at him for a moment, as if she were trying to see through him.

The silence grew between them. And as it grew, he could feel a distance growing, too. She hadn't believed him. He had tried to tell her, and she hadn't believed him.

"You wanted to see me about something," he said.

"I forget what it is now," she said, clearly lying.

He nodded. Then he stood. "I'm glad this impersonator worked out for you, Em," he said, and left.

nineteen

*E*mily rolled over in bed, the covers tangled around her legs. She had been exhausted when she had lain down—earlier than normal—but ever since she had, she hadn't been able to sleep. Her brain kept providing images to her: first of the impersonator, Charles Wolrige, in his Davy Moss regalia; then of Josh as he played in that bar the first night she saw him. And then of Davy Moss himself on all those late-night retrospectives she watched in hotel rooms when she had nothing else to do.

She always watched Davy Moss's fingers.

They moved across the guitar like a lover. They caressed piano keys as if they were touching a beloved. They were long and slender and beautiful.

Like Josh's.

She sat up, pulled her hair out of her face, and clutched a pillow to her stomach. Nonsense. If Davy Moss had lived through that accident, someone would have known. A man that famous couldn't hide forever, could he?

That was the stuff of tabloids: Elvis is alive and living on the Oregon Coast.

She had never seen an article like that about Davy Moss.

Was that because everyone expected Davy Moss to look twenty-two? Elvis had changed over the years. He had gone from dashing to fat, from rugged to middle-aged.

Davy Moss was young forever.

But what would he look like if he had aged?

She clicked on the bedside light. She wouldn't be able to sleep. Not yet. She got up, slipped on a robe, and glanced at the clock. It was only eleven. She had been in bed an hour, thinking. So much for her early—and good—night's sleep. She crossed the hall into the extra bedroom, the one that faced the street, and clicked on the overhead light.

Her computer had dust on it. She hadn't used it much in the last week. She'd been concentrating on the band, probably to the detriment of her work with the casino. These days she did a lot of promotion on-line, through e-mail and the Internet.

God, her e-mail account must be stacked up beyond sanity.

She flicked on the computer, sat in her chair, and logged on. She ignored the chirpy message that told her she had 61 pieces of mail waiting for her, and went to Google.

Then she typed in "Davy" and "Moss." She found several thousand entries. She went to the official club web page. It was all she needed.

There she found several photographs of Davy Moss (Available for Download!) and she studied each one. Davy Moss had been young when he died. His skin was fresh and unlined. He had that round, unformed look often found in young men, and longish black hair—not quite shoulder length, but not quite chin length either.

But it was his eyes that stopped her. They were an intense blue, an electric blue, so vivid that they still seemed alive.

Eyes didn't change.

And in those, she saw Josh Candless.

She sighed and looked away from the screen, rubbing the bridge of her nose with her thumb and forefinger. She was seeing what she wanted to see because Josh had teased her about being Davy Moss, because she had watched a Davy Moss impersonator that day.

Only Josh hadn't been teasing.

He'd been very upset when he watched Charles perform. So upset that Luther, who had once performed with Davy Moss, grabbed Josh's arm and forced him to sit down.

Luther and Josh.

Who seemed like old friends.

You don't understand—

I do.

Luther had spoken with such calm.

I do.

Did he?

She rubbed her face again, then went back to the official website. At the bottom it said it was sponsored by Moss Enterprises, Ltd. Jeremiah Kahn was still managing the Moss estate, covering the information that came out of it. Granting permissions, working with artists.

She went to the section marked *Video* and clicked on the icon. A section of an obscure Davy Moss video filled her screen, a close-up of Moss as he sang, leaning into the mike, his eyes almost alight, they were so intense. Then the camera backed away, and she watched his hands. Long and beautiful like she remembered.

Caressing the guitar like a lover.

She froze the frame. His right forefinger was crooked, his thumbs double-jointed.

Like Josh's.

She unfroze the frame and let the video continue. Then she went to the Davy Moss history section. As if a twenty-two year old could have history. She wondered if there was an official James Dean website and if it was like this. How did people so young do so much with their lives? All she had done at this point was go to school. Julliard was impressive, but hundreds of students went there annually. It wasn't as impressive as climbing to the top of a profession in six years.

My previous manager didn't make any mistakes.

Davy Moss had amazing success.

Fifteen years ago.

I was pretty well known fifteen years ago. That might create a problem.

Davy Moss.

She had said: *You didn't play any pop for me.*

On purpose?

She scrolled down the screen. Davy Moss's background sheet said he was from Minnesota, raised in the affluent suburb of Edina. He'd made his music debut at the age of three. He played every instrument he could by the time he was six, and by the time he was ten, he was performing with the St. Paul Symphony.

He was a prodigy in school, his official biography read, *and his wealthy parents indulged him.*

Josh had said almost those exact words to her that night in his apartment.

How many musicians could play the instruments he did? How many composed? How many were in their mid-thirties with professional experience?

How many had stunning blue eyes and fingers that made love to a guitar?

It went to my head, he had said, *turned me inside out, left me arrogant, stupid, and lonely. And empty. By the end of it, I couldn't write anymore. I was angry all the time, and all I wanted was out.*

I did it wrong before.

I want to know if I can do it right.

Do it right.

Davy Moss.

She knew she had seen him perform before. But he looked so different. Age had added small lines and taken the baby fat from his skin. He had cheekbones now, and a bit of silver in his hair.

And he had muscles. Davy Moss didn't have any muscles.

She turned away from the screen and tilted her head back. Maybe Josh had been so excessively rude to Luther because he had recognized Luther and had seen him as a threat. Maybe they got along like old friends now because they were.

It was preposterous. She had to make several leaps. She had to first believe that Davy Moss lived, and second that he wanted to risk his hard-won anonymity for a comeback.

The official bio said Davy Moss's body had never been found.

He drove his car into a raging river, gorged with spring runoff. It was common to lose bodies in that water. Many were never recovered. They found his car and a ripped windbreaker.

And nothing else.

Davy Moss.

He had lied to her.

She had trusted him, and he had lied.

Like Ricky.

She logged off. Then she picked up her phone.

She didn't know until she dialed that she had decided to call Josh.

twenty

Josh sat at his dining room table, clutching a mug of steaming coffee in both hands. The mug was hot against his palms. It felt good. It made him feel alive.

Emily's phone call had startled him. Her voice, raw and sharp, had come across the line.

"I'm coming over," she had said and hung up.

Nothing more. She didn't need to say any more.

She probably still thought he was crazy. She probably wanted to end her association with the band.

He wasn't sure what he'd do then. The music had wormed its way back into his soul. It had become part of him again. He even dreamed in music now, the notes and chord progressions coming to him in his sleep.

Not that he would be sleeping tonight. He had been pacing when she called, and he would probably pace after she left. How one man could mess up his life like he had messed up his, he didn't know. He didn't even know, really, what had caused it.

The thing he kept coming back to was that he hadn't been prepared for fame, for life, for any of it. All he had been taught how to do was to play music beautifully. And that was all he had done, for twenty-two years.

Then he had driven into the night, on his own, and survived, on his own, for the first time.

He heard her car pull up, but he didn't move. Nor did he question the fact that he now recognized the sound of her car. Sounds were his business. He learned them like he learned faces.

The front door to the building squealed open, and then her footsteps resounded in the tile hallway. Harsh, quick, staccato. She was upset, just as she had sounded on the phone.

He sighed, and brought his head down. Luther had been right and wrong. Josh had to tell her, but only when it became a problem. It hadn't been a problem yet. And if he had worked at it, he might have been able to control his reactions.

The problem was that he didn't want to control his reaction. He wanted her to know about him. He was tired of hiding.

Luther seemed to know that, too.

But Josh didn't want to be Davy Moss anymore. Davy Moss was dead, and he would remain dead. He had to. Josh could never be twenty-two and pretty again. He could not make his living singing only pop tunes, and he couldn't be what Kahn and his associates had made Davy into: an icon. Someone whose dead face covered mugs and posters and T-shirts. Someone who could never change.

Emily knocked, the sound as harsh as her footsteps. He shoved his coffee cup aside and got up, smoothing his hair back with one hand as he went to the door.

He didn't look into the peephole before pulling the door open. He knew it was Emily. Even so, he was surprised when he saw her. She wasn't wearing makeup. Her skin was pale, almost ghostly. Her dark eyes had circles beneath them, and her lips, which he had thought thin each time he looked at them, were actually rather full. It was a trick of make-up that had given her that starlet's face.

If it weren't for her serious expression, he would have preferred this look.

"Come on in," he said, standing aside. She stepped in, her movements suddenly hesitant. Her hair was loose and tangled, trailing in curls down her neck. She wore a blue sweater over a ripped pair of jeans. Her leather shoes were scuffed and water stained.

This was not the Emily of the careful appearances. This was a completely different woman.

"You okay?" he asked, in spite of himself.

She didn't answer. She went into his small kitchen, ignoring the dishes piled beside the sink. "Can I have some water?"

He nodded and grabbed a glass from the cupboard. Then he handed it to her. "It's tap," he reminded her. She didn't flinch, but filled the glass and drained it as if she hadn't had anything to drink in days. Then she wiped her mouth with the back of her hand.

"Thanks," she said, and set the glass beside the others near the sink.

"You okay?" he asked again. He had never seen her like this, so cut off, so cool. It unnerved him.

She raised those haunted eyes to his. "I want you to tell me how Davy Moss died."

He shook his head once. "I was joking—"

"You weren't joking, Josh. I've known you long enough to know when you're serious and when you're not." She pushed curls out of her face. "Tell me how you killed Davy Moss."

He smiled then. "You make me sound like a murderer."

She shrugged. "If you're telling me the truth, you are, in a way."

He had never thought of it that way. He had killed Davy Moss. "If I am, I'm not a very good one. Because Davy Moss will never die."

"We'll see about that." Her words chilled him. He went into the dining area, got his coffee cup, and led her to his ratty living room couch. He sat in the easy chair, sinking down to the springs. He'd been meaning to replace it for months, and hadn't had time. She sat on the edge of the couch, her body barely touching it, as if she were afraid of catching something from it.

"You believe me, then?" he asked.

"I want to hear your story," she said.

"What changed your mind?" he asked.

She tilted her head up, just a little, her defensive movement. "Your fingers."

Whatever he had expected her to say, it wasn't that. "My—fingers?" He held out his hands. They were carpenter's hands, callused, rough, strong. The nails were short, the fingers were long with guitar calluses on the tips, and some scratches and scars along the back, all acquired during a hard day's work.

"They're shaped like Davy Moss's," she said. "You hold a guitar like he does. You move your hands like he does."

"Anyone can learn someone else's moves," Josh said.

"Most of them," she said. "But some can't be imitated, like your damn double-jointed thumbs."

She watched his hands enough to know how he moved. The idea stirred him, made him want to touch her face, smooth away the worry lines. He stood instead.

"Davy Moss," he said.

"His death," she said.

He turned his back on her, went to the window, and lowered the blind. "I've never told anyone this."

"You want me to sign a nondisclosure agreement?" There was sarcasm in her tone. She was angry. That was the emotion she was holding back.

Anger.

His stomach jumped. She might tell. She could tell. If he told her, he was done hiding.

Luther was right. The truth would eventually come out.

"I—" Josh's voice shook. He swallowed. "I had a ranch in Idaho."

"I know. Davy Moss drove his car into the Payette River during spring runoff."

"No," he said. "Let me tell it."

He turned. She was watching him, her hands folded in her lap. She looked prim and disapproving, like his first piano teacher, an old woman who slapped his hands with a ruler whenever he held them in the wrong position.

"I—um—can't explain my frame of mind," he said. "I'm not sure I understand it myself. My folks had died in a plane crash the year before. Kahn was pushing me in directions I didn't want to go. I'd always rebelled, and with my folks gone, the only person I could rebel against was Kahn. Fame came quickly and it isolated me. The women—"

He waved a hand, not having the words.

"Go on," she said.

"The women were interested in Davy Moss the star, not in me. And I didn't know how to make real friends. I didn't know if I could. I hadn't had one since I was a kid. My only friend had been the music."

She didn't move. He had to look away from her. His gaze landed on the wall, on the Magic Marker poster he colored whenever he was on the phone. It was only a quarter done, even though he'd had it since he'd started his trek from town to town. He still didn't talk to many people.

"Somehow I figured out I didn't want it anymore. I don't know how I came to that conclusion. It wasn't an overnight thing. By that spring, I just knew I had to get out. And I'd already laid the groundwork."

He moved to the chair, sat on its arm, and grabbed a marker from the collection he kept near the poster. He didn't color with it. He left the cap on and turned it over and over in his fingers.

"A year before, I'd started sending money to the family of one of my childhood friends, Josh Candless. Josh died when we were ten. He had leukemia. I think it shut me down, his death. We'd been inseparable until then. But I didn't mourn. I just played music all the time. My folks—" he set the pen down, took a breath. "My folks took advantage of that."

He didn't speak for a moment. He never thought about his folks. Never spoke of them. He often felt he hadn't been a child to them, their only child. He had been a trophy, a performing animal, cachet among their prestigious friends. He had been raised by nannies and music teachers. His only contact with his parents had been dinners during which they quizzed him about music, their critiques of his performances, and the occasional praise when he won an award.

"Anyway," he said. "I sent money to Josh's parents. And when I did, I, for some reason, put a lot more in a special account for Josh. I never thought about why or what the money would be for. I got a post office box for a month without letting Kahn know, and the next time I returned to Edina, I went to Josh's grave. I got his birthday, and applied for his birth certificate. Minnesota records still weren't computerized then. They just sent me his certificate. And he became my alias. The first thing I did with it was get a motorcycle license."

"Didn't they recognize you?" Emily was leaning forward slightly, more intent than she had been before.

He shook his head. "Mustache, a long-hair wig, and a baseball cap before they were in fashion. I bought the cycle in Boise. No one there ever thought Davy Moss had come to town. Why would they? I rented motorcycle storage there, and kinda promised myself it would be my freedom."

"When was this?" she asked.

"A year before. Maybe nine months." He picked up the pen again. "Then I canceled the box and threw away the paperwork. And didn't think about it again until a few nights before the accident. I felt—I don't know—disconnected. Acting without feeling."

"What triggered it?"

"I don't know. I don't think the trigger matters," he said. "What happened was one night I was driving my car down 55, the major north-south highway in Idaho, and my car slid on a patch of water—it'd been raining, and I wasn't paying attention. I nearly went into the river then. I pulled over at the next turnout, and sat there until my heart stopped pounding. I knew I had nearly died. I knew I couldn't have survived in that water, in that car, at that point. And that's when I came up with the plan."

He stood again. It felt odd to tell her. It felt odd to tell anyone, but now that he'd started, he couldn't stop.

"The next night, I took my four-by-four to Boise, got the motorcycle, and put it in the truck. Then I drove back to the spot where I had nearly died, and hid the motorcycle in some bushes against a bluff. I figured if the bike was gone when I got there the next day, then I wasn't meant to do anything. But if it was there—well, then, I was free."

Free. The word sounded odd. In some ways, he had become just as much a victim of his death as he had of his life. Only he hadn't minded because he chose it. He chose to travel, to learn how to survive without money, to sleep in bus stations and on roadsides. And each skill he had learned made him the person he was now.

"The motorcycle was there," she said, interrupting him. He hadn't realized he had been silent until she spoke. So much had happened since. He had changed so much.

He had become Josh Candless in those months, those years.

"It was," he said. "It was a dark, rainy night. I put my disguise in the car, along with my Josh Candless papers, and some cash. Then I checked for the bike. When I saw it, I drove back up the road, got my stuff—all of it. I was very careful about that. Then I put my windbreaker in the front seat, put the car in gear, and left the car door open. I pushed the accelerator with my hand, enough to get the car going, then got out of the way. It went down the road, along a steep incline, gathering speed, until it missed the corner and bounced into the river."

His heart had been in his throat. He had stood on the blacktop, resisting the urge to follow the tire tracks to the edge of the road and look down. He had only a moment to decide whether or not to go through with it. One second to choose to remain Davy Moss or become Josh Candless.

"The next thing I knew," he said, "I was running for the bike. I put on my disguise, and my helmet, and I've been Josh Candless ever since."

"They searched for a body," she said.

"I know," he said. "I followed it in the papers. It took months to rule accidental death. It terrified me that they'd find something, that they'd track me. I drove all over the northern half of the country that summer, moving on if anyone so much as stared at me wrong. I didn't settle down for another five years."

Five years. Five years of hiding. Five years while he watched the world he had built fall apart—the unbelievable mourning of his fans, the suicide of a band member, and the sadness—the deep sadness—etched into the face of Jeremiah Kahn.

"Money run out?" she asked.

Josh shook his head. "I still have most of it. I siphoned a small fortune off my very large one. But I couldn't do anything with the money. It would have made me suspicious."

She hadn't moved since she leaned forward. Her hands were clasped together so tight that her knuckles were white.

"A lot of your fans still think you're alive," she said.

"Then they won't be surprised, will they, when they find out that I am."

"You plan to tell them?" she asked.

"I don't want to," he said. "I'm not Davy Moss anymore. I'm not their Davy Moss, and I never was. The music I play is different. The course I'm taking is different."

"Then why tell me?" she asked.

"Because I wanted to." He raised his gaze to hers. "I don't want any secrets from you, Em."

Her gaze darted away. "Luther knows, doesn't he?"

"Yeah," Josh said. "I didn't tell him. He figured it out when he saw the music. He's sharp. He always was."

"Have you told anyone else?" she asked.

He shook his head. "No one, not in fifteen years."

She nodded. "I suppose I should be honored."

He waited. Something in her tone told him that she was not honored at all.

"Shouldn't I, Davy?"

"Josh," he said.

She shook her head. "You lied to me."

"I never lied," he said.

"You never told me." She pushed her hair out of her face. "I asked what you had done before, and you never said 'I was a superstar.' You never said that you were Davy Moss."

"Would you have believed me?"

"Is that the point?"

"No," he said.

She glared at him from under that mop of hair. "I can't do this any-more, Josh."

"Do what?"

"Manage you. Be with you. I can't."

"Em," he said. "I just gave my life to you."

She swallowed, then took a deep breath. "Well, then," she said. "I give it back."

twenty-one

Emily fled. She ran out Josh's front door, down the steps, and out into the night. A mist had started, leaving the air chill. She felt it hard against her face. Strange, but she had never noticed before that the coastal rains tasted like salt.

She stopped beside her MGB and fumbled for her keys. He had lied to her. He had. He had made a complete fool of her.

Davy Moss.

He had forgotten more about the music business than she had ever known. He would have gotten on that stage in July and everyone would have known.

Everyone except her.

She finally found the car key. Her hand shook as it moved toward the lock.

But not everyone had known. The band hadn't recognized him. Neither had the people in the bar. Both bars. It wasn't obvious. He didn't look much like Davy Moss anymore.

And she had even seen the resemblance in his music, in his playing. That first night, she remembered thinking that he reminded her of several musicians, including Davy Moss.

Why hadn't she thought of it before now?

"Emily."

It was his voice. Josh's. Davy's. She turned the key in the lock and pulled the door open.

"Wait, please," he said.

She started to get in when he reached her. He put a hand on the car door. "Please," he said again.

"What do you want?" she asked. "You want me to feel even dumber than I do?"

"I want you to come back inside, Em."

She shook her head. She was cold and wet and she didn't care. She wanted to be as far away from him as she could.

"Em, please."

She yanked herself away from him. "I won't tell anyone, all right? I'll resign tomorrow in front of the band and no one needs to know. I'll even sign something about not revealing your secret identity. Will that satisfy you, Superman?"

"No." He shook his head. "No. I want to go back to the way we were."

"Well, we can't," she said. "Everything has changed now. I can't manage someone like you. I can't deal on that level. I never have. You need someone big to handle Davy Moss's comeback. Someone like his real manager, Jeremiah Kahn."

"I don't want Kahn," Josh said. "I want you."

"You can't have me. You lied to me."

"I lied to everyone, Emily," he said softly. "I told the truth to you."

His words stopped her. She froze in the mist and the dark, shivering in the cold. He had lied to everyone else. And he had told her, of his own free will, who he was.

"Come back in," he said. "Please."

"No," she said. "No."

"It's raining, Em."

She nodded. It was raining and she was cold and she had never felt so odd in her life. Half hopeful and half furious.

"It's not all right," she said. "Just because you told me the truth. It's not all right. Don't you know what you've done, Davy?"

"Josh," he said.

"Josh, then. Don't you know what you've done to the people around you?"

"I can't undo it." His voice was small, plaintive, but always carrying the weight of his emotion. She had never met a man whose voice expressed every nuance of thought—and did it beautifully. "I made my choice fifteen years ago."

"And now you want to come back," she said.

"No," he said. "I want to start over."

"You can't start over." She couldn't believe she was standing in the rain, arguing with him, letting the leather door of her already moldy MGB get even wetter. "You don't need to. You're Davy Moss."

"I *was* Davy Moss," he said, "and I hated it."

"God," she said. The complexities of all this were just starting to hit her. Not of how she felt, but what it meant to be Davy Moss. Davy Moss and Josh Candless, and to have a dream of being in music, of performing, a second time. "You'll run away again. It'll get rough and you'll run away."

"No," he said. "I thought about this for years. I've got to try again. On my terms. No one else's. Mine. I've been straight with you about that."

"Yes," she said, "but Josh—Davy—"

"Josh," he said, with a bit of heat.

"You haven't been on the stage since then. Not really. And it'll come back. All the problems you ran away from will come back."

"I know." He ran his hands through his hair, messing it. It softened his face. For a moment, in the outside light on the apartment building, the outside light and the mist, the edges to his body eased and he looked like the young boy he had once been.

He looked like Davy Moss.

"I've been working through the problems," he said. "Part of the problem was that I hadn't lived my life. I'd been living my parents' life, and then I was rebelling against them. I hadn't made anything with my hands, or seen much of the world. I didn't know what it was like to live from paycheck to paycheck."

"You still don't," she said. "You have money."

"I didn't use it," he said. "I often forgot it was there."

"It's not the same, Josh." She pushed the car door closed and leaned on it. "None of it's the same. You can't start over. You don't need to. You can go back—"

"Davy Moss is dead," he said. "I killed him. On purpose. I can't tell you straighter than that. I don't want to go back."

"But you want to perform again. I told you I could make you famous."

He slowly raised his head. "That remains to be seen, doesn't it?"

"You've got talent—"

"And we both know it takes more than talent."

The confusion had her shaking. "You did it before."

"Did I?" he asked. "Or was I merely going along with someone else's plan? Was it my drive that made me succeed? Or Kahn's?"

How many years had he asked himself that question? Was that why he wanted to try again?

She pushed off the car. "Josh, you say nothing's changed. But everything has. For me. I thought you were a talented man who'd worked nothing jobs all his life, who'd never risen above apartments like this one. Then I find out you've been part of a tiny, tiny subset. Only a handful of people each generation become superstars—"

"I know," he said miserably.

"—and you were one of them. That doesn't reconcile in my mind with Josh Candless."

"Josh Candless never was a superstar," he said.

"But he wants to be."

"No," Josh said. "He wants to be a musician. And that's all."

She put a hand over her face. Her skin was wet from the mist. "If people discover who you are—"

"How can they?" he asked.

"Davy Moss and Josh Candless were friends."

"So?" Josh said.

"Josh Candless died as a child. His parents will testify to that."

"His parents are dead. They passed on three years ago."

"And no one else remembers?"

"So what if they do?" Josh asked. "Where's the proof in that? There can be more than one Josh Candless in the world. I've had this identity for fifteen years. That's pretty established."

"But if I saw the similarities—"

"You saw them after I told you. I won't tell anyone."

"And what about Luther?"

"What about him?"

"What if he tells?"

"Why should he?" Josh said. "He's in the band. And he can leave that if he wants."

"The tabloids pay good money for stories like this."

"Luther doesn't need money. He wants to work with me."

That seemed odd to Emily. She would have to check on it, subtly if she could.

"Em." Josh came closer, put his hand on her shoulder. His touch was warm, and she wanted to lean into it at the same time she wanted to push him away. "If Luther goes to the tabloids so what? It's free publicity. It's a rumor. It's like that whole 'Paul is dead' thing that happened with the Beatles. It may stick, but it will only add cachet, nothing more. No one will know who I am if I say nothing."

"I hope you're right." She put the heel of her hand on her forehead. "You won't tell anyone else, right?"

He smiled. "I've kept the secret for fifteen years. I think I can be trusted to keep it forever."

"I don't know if I'm still going to manage you," she said. "I don't know if I want to talk to you anymore. I've got to think about this."

"Em—"

"No," she said. "Don't. Don't pressure me. You just told me that the sun rises in the west, and I believed you. My whole perception of the world has shifted. I thought you were a nice man. Instead, you tell me that you have lied to an entire nation. Did you know that my little neighbor girl cried for three days when Davy Moss died? I know she wasn't alone. There were vigils for you. People *mourned* you."

"I know," he said.

"And you let them. Do you know what a betrayal that is?"

"Yes." His jaw was set, but his gaze couldn't met hers.

"And after all that, you expect me to trust you?"

"You did before."

"When I thought you were some construction worker with talent. If you can lie about something as big as this, what else can you lie about?"

"You're missing the point, Em," he said softly. "I'm not Ricky Fink."

"I'm not saying you are," she snapped.

"Then give me a chance."

"I gave you a chance," she said.

"No," he said. "You didn't. Davy Moss was an insensitive son of a bitch, I'll grant you that. But I'm not. I've learned. I've grown—"

"It doesn't matter," she said.

"It matters a lot." He took his hand off her shoulder. "I killed Davy Moss so that I could survive, Em. It was like committing suicide without dying. It was a mistake, but it was the kind of mistake that changes your life forever. I can't go back, Em. I can't make it better. I can only make myself better. And part of that is you."

She held up a hand. "Don't."

"I wouldn't be standing here, I wouldn't be trying music again if it weren't for you."

"For me pushing you," she said.

"No. For you believing in me. Not in my image or my marketability. But me." His voice went down to a whisper. "Don't stop, Em. Please?"

She reached out to him. She couldn't help it. She put her arms around him and pulled her to him. How desperate had he been fifteen years ago? Desperate enough to throw everything away. She knew how that felt. After Ricky, she wished she'd been able to do the same thing.

"I'll stay," she said. "But I need to think about what we're going to do."

"Nothing's changed," he said.

"Everything's changed." She buried her face in his hair. It smelled of shampoo and the mist and Josh. It took all of her strength to ease out of the embrace.

The embrace she had started.

"I don't want to be anything more than your manager," she said.

He smiled, but the smile was sad. "It's too late, Em. You're already more. I love you."

She couldn't say anything. She couldn't even move.

He leaned forward and kissed her on the cheek. "See you in the morning?"

"Yeah," she said, and watched him disappear into the apartment building. She stayed in the parking lot for a long time, frozen, not even noticing as the mist turned into rain.

He had caught her, even though she didn't want to be caught. Her heart followed him, bound by the words he had spoken. Not "I love you"—she had heard those before—but "I told the truth to you."

I told the truth to you.

He had her heart, but it was her brain that controlled her actions. It was her brain that got her into her car, her brain that drove her across town, her brain that unlocked her rental.

Her brain reminded her how much her heart had gotten her in trouble before.

I'm not Ricky Fink, he had said.

"Oh, no," she whispered. "For me, you could be much worse."

Part Three

LAS VEGAS, May 1 (AP) – Charles Wolrige won the Tenth Annual Davy Moss Impersonators' contest, held this year at the Luxor Hotel. Fifteen thousand people attended the show. The contest is sponsored by Davy Moss Enterprises and the host hotel.

"I've been doing this for eight years," said Angela Caputo, judge and former Davy Moss fiancée, "and he's the first who actually brought tears to my eyes. He's so like Davy!"

Wolrige, an eighteen-year-old Reno native, received a $5,000 first prize and a one-week performance contract with the casino.

twenty-two

The club was hazy with smoke. Josh leaned against the bar, his elbow resting on the polished wood. Emily was making her way toward the club manager. He watched her walk. In the last two months, he felt as if he had made some headway. He had stayed beside her as much as he could, trying to break down the coolness that had started before he told her he was Davy Moss.

She was afraid of him, he knew it, and not just because of his past. He suspected it was also because of hers.

The attraction remained, though, deep and fine, and once she had gotten over the shock of who he was, she had listened to him about the direction he wanted to take his career. She was willing to try it his way, and willing to protect him as much as she could from his own past.

He couldn't ask for more, even though he wanted more.

He wanted a lot more. Now that his identity was out in the open, he felt comfortable in pursuing Emily. Oddly enough, he felt as if her experience with Ricky Fink echoed his experiences as Davy Moss. They'd both been surprised by other people who controlled their relationships.

They had also allowed someone else to take control of their careers. Now he and Emily were trying to fight back—each in their own way.

The only difference between them, so far as he could see, was that he believed they could fight together, as a couple. Emily, understandably, wasn't so sure.

He hoped to change her mind on this trip. He would certainly try to make the change happen.

Emily was now talking to the club manager and a young woman who happened to be a reporter. Luther stood slightly behind Emily, Peter and Debbie off to her side. Emily had already explained to the band that the first interviews would be with those three. Debbie because she taught in Eugene, Peter because he had played with some national and local celebrities, and Luther because he was a minor celebrity in his own right.

Emily had said she hoped that Josh would be interviewed after the show.

He hoped he wouldn't be interviewed at all. It had always been his least favorite part of the career. But he watched as Emily set up a quiet place for the reporter to take the three, and then he turned to the remaining members of the band.

They had come a long way since March. He was stretching them. He had practiced a wide-ranging repertoire—he wasn't going to get stuck this time as a category artist—and they had kept up. It had helped that Debbie and Lisa had classical training. The only one who had trouble adjusting was Bobby, and it was only because of his youth. He'd also never heard of, let alone played, flamenco guitar. Peter had, but his fingers didn't have the proper dexterity. Bobby could do it, but his work was weak. Josh had spent some late nights teaching Bobby the fingerings and the style. Bobby's flamenco was adequate now, and for this crowd, adequate was all they needed.

Lisa was placing her instruments out in the order in which she'd need them. Josh had designed the music sets. Emily had helped—she had a good sense of how to warm an audience—but Josh also had to consider his band's talents and needs. He couldn't go from difficult guitar part to difficult guitar part. He had to mix styles along with pace. And he had prepared the band to suddenly abandon the play list altogether. The last few rehearsals had been brutal. He'd start them on a set, then toss the set away, and never do so in the same way. Once he'd even brought back a song they hadn't rehearsed since the first week. Everyone except Lisa had coped with that—and Lisa wasn't really at fault. She simply hadn't brought her French horn that evening.

On this night, her French horn stood in the wings—or what passed for wings in this small club—along with her trombone, her oboe, and her flute.

"You ready?" he asked softly.

She paused and rubbed her hands on her thighs. "I've never been this nervous before a concert before."

He smiled at her. "You'll do fine."

She grinned back. "I know I will. But I never cared about a band before. It always mattered more for me to do well than for all of us to do well. Tonight I'm worried about all of us."

So was he, but he didn't want to admit it. This was the first time Emily let them play in public. Josh would have had them play somewhere on the coast, but she wanted a more secluded venue. The coast had too many tourists coming through it. Eugene, which was bigger than any coastal city, was a university town. It had an active music community, but the community only drew from that part of the valley. And the local celebrities, from Mason Williams to the late Ken Kesey, belonged to the '60s. She felt safe having the band perform there. As she had said, if the band failed in Eugene, no one would know. If it failed in Portland or Seattle, the group might not get another chance.

And the coast. She wanted to save the coast for a bash she was throwing at the casino. She hadn't discussed it much with him, but he knew she planned to have both large acts and promoters there. It would be a launch, and she had already started putting it together. He had wanted an approval of who the big stars would be—he was afraid he knew many of them—but she refused. She warned him that he would have to meet old friends as Josh Candless, and he would have to figure out how to deal with them before then.

Sometimes he liked having her know who he was, and sometimes it felt like a burden. She wasn't going to let him run this time.

"You look reflective," Lisa said. "Nervous?"

He grinned. "I guess. It's been so long since I felt this way, I didn't recognize it."

She patted his arm. "We'll do fine."

His grin widened. "We'll do better than fine."

Then he went past her to Bobby. Bobby was practicing his flamenco moves without touching the strings. Josh grabbed Bobby's fingers lightly.

"It's a Zen thing," Josh said.

Bobby raised his head. His cheeks were flushed and his eyes were a bit too bright. "I thought you said the key to performance was practice."

"It is," Josh said, "but on the night of the performance, you must have a Zen experience. You must trust yourself. The practice is done for today. When you're on stage, you have to let the practice come through your fingers."

Bobby licked his lower lip. "I'm afraid I'm really going to mess up."

"All of us are," Josh said.

"Afraid for me?" Bobby asked.

"No." Josh's voice was gentle. He remembered this feeling. He'd had it every time he moved to a new venue. The first time he played rock and roll in a garage, the first time he played in a bar. The first time he played in Madison Square Garden. It all felt the same—at least to his stomach.

"We're afraid for ourselves," Josh said. "It's natural to mess up. And even more natural to worry about it. The key is covering and making sure everything sounds good. That's why I went through so many permutations of so many different things."

"I'm hoping you'll skip that flamenco song."

"I'm hoping you'll enjoy playing it."

At that moment, Debbie came over. Her hair was mussed from running her fingers through it. Josh reached in his back pocket and handed her his comb.

"Bad, huh?" she asked.

"You need to freshen up a bit," he said.

"That reporter," she said. "You'd think she was working for *Rolling Stone* instead of the *Eugene Weekly*."

Instantly Josh froze. "Why?"

"She just asks tough questions. 'Why do you think your band will make it when countless others can't?' She's really grilling Luther. Wondering why he's wasting his talent with us."

Josh swallowed hard. He glanced at Luther, mostly because he couldn't help himself. Luther wouldn't say anything. Luther hadn't so far.

Josh hadn't quite figured Luther out. In the past two months, it felt as if their old friendship had come back, but it was still uncomfortable. Luther had said very little about Davy's death. He hadn't expressed any emotion about it at all. No anger, no sadness, no nothing. And Davy's death had changed Luther's life. He had finished some of Davy's songs, done some studio work for a while, then gave it up and had started writing his own music. He had once told Josh he made enough on the songs and the royalties to live on the coast, in seclusion, forever.

He didn't need the band, but he wouldn't hurt Josh by telling the reporter. Would he?

It was too late now. There was nothing Josh could do except go onstage.

"Well," Josh said. "We'll just have to show her why he isn't wasting his talent on us."

She smiled and headed off to the ladies' room, comb in hand.

Then Peter joined them. He was grinning.

"Good interview?" Josh asked.

Peter shrugged. "I've had better. But Suz is diligent. She works hard."

"You know that reporter?"

"Yeah," Peter said. "I used to go out with her. You'd like her. She never wastes anything."

"I thought she worked for the *Eugene Weekly*."

"She does," Peter said. "But she freelances too. If we make it big, she'll use this interview over and over again. If she likes us tonight, she'll want to talk to the rest of the band."

There was a bit of superiority in his tone, as if he were pleased he'd been interviewed and Josh hadn't. Josh let it slide. Peter gave glimpses of attitude problems, but he never really fell into them. Josh hoped he never would. Attitude was often a screen for greater problems, ones that could create scenes down the road.

"Let's hope she likes us then." Josh glanced at the table. Luther was still talking to her, waving his hands animatedly as he did so. Emily was leaning against a post, listening. She had her arms crossed. When she saw Josh watching them, she smiled.

He felt a curious warmth when she did. He felt that warmth every time she smiled at him—every time she looked at him, truth be told. Yet he hadn't kissed her since that day two months ago, before she learned he was Davy Moss, before she had nearly quit managing the band.

And he hadn't told her he loved her since the night he revealed who he was. She had kept her distance since then. The tentative friendship they had had disappeared, replaced by a strict manager/band leader style. She consulted with him about things, and he consulted with her. They had no personal conversations at all, and she rarely stood near him in a room.

"Don't we have to start soon?" Debbie asked as she came out of the ladies room. Her hair was combed, her makeup was fresh, and her hands were shaking as she handed Josh his comb.

"As soon as Luther gets over here."

"Doesn't our playing take precedence over an interview?"

"Bands never start on time," Bobby said from behind them, then added under his breath, "although I wish we would."

Waiting made everyone nervous. Josh was tempted to walk over to Luther and cut off the interview. Instead, Josh caught Emily's eye and passed a finger across his throat. Emily immediately leaned in, put her hand on Luther's arm, and said something. Luther stood, shook hands with the reporter, and headed for the stage.

"How'd you do that?" Peter asked. "No one can get her to shut up."

"Emily and Luther are pros," Josh said. "They know how to manipulate a situation."

"I guess," Peter said. "If I'd known how to shut Suz off, we'd still might be seeing each other." Then he grabbed his guitar and headed for the stage.

Debbie followed, heading for her keyboard. Lisa picked up her flute, rubbed the mouthpiece with her sleeve, and then approached Debbie. Without being asked, Debbie played middle C and Lisa tuned her flute softly. The movement on stage got the club audience to hush. Peter tuned his guitar, then Bobby went up with his bass, tuning as well. Josh tuned his own guitar offstage. The band didn't start until he joined them.

Luther climbed on the stage and got behind his drum set. There was no name on the bass drum, although Josh had wanted it to read "The Josh Candless Band." Luther had promised to do that if and when Emily put her casino concert together.

The audience grew very hushed. Emily had warned him that this was a listener's club, not a partier's club, but he hadn't believed her. He had hoped for partiers because partiers never listened, they just felt. Listeners could make or break a band.

His throat was dry. It was now or not at all. Either he had a music career as Josh Candless or he didn't have a career at all. Emily looked at him from across the stage. She nodded, rather questioningly, and he nodded back. She rubbed her hands on her jeans, looked as if she had gone slightly pale, and took a deep, visible, breath. Then she bounded up to his microphone.

"Good evening, ladies and gentlemen." She had a stage voice that was dark and sultry. "We have a special treat for you tonight. Fresh from the Oregon Coast, the Josh Candless Band!"

She almost ran off the stage as Josh walked on. The sound of their passage was covered by polite applause. He immediately turned his back on the audience and counted a three/four rhythm to Luther. It sounded spontaneous, but it wasn't. They had planned their opening number very carefully, a piece of good old rock and roll that would get the place shaking. First they had to capture the audience, and then they had to woo them.

The music started around him: Bobby's bass, Peter's guitar, Debbie's keyboard, Luther's drums. Josh turned and faced the microphone half a beat before his opening note. He saw fifty faces, half-lit by candles, raised to the stage. Their eyes were open, their mouths closed, and they all seemed attentive.

Then he closed his own eyes, forgot them, and began to sing.

Thirty-Three

Sweat plastered Josh's shirt to his well-molded chest. His black hair was damp and slicked back, and his electric blue eyes flared like neon across the room. The music rocked and rolled, and the entire club shook. Women leaned forward and men were tapping their feet. And Emily sat at her table in the back, her heart in her throat.

It was working. The music was gorgeous. Somehow it sounded louder, fuller, better in front of an audience. With an effort, she wrenched her own gaze from Josh and looked at the other band members. Bobby was grinning and swinging his bass guitar as he played. Peter was bouncing back and forth as if he were at a Dead concert. Lisa had switched from flute to trumpet, holding its bell aloft as if she were a herald announcing a king. Debbie was pounding on her keyboard and Luther—

Luther was grinning like a man who had finally achieved nirvana.

But Josh, Josh was the center of it all. Emily had never felt such power coming from one man. The hint of it she had had that night in January, the night she first met him, was as faint as a radio signal two apartments away. This was full wattage: Josh on *high*. And, it seemed, no one was immune.

The women in front of her were swaying and clapping to the music. A girl toward the back was standing and dancing all by herself. A group of men near the front were bobbing their heads in time to the music. Even the bartender was watching as he mixed the drinks and guided the cocktail waitresses.

Everyone was involved. It was impossible not to be.

Emily sat back, remembering one of her first concerts as a teenager, with music so loud it was part of her. It was there she learned that music was a physical thing that could evoke more than the soft emotions. It could imitate anger and fear—and sex.

The pounding beat sent a flare of heat through her. At that moment, Josh's gaze found hers and she flushed. She doubted he could see it in the dark, but she couldn't pull her gaze from his. He was stunning when he played. His entire body was a poem. The hard angles on his face softened, and his eyes were like windows into his heart.

And every chance they got, those eyes found her.

She grabbed her Diet Coke and clung to the sweating highball glass the bartender had put it in. She had forced herself to stay away from Josh. Day after day, night after night, she kept herself as far from him as she could. She never spoke to him on the phone except about business and she never stood near him when she spoke to him in person.

It had taken her a while to get over his revelation. She still thought of him as Josh, not Davy Moss. In fact, after that night, she hardly thought of Davy Moss at all. Josh was right: His past didn't seem to make a difference.

Yet.

A shudder ran down her back. The main difference it made for her was a feeling of impending doom, as if one day everything could be taken away from her. This was probably how Josh had felt every day for the last fifteen years.

So far, nothing had happened. So far no one had said a word. She had spoken with Luther and they had made a pact to keep everything quiet, and, except for an occasional comment, that was all.

Josh never said much about it. And he never again told her he loved her. He had just watched her with those intense eyes, and she knew that if she got close, he would burn her with his heat.

She could avoid him during the day, but she dreamed about him every night: erotic dreams, with his hands on her skin, his body pressed against hers, kissing her like he had that first day in the Eagles, his mouth soft and exploring, his taste filling her, the warmth of his body warming hers.

I told the truth to you.

She groaned and made herself drink the cool soda. Those were the dreams she had after rehearsals. Imagine the dreams she would have after tonight.

They finished the song and had a music bridge into the next. The music bridge was Josh's idea; she'd never heard of doing it that way. In this particular bridge, he had Bobby, Peter, and Debbie take the crowd from hard rock through R&B, jazz, and into a popular song mood, all through the weaving of motifs and musical lines that Emily hadn't heard outside of Broadway musicals.

And while they were playing, Josh set his guitar down, grabbed the cordless mike, and sat on the edge of the stage.

His theory of concerts was so simple she wondered why she hadn't thought of it. He believed that concerts evoked a mood in an audience, and that the band controlled the mood. It wasn't right to go from energetic rock and roll to a sad love ballad any more than it was right to go from screaming at someone to kissing them lightly on the cheek.

Most professionals knew this, of course, but she would wager it was instinctual rather than anything taught. And Josh, being Josh, took it to another level. If he wanted to switch moods, he didn't make the change and expect the audience to follow. He led them through a series of moods as if they were traffic lights, and let them arrive at the same mood he did, at the exact same time.

By the time he was ready to sing again, it seemed as if he had brought a big band with him. Debbie was using the keyboard to provide violins, pianos, and harp sounds. The drums came in softly, so faint they seemed nonexistent. Then Lisa's flute floated above the group. Peter and Bobby blended into the shadows, and if Emily closed her eyes, she could imagine herself in a 1940s nightclub toward the end of the war.

Then Josh started to sing. His voice was warm, with elements of Nat King Cole, Harry Connick, Jr., and Frank Sinatra. And yet he still sounded like Josh. She didn't know how he managed that. The music was melodic, the melody singable and almost familiar, the lyrics haunting. She loved the piece, although she'd never told him. It was a song about a man who watched others love and who had never felt that emotion himself.

The piece was filled with such longing—and the music promoted that with the violins, the sustained chords, the sweeping flute line—that every time she heard it, she wanted to go onto the stage and put her arms around him.

And she was not alone. The women in front of her were sighing. Couples had put their arms around each other and were holding each other close.

Then the song ended. Josh bowed his head as the band finished its last sweeping chords.

There was a moment of silence, followed by deafening applause. The entire place shook with the force of it. Emily herself was clapping so hard that her hands hurt. Josh stood and held his hands over the crowd like he was giving them a benediction.

"Thanks," he said, and at the sound of his voice, the applause slowed.

"Thanks," he said again, and the applause died. "You're a wonderful audience."

Some woman shouted from the back and Josh smiled at her.

"We have to take a break now—" he sounded regretful "—but we'll be back in fifteen minutes or so. We hope you will too."

Applause rose around him as he disappeared down the side of the stage. Luther, Debbie, and Lisa followed. Peter and Bobby were already at the bar, getting their complimentary drinks. Emily had arranged drinks and food with the manager, but she had stressed no alcohol. The bartender and the band knew that, and she expected no trouble. They all understood the importance of this first performance. Besides, she had seen too many wonderful bands go the route of addiction after addiction, until both the unity and the music were gone.

It seemed as if the entire club were thronging toward the bar. Emily stood as well, tottered a little on her heels, and then shoved her way through the crowd. As she went, she eavesdropped:

"…never expected anything that good…"

"…what are they doing in Eugene? Man, if…"

"…lead singer remind you of someone?…"

"…hope he's single…."

"…gorgeous…"

"…drummer's been around. I've seen him before…"

"…quite a gig for Peter…"

"…didn't know five people could achieve such diverse sounds…"

She managed to reach the bar with little damage. Luther grabbed her arm and pulled her closer to the band. His skin was damp with sweat, and his hair glistened. Bobby was talking to two young girls who didn't look old enough to be in the club. Debbie was talking to some friends, and Lisa was surrounded by a crowd of young men. Peter was in the corner, talking to a group of people with familiar faces: the local professional music community. Emily recognized most of them, and nodded at them amiably. She knew better than to acknowledge them in this crowd. Most of those folks had moved to Eugene for its anonymity; they had discovered it during the Grateful Dead's heyday and had used it as a base ever since.

But she sought out Josh, and when she found him, her heart sank. He was leaning against a wall, one hand resting casually on a woman's shoulder, another woman standing so close to him that her breasts were nearly touching his chest. Women, five deep, were waiting to talk to him.

His smile was gentle, his mood casual, and he appeared to be having a good time. He clearly finished a story and the women laughed.

"Better rescue him," Luther said in her ear.

"Me?" Emily said.

"If you don't, he'll be stuck there forever and will pass out from heat and dehydration."

"Sounds like you speak from experience."

Luther grinned. "The kid's got it. He always has."

"I don't think Josh is a kid," Emily said.

"Tonight he was," Luther said. "Wasn't he great?"

She nodded. He was marvelous. The women around him laughed again. "You get him. You sound experienced."

"And you sound jealous." Luther peered at her, a light in his dark eyes. "Managers never balk at chick duty."

The flush that had never really left her cheeks grew warmer. She didn't like seeing all those women around him, but she wasn't going to admit that to Luther.

"You just know the way to rescue him," she said.

Luther shook his head. "Kahn always did that."

"Kahn." She was beginning to hate the name. The man was mentioned over and over again in tones mixed with awe, respect, and something darker, something she hadn't been able to put her finger on.

She took a deep breath. The air tasted of smoke and beer, and she nearly coughed it out. Then she tried again. She had to calm herself somehow.

She was Josh's manager, not his girlfriend.

Funny how that plagued her no matter whether she slept with her star or not.

"Joshua!" she snapped, her voice cutting across the crowd noise. The conversation around him died, and he looked at her, a smile in his blue eyes.

"We need you over here," she added, her tone just as sharp, but she had lowered her voice slightly. She hadn't needed its full power.

Josh leaned forward. She couldn't hear him, but she recognized an apology when he saw it. Then he extricated himself from the women and moved toward her, pausing to answer questions along the way.

"You get him outside," Luther said, "and I'll bring drinks and snacks. But hurry before someone sees where you're going."

It sounded as if Luther *had* done this before, but she wasn't going to call him on that. It was too late, anyway. She'd already had the conversation with him.

Josh approached her and took her arm. "Wow," he said as he led her outside, "that was some set, huh?"

"People are talking," she said.

He was warm and damp and smelled of soap. She resisted an urge to run her hand along his arm.

They made it through the crowd slowly, Josh nodding and thanking people for their positive comments. He was smiling like she had never seen him do before—the term *full wattage* came back to her—and that seemed to melt the women around him. He kept moving forward, though, never stopping no matter what comment or question was thrown at him.

When they got outside, the cool air hit like a fan. They were in the Fifth Street Market area of Eugene. The lights here were as bright as day, and the shops, even though they were closed, were brightly lit as well. The trees had white Christmas lights on them year-round, and it gave the area a festive air.

Josh didn't let go of her arm. He hurried her away from the door to the side of the building. They went up half a block toward Skinner Butte. The bed-and-breakfast at the top of the hill was also brightly lit, and the Victorian looked like something out of a movie.

The sky was clear, and she could see the stars glowing faintly against the well-lit darkness.

Somehow Josh's arm had slipped behind her back.

"Em," he said as he turned toward her, pulling her close, "it was so wonderful in there. I'd forgotten."

Then, before she could answer, he bent down and kissed her—the very kiss she had imagined night after night; the kiss she remembered, gentle yet demanding, his mouth holding hers, tasting hers.

Her hands went into his damp hair—she couldn't help herself—and she pulled him close, answering his kiss with her own. He tasted like soda and Josh and she couldn't get enough—

Behind her someone cleared his throat.

She and Josh jumped apart like guilty teenagers. Luther was standing there, holding a can of pop and a bag of food.

"Sorry to interrupt," he said, "but we only have five minutes until the next set."

"It wasn't—" Emily started. She could feel the panic build. She had given in and been caught by a band member. It was the worst thing she could think of. "It isn't what you think—"

"Too bad," Luther said. "Don't you think that's too bad, Josh?"

Josh was standing beside her, his long hair messed, his eyes half closed. He looked like he'd been awakened from a particularly good dream.

He took the can and the bag from Luther. "Thanks," he said hoarsely.

"I'll make sure you have some bottled water on the stage," Luther said, and then left.

Josh set the bag on the sidewalk beside the brick building, then he opened the can of pop.

She stood in the same position, watching as Luther disappeared around the building. Her heart was pounding from fear and arousal. She wanted Josh to put his arms around her, and she wanted to run. It was starting all over again.

He put the can in front of her. "Drink?"

She shook her head.

"Last chance," he said.

She shook her head again.

He tilted his head back and drank like a man who had just come out of the desert. When he set the can down, it was clearly empty.

"I'm not going to apologize," he said. "I could plead the moment, but I won't. I wanted to kiss you, Em."

"I know," her voice came out as a whisper.

"And you wanted to kiss me too."

"Yes." There was no denying that. She had nearly thrown herself at him.

"Then let's just deal with it, this past of yours," he said. "Like we're dealing with mine."

She turned then, and looked at him. Those electric eyes seemed dark in this light, and his face was in shadow. The angles had come back. Her Josh was back: not the performer, but the man.

"You don't know what he did," she whispered.

"Oh, I think I do." He ran a hand through her hair. "I promise that I will always respect you, that I will always listen to you, and that I will do the best by you I can."

"Great words," she said, "but I've heard words before. I can't trust you. Especially after—"

"Davy," he finished for her, letting his hand drop.

"I'm sorry," she said.

He sighed. "I can't change it, Em, and I can't change what happened to you. All I know is that I've never felt this way about anyone before."

"Neither have I," she whispered.

"Then let's give it a chance," he said. "Take it one day at a time. No promises. Either one of us can end it if we want."

"No promises?" she asked.

"No promises, and no expectations. It'll be a start, at least. What do you say to that?"

She couldn't say anything. Not yet. She had to think about it.

He stroked her cheek with his knuckles. She was motionless, knowing that everything was changing here and she didn't quite know how to stop it.

Then he bent down, just enough, his gaze remaining on hers as he silently asked permission to kiss her. She tilted her head slightly, and his mouth came down on hers. He wasn't gentle this time. His kiss was fierce, demanding, asking as much of her as he gave. She melted into him with a sigh and pulled him close.

She had wanted to do this from the moment she saw him, and now she was, and it felt so good.

It felt right.

twenty-four

He'd never wanted a woman like he'd wanted her. She felt so good in his arms. He pulled her closer, wishing they weren't outside, weren't in Eugene, weren't near the club....

The club.

He groaned and broke off the kiss. "Em, I have to get back."

Her eyes were open and bright, her cheeks flushed in the pale street-light. Her lipstick was smeared all over her mouth, and her lips were swollen. She looked well and thoroughly kissed.

He cupped her face in his hand. "I have to go."

"I know." She stood on her toes, kissed him, then wiped her lipstick from his mouth.

"I don't want to," he said.

"I know that too, you liar." She smiled and softened the words. He was amazed how she caught his mood. He didn't want to leave her, didn't want to stop kissing her, but he had to. The call of the stage was too great to walk away from.

"Wait for me, Em," he said.

"I'm not going anywhere," she said, and her smile grew. "I'm your manager."

"No," he said, playing with a silken strand of hair. "Wait for me. Like this."

In response, she kissed him again. It felt as if he had been starving and had finally gotten food. She was so warm, so fragile, so right in his arms. He'd never held a woman who fit against him like she did.

So perfectly.

"Em," he said against her mouth.

She put her hands on his chest and pushed him slightly. Their lips were the last thing to part. "Go."

He did because if he didn't, he would grab her arm and haul her to that bed-and-breakfast up the hill.

He hoped she would wait for him. They had finally made a breakthrough. Finally. He didn't like the terms, but he understood how to approach someone as injured as she was.

One day at a time.

He could do that, for a while. Eventually he would want more. He hoped she would, too.

The key was to keep her in this mood now, not to let her back away. And he wasn't sure how to do that, especially with the second half of the concert ahead.

He went around the building. Luther was standing outside, arms crossed. "About time. Fifteen minute breaks should never go thirty."

"I thought I was in charge," Josh said with a grin.

"I thought you and Emily were in charge until I walked around that corner." Luther clapped a hand on Josh's shoulder. "About time, man."

Josh didn't want to explore that. He glanced at the wall. Emily was coming around the corner, carrying the food he hadn't touched and the pop.

"Nope," Luther said, seeing where Josh's gaze went. "You got work." He pushed Josh toward the door.

Josh pulled the door open and found himself in a hazy, smoky crowd of people. Women touched him, men asked him questions. The band was hovering near the stage, watching for him.

It was like the early days. People didn't know who he was, but they wanted to be near him. Later, it got crazy. He couldn't go anywhere without someone screaming or launching herself at him, or feeling she had the right to kiss him without asking his permission. It got to the point, at the end, where dinners out were in small back rooms of restaurants or in closed restaurants or while he wore a disguise. Otherwise some well-meaning fan would interrupt his dinner asking for an autograph and then others would start. His meal would grow cold, his companion angry, and he would be exhausted.

Even performers needed to get off the stage sometime.

He excused himself as he passed through the crowd—that habit was still as natural as breathing to him—and made it to the stage. As he picked up his guitar, applause started.

The audience was ready.

It was past ready.

He nodded to the band and launched into an rhythm-and-blues number that had both energy and swing. And as he played, he watched for Emily.

She came inside after the second song. Her hair was still mussed but she had somehow repaired her makeup. Her movements were a little slow, as if she were underwater, and she had a slight grin on her face.

The grin reassured him.

She had been so frightened, so worried about any hint of impropriety. During the last few months, he had had Luther check on her and Ricky Fink. The story Luther got wasn't pretty.

Fink—how a man could chose such an accurate stage name was beyond Josh—had gone on a steep decline after Emily left. Much of his career, if not all of his career, had been based on her management. She had created something out of nearly nothing, a grunge band that probably should have stayed grunge. A few records, a few good concerts, and Fink was on his way to a solid national career.

But he had a habit of using women like Kleenex, and somehow Emily had missed it. Luther suspected she had really loved the guy, and Josh figured he was right. Love seemed to do that to people, blinded them to the faults in others.

Fink had used Emily, and then when he had gotten that first taste of the egotism that went with early fame, he had gotten rid of her. Then, when his career went into immediate decline, he had used the press and the tabloids to blame Emily.

She hadn't sued, even though the entire industry knew the problem had been Fink's and not hers. Curiously, that made folks in the notoriously cutthroat business respect her more. It was as if she had set a new standard by refusing to sink to Fink's level.

But Fink had damaged her career. She couldn't get another management job. There were too many rumors, too many risks for a new band to get involved with. She had turned her attention to promotion, and had seen the niche of building local casinos into Vegas show palaces. They hadn't the skill to hire the right kinds of acts—and so many of these places were unwilling to hand the management of their entertainment lineup to an outsider. She saw the opening, and instead of permanently working for a casino, she trained them to be their own promoter.

It was working. Her reputation was solid here—partly, Luther said, because she hadn't had a relationship since the now-passé Ricky Fink.

The crowd was applauding and Josh realized he hadn't paid much attention to the last song they did. Amazing. He had been looking forward to this for weeks and touching Emily had blocked the music out.

Or enhanced it, he wasn't sure.

They had been doing beat-heavy music since they started. It was time to shift. He gave the band a signal that he thought he wasn't going to use—a signal to let him do a solo piece. He had thought he would need that signal in case the audience was cold.

He hadn't realized he was going to use it because he needed to communicate to Emily.

"We're going to slow things down for a moment," Josh said. "Cuddle up to your sweetie. I'm going to play you a love song."

Out of the corner of his eye, he saw Luther start. The only love songs that Luther knew of were Davy Moss songs. Emily, in the back of the room, looked up in fright.

Bobby brought him a stool from the bar, and Lisa put a mike stand in front of the chair. They did that in a heartbeat. Josh sat on the stool, put his feet on the rung, and signaled the bartender to lower the lights. The stage had a single spot. He planned to use it.

He went up to the keyboard, played the C below middle C and hummed as he made his way back to the stool. Then he did something he'd never done—at least not seriously—since he started performing.

He covered someone else's material.

A cappella.

He found Emily, who had her arms crossed and was leaning back in her chair. Then he smiled at her, and started into one of his favorite old standards, "A Kiss to Build a Dream On."

He sang the first verse slowly, emphasizing the words, singing about the importance of a single kiss.

The audience started to applaud with the familiarity. He nodded at them as he continued into the second verse.

And then he looked at Emily.

Her mouth was open, and she brought her fingers to her lips, as if remembering the very kiss he was singing about. When he finished the third verse, a trumpet came in over the refrain—and he turned to see Lisa doing the Louis Armstrong version, the difficult trumpet line, and doing it well. Luther came in using brushes, and then Debbie brought in a piano accompaniment. Bobby shrugged at him, and Peter stayed out of the way.

Josh smiled at them, and let them build the music bridge into a jam session, something that belonged in the hot, smoky club. They had gone from a six-piece rock band that played odd music to a four-person jazz band in the space of a heartbeat.

Then he turned back to Emily. She was standing, her fingers still on her lips, and he didn't know if she was watching as his manager or as the woman he had kissed a moment ago.

The trumpet soared and the drum beat was sure and steady. Debbie's piano was soft, as if they had practiced this a hundred times before. The spotlight had moved to Lisa for the moment—Josh wasn't sure how the bartender did that—and she stood in the back of the stage, a tiny goddess doing Armstrong's part justice.

They played for about six minutes, building on each other. He didn't move from his stool as they moved easily into jazz improvisation. Then, after they had played for a few minutes, Lisa returned to the melody, playing it once. Debbie followed, and so did Luther. As they hit the refrain, Josh nodded to them. Lisa played it, complete with glissando, then with a flourish brought her trumpet down.

The spot swung to Josh just in time, just as he repeated the vocal bridge—the center of the song—singing about how he'd remember the kiss whenever he was alone.

Together the four of them wound the song down. He finished the final verse, and then the trumpet, keyboard, and drums built to a finale.

At the end, the audience was on its feet, clapping and whistling and cheering. He couldn't see Emily anymore, but he could sense her, that stunned surprise and that fear on her face.

"Now what, Romeo?" Luther asked him in a normal tone, a voice that couldn't carry to the audience.

"'Swing Town,'" Josh said, signaling Peter and Bobby to get back on stage. He took the stool away himself while the audience continued to applaud. His lack of attention seemed to make them even more frenzied. The only way to stop it would be to play.

And play he did. He came back with his guitar, using its back to give the others the beat, and then, instead of playing, he started scat-singing the opening of "Swing Town"—something he'd done at home, but never in rehearsal. It threw Bobby—Josh could hear the bass pounding to catch up—but the others followed just fine.

That quieted the audience, and they were his, song after song, number after number.

He played until his fingers were sore and his throat was parched. The place had become a heat factory, and some of the audience members had moved tables to create a dance floor. No one left, and more people arrived, and he suspected they were way over fire code, but no one seemed to care.

He played until the bartender stopped it all by shouting last call and getting booed by everyone in the place.

"No, no," Josh said, chastising them. "It's time to call it a night."

Then he signaled the band to start what was going to be their final number, a lullaby waltz called "Sunset on a Summer Evening."

When they finished, they bowed in unison and the audience whistled, and cheered, and applauded and applauded and applauded.

"They want more," Bobby said.

"I know," Josh said, but he couldn't do anything. The club was closing. Instead, he waved and bowed again, then shouted, "Thank you! And good night!" and hustled off the stage.

This time, he used the door into the storage room, knowing he had to escape the crowd.

Luther and the rest of the band followed him in.

"Man, oh man, oh man," Peter said, "that was a hell of a high."

"I didn't screw up too bad, did I?" Bobby asked. "I never heard you sing like that on 'Swing Town.'"

"I hope you didn't mind the trumpet coming in on your solo," Lisa said.

"That was brilliant, just brilliant," Luther said.

"The moment that defined us," Debbie said.

Peter shook his head. "They were with us before that."

"They were with us from the first song." Luther clapped Josh on the back. "You haven't lost it."

"Lost what?" Bobby asked.

Josh flushed.

"That boyish charm of his," Luther said, as if he hadn't blundered at all.

"Now that's a reference that eluded me," Bobby said, "but then I feel as if half this concert eluded me, and I was part of it. When you said be ready for spontaneity, I never thought we'd jam."

"I did," Lisa said. "And I'm glad that we had the chance."

"I never expected you to do a cover, though," Luther said. "An inspired, romantic choice, I thought."

Josh smiled, the awkward moment past. "Thanks."

"But I gotta tell you, that's not a love song."

Josh raised an eyebrow. "Here we go again."

"I mean it," Luther said, and as he spoke the room got quiet. Somehow the others sensed the change of mood. "It's not a love song."

"You mean the Hammerstein?" Debbie asked. "'A Kiss to Build a Dream On?'"

Luther nodded.

"He's right," Debbie said. "It's not a love song. It's about the possibilities of love."

Luther nudged Josh. "At least it's not about sex."

Josh looked at him and shook his head. "Are any of the songs we're doing about sex?"

"Lyrics or rhythm?" Luther asked.

Bobby blushed as the door opened and Emily came in. Her hair was still disheveled from her encounter with Josh earlier. She looked at him first, then looked away, then looked at him again.

"No one wants to leave," she said. "The bartender is conferring with the bouncer on how to get people out of here. They want you on stage some more."

"If we stay here, they'll go," Luther said.

She nodded. "But you have to wait. One view of you guys, and they'll go nuts. I've never seen anyone wow a crowd like that."

"I have," Luther said quietly.

She gave him a warning look at the same time Josh did, but none of the other band members seemed to notice. They were all crowded around her.

"So they liked us?" Bobby's voice rose a little on the last word.

"They didn't just like you," Emily said. "They loved you. If you play like this every time you go out, I can sell you anywhere. They didn't care what kind of music you played. They just wanted to hear it."

Josh grinned. He had known he could trust an audience to go with him, as long as he eased them through the transitions. No one liked to go from Metallica to Chopin. But Metallica to Beethoven wasn't as much of a stretch, if the players picked the right Beethoven piece.

"This is marvelous," he said. "Just marvelous."

Then the door opened again, letting in a roar from the crowd, and the reporter popped her head in. She saw Josh and two spots of color rose on her cheeks. The bartender's head appeared above hers. He looked harried.

"I couldn't keep her out," he said.

"It's fine," Emily said. Then to the reporter, she added, "Get inside."

The reporter came in and the bartender slammed the door shut. There was yelling outside as they tried to clear the club.

"What are you doing in here, Suz?" Peter asked, with the tired weariness only a longtime lover could sustain.

"I need to—I—I—" She smiled at herself, then shook her head. "I had said I might want to interview the rest of the band depending on what I saw. Well, I saw a near riot out there. You have something, Mr.—Candless, is it?"

Josh nodded. The nerves that had plagued his stomach all day had returned.

"And I'd like to talk to you about it." In the full light of the storage room, he realized she wasn't as young as she had appeared out front. Her eyes were sharp; she seemed to miss nothing. He wondered what she was doing as a reporter for a such a small local paper, then remembered something Peter had said about freelancing.

Josh swallowed. He glanced at Emily. She shrugged, then helped him out.

"You said the rest of the band?"

"Well, Mr. Candless at least."

"If you interview four of the six," Emily said, "you may as well get the rest."

"Right," the reporter said. "But it's really Mr. Candless."

"It's okay, Em." Josh had to face all sides of this job sooner or later. Better now.

"They'll want us out of this club pretty soon," Luther said.

The reporter shook her head. "The staff has about an hour's worth of cleanup after the last customer leaves. They said we can stay through that."

"Lucky us," Peter muttered just loud enough for her to hear.

"It's all right," Josh said. "You can start with me, but I'm afraid it'll have to be in here."

She smiled at him. "That's fine, Mr. Candless. Come with me, so that we can have some measure of privacy."

Emily raised her eyebrows. Apparently the reporter hadn't asked this with any of the others. The reporter headed toward some crates near the side of the room. As she did, Josh turned to Emily and made a gesture they'd already agreed on. It meant: *Help me keep this short.* She nodded once, and Josh followed the reporter to the crates.

He sat down across from her, and as he did, she touched his hand. "You were electric, Mr. Candless."

Her fingers lingered a moment too long.

"Thank you," he said, then eased his hand out of her reach, slowly, as he had been taught years ago. The slow movement seemed casual, less likely to give offense.

"I'm sorry," he said. "We were never properly introduced."

"Suzanne Phane," she said. "I write for the *Eugene Weekly* and I've freelanced for such publications as *Rolling Stone* and *The LA Trib.*"

Wonderful. She was a concert reviewer. He wasn't sure how he felt about that.

"I'm sorry I didn't interview you earlier," she said. "It's just that I see so many bands, and most of them are—you know—local."

"We're local, Ms. Phane," he said.

She shook her head. "Not with Luther Tigoro, you're not. And Peter could always have done more if he really wanted to. And you, Mr. Candless. You're quite a surprise."

"I am?" he said.

She nodded. "A man like you—a performer like you—undiscovered at your age. It seems odd, doesn't it?"

He swallowed again, and hoped she didn't see the nervous bobbing of his Adam's apple. "Not when you consider I spent most of my adulthood as a contractor."

"Yes, that's what Luther said. Forgive the rude question, but how does a blue-collar worker gain the musical knowledge you have?"

He and Emily had decided he wouldn't lie. He would just express the truth sideways, and leave out much of it. "My parents thought I was musically gifted. They pushed me at a young age."

"And then?" she asked.

He shrugged, made the movement seem casual. "I thought it wasn't for me. I came out here, learned a real trade. It wasn't until I met Emily Lukovich that I even thought I had a chance, at this age, with my background."

"And that was in January?"

He nodded.

"You came this far since January?"

"I've always played music," he said. "It's kind of like a drug, you know? You can't really give it up. So I had a music room at home. It was just for me."

"Then how did Ms. Lukovich discover you?"

"I got mad," he said. "In a bar. I decided to teach a bad lead singer a lesson. Emily was there. And she talked me into this."

"Such a story, Mr. Candless." She said the sentence with just enough sincerity to make him nervous. He couldn't tell if she was being coy or honestly surprised. He almost asked, *Don't you believe me?* and then bit the question back.

The silence was momentarily awkward—and then he stood. "I'll bet you want to talk to the others."

"Actually—" she started, but he turned away before she finished, signaling Bobby to come on over.

He did, and as Josh passed him, he whispered, "First interview, kid. Good luck."

"Thanks," Bobby said and continued forward.

Emily was standing by the door. She had it partially open and was peering out. "Coast is clear."

"Good." Josh took her hand and escaped the storage room. The club was empty except for the bartender, the cocktail waitresses, and the bouncers. He took her to the side of the stage, and then he kissed her, slowly and thoroughly.

"God," he said pressing his forehead against hers. "I've wanted to do that since the start of the second set."

"Mmm," she answered, and kissed him back. Something had changed in her, and he welcomed it. It held a promise that he liked, a promise of more than simple kisses in the dark.

"What do you say we head back to the hotel?" he whispered.

"The others—" she said.

"Can find their own way back. It's only a few blocks from here."

She closed her eyes, and he could feel her emotional shift as if it were his own.

"I can't," she said, and her voice held weariness, as if she had expected this from him and was disappointed he had done it. "It's my job."

His heart leaped into his throat, but he didn't allow himself to panic. Instead, he kept his voice calm and didn't apologize. Apologizing would be bad.

He stroked the side of her face. "I get ahead of myself. Why don't I walk back, get a little air to clear my head, and meet you in my room?"

"Your room?" She sounded startled. And her startlement made him suddenly less sure of himself.

"If you want," he said.

There was a heartbeat, a small heartbeat, where he wondered if he had misinterpreted everything, if in his high from the concert he had suddenly forced her into a position she didn't want to be in.

"I want," she said softly.

He smiled. "Meet you there," he said, kissed her once for luck, and then left the club.

twenty-five

It took Emily fifteen minutes to get the excited band out of the club. She wasn't trying to hurry them.

She needed time to think.

She had said yes to Josh so quickly, as if the idea were already planned. And she wanted to go back with him.

She wanted it desperately.

She was just so afraid.

But he had said one day at a time. He had promised no expectations. And if she kept that in mind, she might be able to go to him.

The band took the van back to the Hilton. The van was stuffed full of people and equipment. After a good night's sleep, they would drive back to the coast, and they would practice more while she found them more performing venues.

This one had been a huge success.

Her hands were damp and they slid on the wheel as she drove. It was ridiculous to drive the few short blocks to the hotel, and if she didn't have all the equipment, she wouldn't have.

Behind her, the band was chattering amiably, Bobby complaining that he never got to use the flamenco guitar parts he had learned, Lisa ribbing him about learning a new instrument, Debbie teasing Lisa about how her talents were wasted on the tambourine.

Emily was too preoccupied to participate. She drove into the parking structure beneath the hotel, and parked beneath a light, wishing that the van had a security system. She reminded the members to take their valuables with them, then tossed Peter the van keys, and she went inside without saying another word.

Her heart was pounding as if she were going to a job interview. She had never had an assignation like this. Her dates before Ricky had followed a traditional pattern: She had gone to dinner or dancing or whatever, and then passion had swept her to bed with the man—or the lack of passion had stopped her, which was more likely. Ricky had seduced her after rehearsal one day in the dressing room of a large theater, and from that moment on, she had spent many of her waking hours with him.

Things were different with Josh.

So different.

She had never been so thoroughly and erotically kissed, and then had to wait—or wanted to wait. She had never realized how anticipation could build.

And fear.

And doubt.

Her heart was ready.

Her mind was holding her back.

As always.

The lobby of the hotel was empty except for a sleepy-looking clerk and a maid who was vacuuming the red-and-black carpet. Emily ignored them and got into the elevator banks. She knew where Josh's room was; she had booked it herself. The band didn't know and didn't ask where the money was coming for this. She knew that it was coming from Josh's savings.

The Josh Candless Band was being funded by Davy Moss.

She wondered if he appreciated the irony of this.

She got on the elevator and hesitated a moment. What if Josh had changed his mind? What if he had only been caught up in the moment, and had decided that he didn't want her after all?

Then she realized she was being silly. He had made his intentions clear from the beginning.

She was the one who'd been stopping anything from happening.

And she would have continued to if he hadn't said, quite seriously, *Then let's just deal with it, this past of yours, like we're dealing with mine.*

Were they dealing with his? The two of them? They hadn't talked about it much since the day he told her, and she wasn't sure if she had factored it in. Josh seemed like Josh to her, not some former superstar. He seemed too normal for that.

But still, his words had resonated within her. They were right. She couldn't run forever, and she was clearly attracted to musicians. She would have this problem until she solved it.

Better to solve it with Josh.

She wanted to solve it with Josh.

He made her feel like no one had before, not even the great Ricky Fink. Josh made her feel alive in a whole new way.

She got off the elevator and walked down the hall to his suite. Hotels had a different feel late at night, almost as if a person could hear the other patrons sleeping. The silence seemed to make their presence stronger.

She wondered if they knew who was staying in the corner suite, and if they did, if they cared.

Or if they knew why she was walking down the hall right now.

By the time she reached his door, she was breathing shallowly and her fists were clenched. Her nerves were so taut she wondered if her body was warning her away. But the rest of her didn't feel that way. The rest of her wanted to be with Josh, to finish what they had started in the club.

She knocked.

There was a pause, and during it, she almost turned away. What was she doing there, anyway? Then the door opened, and Josh was standing in front of her.

His hair was wet and slicked back as if he had just showered. He was wearing a blue shirt and clean jeans. A wave of steam and soap floated into the hallway.

She touched her own clothes, nervously. They smelled like smoke and the bar. She hadn't thought of cleaning up.

"I didn't—I haven't—"

He smiled, but didn't say anything. He held out his hand. She took it, her fingers shaking slightly, then he led her inside the room.

The suite was big, with a wet bar and a glass dining room table near the door, and a couch and chairs around a large screen television set. The bedroom was through another door. The place was full of flowers. A bottle of champagne was open and breathing on the table, two crystal glasses beside it. There was also a plate of cheeses, another plate of crackers, and a plate of chocolates on the table.

He closed the door with his foot and kissed her. She turned her head toward his. He was slightly damp from the shower, and very warm. She hadn't realized how cold she was until he held her in his arms.

Then he pulled back. "Chocolate? Champagne?"

She shook her head. He looked uncertain, almost young, as if he were sixteen and this was a first date.

"Maybe later," she said. Then she took his hand and led him into the bedroom.

The lights were off, but he had lit candles all over the room, giving the room a soft glow. He had sprinkled rose petals all over the king-size bed. The room had the faint scent of crushed flowers.

"Josh…" she said, her voice thick.

"Is it all right?"

She nodded, her grip on his hand tight. "No one has ever done anything like this for me before."

He smiled, and it seemed to light his face from within. "Good. I wanted to…"

He didn't finish the sentence. Instead, he kissed her softly and ran his hands along her side. Tingles ran through her, and she pulled him closer. His kiss deepened and became all consuming. She had never felt like this, as if the nerve endings all through her body were on fire. She had to touch his skin, she wanted to touch his skin, she wanted to feel his skin against hers.

She tugged his shirt from his jeans. He reached down and caught her hands in his.

"Not yet," he said.

"Now," she whispered against him.

He smiled. She could feel his lips move. The skin around his eyes crinkled, too, revealing fine lines she had never seen before. He wasn't young, not really, but he seemed that way.

She slipped her hands away from his and unbuttoned his shirt. His chest was hard and muscular. She slid the shirt off his powerful shoulders, trapping his arms in the sleeves. Then she kissed his lips, his neck, and let her lips trail down his chest. He groaned and struggled free, undoing her shirt and stopping when he reached the lacy teddy beneath.

He slipped his finger under the lace, brushing her nipple and sending heat through her. Then he pulled the teddy over her head and cupped her breasts. They felt sensitive, almost like someone else's. He ran his callused thumbs over her nipples and the sensation was exquisite.

"Josh," she said, and pressed her body against his. The sensation of skin against skin, soft against hard, was almost more than she could bear. Somehow her pants came off, then his jeans, and she stepped back, wanting to see him naked for the first time.

He was perfect in the candlelight. Broad shoulders tapering to narrow hips. His legs were long and muscular, his arms corded and strong. Combined with his dark hair and his brilliant blue eyes, and she was beholding the man of her dreams.

"God, you're beautiful," he said, and it took her a minute to realize that he had even spoken. She had been thinking the same thing about him.

Then he wrapped himself around her, his hands roaming from her back to her buttocks. His touch made her frenzied, his fingers—their mixture of strong and callused—were like an aphrodisiac. She moved into them, arched into them. He eased her onto the bed, and she pulled him with her, opening her legs for him. He hesitated for just a moment above her. She wrapped her arms around him, pulling him down, putting her mouth on his as he slipped inside her.

Electricity flared between them, and just when she thought she couldn't be any more sensitive, she became all liquid sensation. He moved within her and she moved to match, her mouth all over him, his mouth all over her. Almost instantly she had a small orgasm, and he paused, looking down at her.

It wasn't enough. The sensation was all she lived for, having him inside her was overwhelming. She started moving again, and so did he, and it built and built and built until she couldn't stand it anymore. He kissed her breasts and she climaxed again, but even that didn't satisfy her. She put her legs around him, pulling him closer, driving him deeper.

She had never been touched this way. She had never been held this way, with this mixture of passion and gentleness, urgency and consideration. Each touch, each movement aroused her more. He moved inside her and she made him move harder, faster, harder—they were following her rhythm, not his. Then she built to a place she had never been before, a place that felt as if she were on the edge of something greater than anything she had ever experienced, and she could only feel it with him, she could only be with him. She moved harder and faster beneath him, and he moaned in her ear. He was whispering her name as if it were sacred, as if he couldn't say it enough—

And then she shuddered into a climax. She arched and he arched to meet her and his body emptied into hers, and they cascaded into oblivion—together.

twenty-six

He was giddy and exhausted and exhilarated all at the same time. He pulled Emily closer. Rose petals stuck to his back, and in the dim recesses of his brain he decided that what was romantic wasn't always comfortable. Then he realized it might be fun to pick the petals off each other.

She felt so good against him. This was the feeling Luther had tried to describe to him so long ago. This fear mixed with joy mixed with a warmth he had never felt. He almost—almost—told her he loved her, but he couldn't. Not again. She wanted to go slow. He would. He didn't want to scare her.

Especially tonight, especially after the first concert, after the first time they were together. Showing her how he felt had to be enough.

He stroked her hair. She looked marvelous in the candlelight. Her breasts were fuller than he expected, her waist narrower, and her legs as spectacular as ever. She was the most beautiful woman he had ever seen.

He pulled her closer. She sighed and rested her head on his chest. He still wasn't ready to sleep. Even after the concert, and now this, he felt curiously energized, as if touching her had somehow made him stronger.

"You hungry?" he asked.

"Yeah." Her voice was soft.

He didn't want to move to get the food. But he did. He kissed the top of her head, then stroked her hair away from her face. Then he slid out from beneath her. She leaned up on an elbow and kissed him on the lips, then watched him walk into the suite's other room.

She had insisted he book a suite—especially when she learned he could afford such things—because she wanted him to try all the trappings of his past life. She wanted to catch whatever problem that was going to arise before it arose on a national scene, and she thought the smallest things might be a trigger. So he booked a suite, not bothering to tell her that the suites in Eugene, Oregon, were small compared with the ones he'd stayed in, the places the size of apartments, in New York, Los Angeles, Sydney, and London.

He grabbed the plate of cheese and the plate of crackers, then brought them in and set them in front of her on the bed. She grinned at him. He held up a finger and went back to pour them both glasses of champagne.

When he came into the bedroom, she was already eating a small cracker sandwich. She wiped the crumbs off her fingers onto her leg, and then shrugged.

"Hungrier than I thought," she said around the cheese. He laughed and handed her a glass of champagne.

"To us," he said, knowing it was a bit daring, but unable to keep completely silent.

She took the glass, stared at the bubbling amber liquid for a moment. His heart stopped. Mistake, he thought. He'd made a mistake and this night would crash around him.

Then she raised the glass. "To us."

He clinked his glass against hers and they both drank.

"Mmm," she said. "Good champagne."

He smiled at her. "Only the best," he said, mirroring her words in planning this trip.

He brushed some more rose petals aside—they both were covered in them—and then sat on the bed. He took one off her, crushed it, and smelled the combined scent of Emily and roses.

"I'm glad you came up here," he said. "I wasn't sure you would."

She smiled. "I wouldn't have if you hadn't said we could go day by day. I needed to hear that."

Some of his elation faded, but he didn't allow himself to show it. He had said they could go day by day. He meant it. He also meant to make each of those days worthwhile.

She wasn't looking at him. "And then you said we needed to deal with my past, too. I hadn't thought of that. Here I was telling you to deal with your past and then you say it to me. I hadn't realized I was—hiding—behind it."

He kissed the hollow between her shoulder and her neck. "Were you?"

She nodded and buried her face in his chest. "You scare me, Josh." Her voice was a bit muffled. He could feel her breath on his skin. "Your past, your secrets. Your talent."

His hand shook as he stroked her hair. "*I* scare *you*?"

She nodded.

He leaned his cheek against the top of her head. Her hair was damp and silky. "Em, I haven't been myself since I met you. I was content to work and play my music in secret."

"You were playing before a crowd when I met you."

He smiled and ran a hand down her back. "I did that sometimes when I couldn't contain myself any longer, but I had myself convinced it was an aberration."

"Wasn't it?" she asked.

"No." His forefinger traced her spine. She shivered and snuggled closer. "It was as if I were a pressure cooker, releasing steam so that I wouldn't blow."

"You didn't blow, Josh," she said. "You were sane and strong when I met you."

"No," he said. "I would have snapped eventually, and done it in typically messy fashion. You coaxed me out of my shell. You gave me my music back in a way that I can live with for the rest of my life. And you did it gently."

"I just like nurturing talent."

"And that was something that Ricky Fink nearly stole from you," he said. "I hope I never meet him."

She sat back enough so that she could see his face. "You might. He's on the downward slide. You play clubs on the way up and on the way down. And he likes the Pacific Northwest."

"Well, try to avoid booking us in the same place, all right?"

Her smile was soft. "Deal."

He nodded, then took another sip of champagne. "He's not going to be in the big concert, is he?"

He was asking about the concert at the casino, the one she was planning. She hadn't been willing to tell him much. She wanted to let the whole band know together. All she had told him was that she was going to book some major acts as well as some unknown ones, and bring promoters in. The pretext was to get the promoters to see the casino's performing space. In point of fact, she wanted them to see the Josh Candless Band.

"When I said big acts, Josh," she said, taking another cracker, "I meant big acts. Not someone with a name who's on his way out of the business."

He sighed softly. He had been a bit worried about that. He know that Rolling Waves was a small casino, and he knew that sometimes the best laid plans didn't take that into account. He also knew she'd been working her tail off on this concert, putting in twelve-hour days between it and the band.

"You really think we're good enough for this?" he asked.

"After tonight, I think you're more than good enough. After tonight, I think this group has the potential of going all the way." Then she winced. "If we didn't screw it up."

"We?" he asked.

Her expression was fearful. She put her hand between them, moving the fingers back and forth. "You, me. This."

"You're the manager, Em. Nothing will change that."

"They won't think as much of me," she said.

He smiled. "They already think we're lovers."

"What?" she asked, and he could feel her shock.

"I overheard Peter and Debbie one afternoon. Debbie was complaining that she couldn't meet men through the band."

"She should wait. Now that you're doing concerts—"

"I know," Josh said. "But she didn't. And Peter asked her about me, why she wasn't interested in me."

"And why wasn't she?"

"Because, she said, I'm already spoken for. Couldn't he tell? And he said, you mean Emily? And she said, is there anyone else?"

"They didn't," Emily said.

Josh nodded.

"When was this?" she asked.

"The second week of rehearsal."

She leaned back and set down the cracker she'd been holding. "That long? Honestly?"

"Honestly." He waited. He wanted her to see that it had made no difference.

"They thought—did you say something?"

He shook his head. "Not a word."

"And they don't mind?"

"Why should they?" he asked. "As long as the work gets done, as long as the rehearsals go well, the concerts go well, and we can all do what we want."

"But if they have problems, they should feel free to come to me."

"I think they will," he said. "But they've known from the beginning it's the Josh Candless Band. You and I started it. We were a team before they joined us. I think they still see us that way. Whether or not we sleep together is our business, not theirs. And if we keep things in business at a strictly business level, then they should be fine with that."

"And treat all band members equally?" she asked.

"More or less," he said. "In all the bands I've known, the band leader gets slightly different treatment."

She grinned. "In all the bands I've managed, the band leader *expects* slightly different treatment. He doesn't always get it."

He smiled back, then took her hand. "What I'm trying to tell you is that we'll be all right."

"I hope so," she said. "It didn't work that way with Ricky, and I got burned."

"It seems to me," he said slowly, not sure how defensive she would be on this topic, "that Ricky manipulated you and his band. He didn't play fair with any of you, from what you discussed. That's bound to burn anyone, but it also puts you in a no-win situation. If you're close to him, you're part of the problem. If you're not close to him, you're also part of the problem. A man like that can't take responsibility for anything. He manipulates others into taking that responsibility for him. You did. You still carry it. You blame yourself."

"I do not," she said.

He raised an eyebrow at her.

She sighed. "All right. I do. But I was his manager. I should have seen the problems coming."

"I thought you did see them," he said.

She ran a hand through her hair. "I did."

"And at that point, your relationship with Ricky went sour, from your point of view."

She raised her eyes to him. They were open and vulnerable, a way he had never seen her before. "How did you know?"

"Logic," he said. "You told him something he didn't want to hear. What was worse is that you believed it. He knew, deep down, he would either have to listen to you or he would have to change your mind. You're a strong woman, Em. Changing your mind, especially when you *know* you're right, is very difficult. He decided instead to discredit you."

"Which you could do," she said, "just as easily after tonight."

He shook his head. "Not without discrediting myself, and that's what Ricky didn't understand. He lost all his credibility when he destroyed yours. That, and his unwillingness to change his musical style, is why he's on his way down."

"Not everyone goes up," Emily said. "And no one goes up all the time."

"I know," Josh said. "I'm ready to ride the wave. Now."

She nodded. "We have some things to do this next month."

"Business already?" he asked.

She flushed, then shrugged. "One day at a time," she said, and there was a pleading tone in her voice. They had strayed perilously close to discussing their future as a couple. It was clearly more than she could handle.

He was lucky she was still here, lucky she was still talking with him.

Lucky she hadn't followed her instincts and run.

"One day at a time," he said, trying not to sound reluctant.

She smiled. "We have some things to do. More performances in towns like this. Close enough to drive to the casino, but far enough away that we don't hurt the local draw."

He wondered if she knew how beautiful she was, sitting there naked, talking business to him, cracker crumbs and rose petals on her skin.

"Sounds good," he said.

"And I want you in a studio. We need to produce our own CD."

That got his attention. He leaned back. "Em, shouldn't we wait until someone approaches us?"

She shook her head. "This is the part of the business that has changed, Josh. We can produce our own in Newport and sell it at our concerts. If the CD is good enough, it's another open door. You want a major label to distribute your work. And they will if they like what they hear."

"I suspect this will be expensive," he said.

"Not nearly as much as it would cost in LA," she said.

"Small comfort." He took her in his arms. He loved touching her, loved the feel of her against him. "You like to spend my money."

"Actually, I hate it," she said, "but it's a necessity early on."

"And getting me into the studio is one more test," he said.

Her arms wrapped themselves around him. "One more test," she said, "before the big one."

"The casino concert is just a concert," he said.

She sighed. "Josh, you might know some of the performers I book. And you don't know who'll be in the audience."

He had thought of that, but only in passing. Never with a firm concentration, almost as if his mind skipped over it.

"I'll handle it," he said, and wondered if he lied.

Part Four

SEATTLE, June 20 (AP) – Grunge musician Ricky Fink was arrested this weekend for inciting a riot. Fink, former leader of the Ricky Fink Band, was asked to leave the stage of the Sweat Heat Club. He refused, and punched the club's bouncer. Then Fink appealed to the audience for help. Fighting broke out, damaging furniture, equipment, and fixtures. The club's owner says repairs will cost nearly $100,000.

Fink, whose real name is Chet Rickman, was released on bail. A court date has not yet been set.

twenty-seven

$\mathcal{E}$mily sat at her desk in her rented home, computer humming beside her, pen in hand. She was bent over a yellow legal pad, scratching figures. She had finally decided to forego her computer program and try the math by hand. Sometimes that led her to find mistakes in her calculations.

She raised her head. The sun was setting over the ocean, bathing the town in orange and pink light. Oceanlake's beauty was amazing and seductive. Especially in June. The entire month had been beautiful. She could see how Josh had lived here for so long.

Josh. She braced her chin on the palm of her right hand. He had been right about the band. They hadn't cared that she and Josh had become lovers. They didn't even seem to notice the difference.

Except Luther, of course. He had smiled gently and had murmured his approval—to both of them.

She had been content to go day by day. Josh had put no pressure on her, never repeating what he had said before, and she had never told him how she felt.

She hadn't even told herself.

If she didn't pay attention to her feelings, she figured, it would be easier when the end came. And there would be an end. There always was.

It would probably come after the big concert a few days away.

Josh would get offered a contract, and he would find a new manager, someone with more experience.

He would leave.

Or she would. Her job at the casino was done after this.

But right now, she had more pressing matters than her relationship with Josh. She had to figure out who to substitute for the fifth act.

Singlet Seven was one of the hottest bands in the country, and replacing them wouldn't be easy. She had what she had thought was an iron-clad contract with them—she had been warned about their propensity for canceling at the last minute—but she didn't have the time or the energy to take them to court for breach of contract. At least, not right now, not in the last few days of concert planning. She would when this whole thing was over, and she told their manager that in no uncertain terms. He seemed unconcerned. He apparently got those kinds of threats all the time.

Especially with a band that irresponsible.

What they didn't realize was that each time they canceled, they offended fans all over the country. Fans tended to get more irritated when they planned their vacations around an S7 concert, as so many had here. Anger the fans too many times and they would stop buying the group's CDs. It was only a matter of time.

She had decided long ago not to manage bands like that. Their career trajectory was usually a sharp upward peak followed by a long and painful downward spiral.

She sighed. Darkness had fallen on Oceanlake while she'd been thinking about Singlet Seven. She reached up and closed the blinds, then flicked on the overhead light.

Managing S7 must be a nightmare, but it wasn't hers. What S7 had done to her was hurt her credibility with the casino and make a potential wreck out of the concert. She had four other headliners: Marbles, the hottest R&B band in the country; Jennifer Shin, country music's Singer of the Year; old favorites Shaul, on their reunion tour; and the Country Kitten Band, an eclectic folksy country group that had been together for thirty years. S7 was supposed to bring in the pop crowd. Without them, she was stuck.

She didn't know any group that wasn't booked months, sometimes years in advance.

She scratched her head with the pen. The math had her head swirling. She had billed this concert as a day of music, gambling, and fireworks. In addition to the five main acts, she had planned four minor acts and one unknown—the Josh Candless Band. She knew she was risking everything by putting them in such company. What she was communicating was this: The Josh Candless Band could compete *when it started* with performers that had been on the stage for thirty years. One promoter had already applauded her arrogance when he saw the publicity, and his tone had led her to believe that he thought she was crazy.

He'd see how crazy she was.

She stood and took a deep breath. The computer and the sun had heated the space until it felt like an oven. She reached under the blind, slid the window back, and let the cool ocean breeze correct the situation.

The gamble was what the dealers at the casino called a smart bet. She knew how talented the band was. She knew Josh and Luther could match the other performers in both talent and experience, and they wouldn't let the performance get out of hand. She also knew that, even if most of the promoters she had invited didn't show, word would still get back to them. The managers of the various groups might actually try to steal the Josh Candless Band from her, and a few of those managers acted as scouts for studios as well. She was doing her best, with her limited resources, to launch Josh right.

And she wanted nothing to go wrong with this concert, so of course something went wrong right before the thing started. The cancellation of S7 made things hard for her. She couldn't get another band of the same quality—unless there was a fluke—and even if she did, there was the matter of the upfront fee she had paid to S7. She would get the money back. If she didn't, she would definitely take them to court and win; their business manager understood that much. But that didn't help her in the short term. The casino had money, but wouldn't give her enough up front until she had proven herself.

This concert was supposed to prove everything she had been saying. The cancellation had reinforced the casino's prejudice against-large name acts. She hoped she could rectify that—and soon.

Her other option was to issue partial refunds. She had done the math on that, too, and with the upfront fee (and subsequent loss of interest) paid to S7, a partial refund would cause the concert to lose money. She could ask Josh to forego his fee, but even doing that wouldn't make much of a financial difference.

"Still doing math?" Josh was standing behind her. She hadn't heard him come in. Not that she minded. She had given him a key about a month ago.

For business reasons, she had thought at the time, even though he rarely used it for that.

She turned to face him. She knew she looked a wreck: her hair tangled and her eyes lined from lack of sleep. He, on the other hand, had a vibrancy that seemed to grow the more music he played. The closer the concert came, the more Josh seemed to shine. That charisma—that *Joshness*—that she had first seen in Eugene had become a part of his everyday persona, almost as if the light that flickered within had grown to a flame.

She stood and slipped into his arms. He held her tight. He felt good; his strong shoulders were perfect support for her head. She could fall asleep standing up, secure in his arms.

"You need to get more rest," he said.

"I can't rest until I get this figured out."

He stroked her hair and pulled the pen out from behind her ear. "Luther's here."

She blinked, at first not able to understand what he said. Her mind was whirling with numbers and percentages and grosses. "Luther?"

Josh nodded. "He's been doing some calling around. I hope you don't mind."

"I don't mind," she said, wondering what Luther could do that she couldn't.

"Good," Josh said. "Luther, in here."

He came wandering back. He had shaved his head especially for the band, wanting a new look for the new century, he said. Curiously, his bald, shiny scalp made him look younger. "This is some spread."

"Wish it was mine. The casino's giving it to me while I'm here."

"They need to update the furniture, slap a little paint on it, and it'd be a perfect bungalow."

She nodded, waiting for whatever Luther had come to tell her.

"You've been spending too much time in this room," he said. "I gotta bottle of wine out front. Come relax with us."

"Luther, we've only got a few days until the Fourth. I'll relax on the fifth."

"She'll collapse on the fifth," Luther said to Josh. "You need to make her slow down."

Josh grinned. "I can't make her do anything."

"You'll work yourself to death, girl," Luther said, "and then you won't enjoy the show."

"I won't enjoy it anyway," she said. "Not unless we can get an act as big as S7."

"Big, but not good. Don't know if I can help you there," Luther said.

"She means box office," Josh said.

"I know what she means. I think that band would've screwed us one way or another anyhow. Better to be rid of them now." Luther didn't enter the room, but instead stood back and pointed to the hallway. "You coming for that wine?"

Emily smiled. "I'll leave the computer, but I won't drink."

"You'll drink," Luther said. "This is hundred-dollar-a-bottle wine. I don't open it unless we all taste."

"Spendy," Josh said.

"What are we celebrating?" Emily asked as she followed them into her living room.

"Good friends, good times, and good opportunities." Luther went to her cabinets as if he'd been in her place before and pulled down three wine glasses.

"Luther " Emily started, but he glared at her, and she was quiet.

The bottle was small and the label colorful, but she couldn't read it from that distance. He poured the amber liquid into the glasses, then brought one to her.

She was going to just hold it, but the fruity bouquet of the wine tempted her. She'd had expensive wine before—hundred-dollar bottles and up—and they were always exquisite. Wine was one of many things in life that improved with price.

She sipped and Luther clapped. "Step one," he said to Josh.

Josh nodded, then sipped himself. "Wow."

"Wow" was a good term. The wine was fruity and tart at the same time. It started dry and had a sweet finish that was so smooth she could almost swear she was drinking nectar.

Luther took a sip himself. Then he smiled. "Excellent."

He swirled his glass, took another sip, and topped it off. Then he came to the couch and sat beside Emily.

"Did Josh tell you what I did?"

"He said you made a few phone calls."

"More than a few," Luther said.

"I've been making calls for days," Emily said. "I can't find anyone."

"Of course not," Luther said. "You're in the wrong position now. No one's going to tell you they've been rained out of July 4th. They want to sound busy, involved, *wanted*, if you know what I mean."

"I know what you mean," she said, more annoyed than she expected to be, "and I called old friends. They'd be up front with me."

Luther leaned back. The couch squeaked beneath his weight. "Would you have been up front with them? In the same position, I mean."

"Sure," she said. "They're old friends."

"So," Josh said. "You told them how you were planning to launch the band."

"No, of course not," she said, and then paused. She took another sip of the wine to hide her sudden embarrassment. "All right, you've made your point. What'd you learn?"

"That three rather large bands are available for the right price," Luther said.

"The problem is none of them are pop," Josh said.

"And only one appeals to young adults."

"Who's that?" Emily asked.

"Kassidy Four," Luther said.

Emily smiled at him. "You almost had me going. I thought you were on the up-and-up."

"I am," he said.

"Kassidy Four's been booked for nearly a year."

"That's right, and the venue they were performing in got sold and is now being torn down. The concert's canceled, Emily," Luther said.

"Who're the other two?" she asked.

Luther and Josh exchanged glances. They almost seemed as if they were trying to decide to tell her.

"Josh?" she asked.

He tilted his head toward Luther.

"Luther?"

"The other two bands are New World and Modern American Diplomats."

She shrugged, seeing nothing wrong with either band. "They're both very good."

"Yes, they are." Josh spoke quietly. He had set his glass of wine on her scarred coffee table. "They also have former members of the Davy Moss Band."

Her stomach jumped and then turned. This was a problem they were going to run into—they were always going to face it. She had to get used to that.

"And you think they'll recognize you?" she asked.

"We don't know," Luther said. "We just don't want it to happen at the first concert."

She rolled her wine glass between her palms. Its smooth glass surface felt good against her skin. "Obviously I'll contact Kassidy Four first. But if they can't perform, what then? Are you asking me not to call these other two bands?"

"No," Josh said, a touch too quickly. "But we want you to know the potential problem."

"We can't avoid members of the Davy Moss Band forever," Emily said. "We will encounter them if they're in the business."

"I know," Josh said.

"I think this first big concert is going to be difficult enough without Josh being distracted," Luther said.

"He'll be distracted." Emily took a sip of the wine. It didn't soothe her, but the rich taste was a distraction. "But the issue isn't the concert. It's the old band members. Josh, you attacked Luther when you saw him in an attempt to make him go away."

"I won't do that," Josh said.

"You've done it before."

Josh leaned back in his chair and put his feet on the coffee table, narrowly missing his glass of wine. "I won't, Em. I promise. I'll have myself under tight rope."

"But not too tight," Luther said. "Otherwise the music will suck."

Josh didn't even acknowledge the comment. He was watching Emily. She sipped her wine again, trying not to let him see that his gaze was making her uncomfortable.

"You'd like to call them, wouldn't you?" Josh asked.

She nodded. "We need a headliner. We can't afford the refunds. I don't want this concert to be a bust."

"But if the band performs well," Josh said, "it won't matter what the casino thinks of your job performance."

"It matters," she said. "I do the best job I can. Right now, I'm being pulled. I can't do a good job for the band and a bad job for the casino. I have my own future to think of."

"What does that mean?" Josh's voice had a bit of an edge.

"Mmm," Luther said, standing. "I need to get rid of some wine." He left the room.

Emily waited until he was down the hall. "It means that if, for some reason, I'm no longer managing the band, I have something to fall back on."

"Em, I'm not Ricky Fink."

"I know." She finished her wine. She had drunk slightly too fast and she was a bit dizzy. Although that could also be the exhaustion. "But we could have creative differences down the road, or we might decide—together—that I don't have the skills to bring you to the next level. In those cases, I might want to go back into consulting. And I want to have left on a high note, not on a failure."

"The concert won't be a failure."

"Not for you, or Luther, or the band. Probably not for the others as well. But if we don't have a headliner, the casino could lose some substantial revenue. And if it does, it might affect our case against S7."

"You're suing them?"

"If I have to," she said. "They're already expecting it. But I've looked into S7 cases before. When they've pulled out, the promoter has lost revenue, and S7 has successfully argued that they pulled out because their percentage wasn't going to earn them enough money in the first place."

"Ouch," Josh said.

"I need a good group," she said. "Luther's three are good, and they solve part of my problem, but not all of it. S7 appeals to kids. None of these groups do."

"Kids can't go in that part of the casino anyway," Josh said.

"They weren't going to, remember?" she said. "They had the beach concert during the day, and they were going to do a second concert that evening that was closed to kids."

"I don't think I ever knew that," Josh said. "You're right. None of these groups will bring in the preteens."

"Too bad we can't reassemble the Davy Moss Band," Luther said from the doorway. Emily looked up. She wasn't sure how long he'd been standing there. "That would appeal to kids."

Josh didn't look bothered at all. But Emily was. "You like living dangerously, don't you, Luther?"

He grinned at her.

Josh saw her distress, and said, quite seriously, "It doesn't matter, Em. Even if we put the Davy Moss Band back together, it wouldn't bring in the kids. It would bring in their parents. And that doesn't solve your problem."

She smiled at him. "Thanks, Josh."

He shrugged. "It's just the truth."

"You realize that after this concert, we won't be able to make jokes about Davy Moss anymore?" she said, more to Luther than anyone.

"Afraid we'll be bugged?" Luther asked.

She shook her head. "Afraid we'll get careless. If everything goes the way I plan, we'll have to watch everything we say because it'll get reported."

"That won't be the first time." Josh picked up his wine glass and took another sip.

"It's your last chance, Josh. You can back out now, and no one will complain. You can say the casino broke its agreement with you when S7 canceled."

Luther straightened behind him. His face, usually animated, had frozen.

"I'm not going to cancel," Josh said. "I want to do this. Did you know that the concert in Eugene was the first one I ever did on my terms? And all the others since—it feels as if I've been set free. I've been looking forward to the Fourth like I've never looked forward to anything. I've finally claimed music for *me*. Not for Kahn, not for my parents. But for me."

"What about Emily?" Luther asked.

Josh gave her a fond gaze. "Emily's sharing this with me. She's not controlling it."

"I should hope not," Emily said.

"Call the groups, Em," Josh said. "We'll deal with whatever comes—together."

twenty-eight

Typical casino planning, Josh thought as he stood backstage, his hands on his hips. Out front, he could hear the drone of a single voice as it called out bingo numbers.

B3

I27

O70

Emily, who hadn't slept at all the last three days, was looking even more frazzled than she had a week earlier. She had found a practice venue, but even she knew that wouldn't be the same. Bands wanted time to test the acoustics and the lighting, to get a sense of the stage.

And the casino insisted on running two bingo tournaments opposite the concerts. In fact, the management had set up the tournaments without regard to the concerts at all. They had avoided performance times, but they had allowed no rehearsal, no chance to get to know the stage.

When Emily had found out, she had been livid. He had never seen her so astonishingly mad. She had come into her house—they'd been spending most of their time there—and had proceeded to launch into a tirade about the stupidity of people who didn't know what they wanted.

Josh had let her go. She had already gone after the casino staff and it had done no good. Then she had used their money to rent the rehearsal hall, and received their permission for the bands to practice after bingo ended both nights. All of this before she saw Josh.

It still hadn't been enough. She fumed over it and worried it as if it would make or break the concert. He knew better. He also knew that she was avoiding a look at the larger picture, at what success or failure meant for both of them.

"Hey, Josh!" Bobby stopped beside him. The boy was covered with dust. He'd been helping the casino clear out a storage room to accommodate some of the bands' equipment. "Did you see we got eight o'clock? That's good, huh?"

Josh shrugged. "Emily thinks it's all right."

An eight o'clock performance would normally have been quite good, but with ten bands and a lot of excitement, Josh wasn't so sure. It gave people time to slip away for gambling or dinner or to play in the big poker tournament that started at eight-thirty. The Fourth of July weekend had initially seemed like a good idea for the concert, but as the date closed in, he wondered. The tickets were mostly sold out—the numbers remaining would go at the start of the weekend most certainly—but that wasn't his concern. His concert was free. Those who wanted tickets got them as a bonus when they bought one of the package deals. The remaining seats would go on a first-come, first-serve basis. And Emily had reserved the entire middle section of the theater for special guests, including the other bands, their managers and roadies, and the promoters and studio executives she had invited.

"You don't sound too thrilled," Bobby said.

Josh brushed some of the dust from Bobby's shoulder. "Nerves."

"You can't be nervous. All the rest of us are. One of us has to be calm."

"And you've all elected me," he said, smiling.

"No choice," Bobby said. "You're the leader."

Josh glanced around the backstage area. Three roadies were talking in a corner. Another roadie was carrying an amp half his size. Four of the performers had gone by, but so far, Josh saw no one he recognized.

"I should have thought that through before I signed up for this job," he said.

"Did you hear who's here?" Bobby asked.

Josh shook his head. "I know who we're performing with, if that's what you mean."

"Emily's got two guys here from Universal." Bobby frowned. "How come you haven't heard? I thought she told you everything."

"I asked her not to tell me much this time," Josh said. "I just want this to be a concert."

"Fat chance," Bobby said. "Do you think bingo will be done soon?"

"I hope so," Josh said. "We've got a lot of practicing to do."

"Makes me wish we'd practiced here before," Bobby said.

"We tried," Josh said. "They didn't want us in here before the concert."

"Is it always this hard?" Bobby asked.

"It's usually something," Josh said.

"Man." Bobby brushed some more dust off his clothes. "I'm going to clean up. I hope they're done by the time I get back."

"Me, too," Josh said. Bobby went out the side door into the bingo area. There was a rustle of paper, and some woman shouted *Bingo!* so loudly that it reverberated in the back.

A woman wearing a midriff top, short-shorts, and a car coat sweater over them stopped beside him. She had wild blond hair teased and sprayed into position. On her, it looked natural.

"No one told me it'd be cold over here," she said, her voice warm and musical, her accent deep Texas. She stuck out a hand. "I'm Jenny Shin. The guys in the back say you're Josh Candless."

Jennifer Shin, the country singer. Now he recognized her. She looked younger and dumber in her publicity photos. In life, she had fine lines around her eyes and mouth, and an intelligence that fairly radiated off her.

"I am," he said, taking her hand. Her fingers were ice cold. "You might want to change into coastal clothes."

"Oh, I plan to," she said. "When the bus pulled into Portland, it was a hundred degrees. I did not expect a forty-degree difference over here."

"Welcome to the Oregon Coast," he said.

"Thanks." She pulled the sweater tighter. "Tell me, honey, you banging that sweet young thing who organized this shindig or are you really talented?"

A shiver ran down his back. He'd forgotten about this part of performing. Actually, he hadn't really forgotten it. He had merely put it out of his mind.

"Guess you have to wait until tomorrow to find out," he said.

She put a hand on his arm. Her nails were long and red. "I didn't mean to offend by askin' that. It's just everyone's wondering why there's one unknown among this group of performers. Normally things like this have a contest with 'em if anything. Not some pre-chosen band."

"How do you know there wasn't a contest?" he asked.

"I don't," she said. "I just find unusual things fascinating, don't you?"

"Sometimes, things are less fascinating when you meet them in person." He took her hand off his arm. "Excuse me."

He left her and wandered back to the converted storage room. Luther was standing outside it.

"You met Jennifer Shin yet?" Josh asked.

"That's one mean piece of work, isn't it?" Luther asked.

"I'll take that to be a yes," Josh said.

Luther grinned. "I talked to her manager. When she found out how small Oceanlake was, she tried to break the contract. I guess Jennifer Shin thinks she's too big to play small venues, even when the money's good and the audience is large."

"The lady's got an attitude problem," Josh said.

"And an ego problem," Luther said. "Did you know she was shocked when she saw you?"

Josh's stomach fluttered. "Why?"

"Because you were 'gorgeous.' I don't know what she expected, but gorgeous wasn't it."

"Great," Josh said. "So she doesn't know if she wants to screw me literally or figuratively."

"You got it," Luther said. Then he lowered his voice. "The band is nervous. I thought Bobby was going to blow a blood vessel when he saw Kassidy Four's bus pull in."

"We're in the big leagues for the next few days."

"Yeah," Luther said, "but you and I are the only ones who've been here before. Debbie is so nervous that she can't eat, and Lisa is systematically practicing each instrument she plays."

"My God," Josh said, "that'll take days. Where's Peter?"

"He's got an old buddy in Shaul. I suspect they're in the buddy's room, doing some experimentation."

"Musical, I hope," Josh said.

Luther shook his head slightly. "Once you've jammed with the Dead, I suspect the party lifestyle infects you."

"You'd think smart people would learn from Jerry Garcia's death."

"Garcia never learned," Luther said.

"Well, I'm not going on stage with a loaded band member," Josh said. "Find him, and clean him up."

"Isn't that Emily's job?"

"Yeah," Josh said, "but she's got enough to handle right now, and if I find him, I'll kill him with my bare hands."

"And if he doesn't clean?" Luther asked.

"We go on without him," Josh said.

"We can't do some of these pieces with only one guitarist."

"Oh, yes we can," Josh said. "And we will. Hell, if we have to, we can perform with just you and me. Me on keyboard and you on drums."

Luther took a deep breath. "I don't want to do that."

"Me, either," Josh said. "But it's better than imploding on stage."

Luther nodded. He rubbed a hand over his newly shaved skull. "I hate pre-concert jitters. I'd forgotten about this."

Josh grinned. "I hadn't. I kinda missed it."

"I didn't," Luther said. "Hell, I'm rich enough. I didn't have to do this. Why did I?"

"Something about long-lost dreams," Josh said softly.

"For both of us, I think," Luther said. They stared at each other for a moment. It was odd, Josh thought, that Luther had never yelled at him. They had been friends in the old days, better friends than Josh had wanted to admit, and Luther had stomached Josh's return and his non-death better than anyone else would have. It was almost as if Luther had known that Josh had never died.

"Where's Emily?" Josh asked, not wanting to delve into this any deeper, especially here, backstage.

"There was some problem with Marbles' hotel suites. She went to sort it out."

The poor woman. She had so many details to coordinate. And her assistants from the casino box office were little help. Mostly they saw their job as ticket sales and venue setup and nothing else. She hadn't argued. She had simply set things up herself, taking more and more of the load until she was coordinating a thousand details a minute.

Josh thanked Luther, and headed out the backstage door. The air outside the casino was brisk, just as Jenny Shin had said. The sun was out, but the breeze was off the ocean, making the temperature about sixty-five. He preferred the cool weather. So did most of the tourists who flocked to the coast at this time of year.

The casino had been built on land near the Sea Grotto, one of the largest resorts on the coast. The hotel complex had three parts: the old section with single rooms that overlooked both the ocean and the parking lot; he newer main section, that included the convention center, the restaurant, and the entertainment area; and the newest section, a three-story building composed only of suites. It had been finished just before Josh came to town and he was glad he hadn't worked on that project. The suites were so poorly constructed that laughter in one room could be heard through the walls of another.

Of course Emily was having trouble. She had booked the artists in the suites, and they wouldn't have enough privacy. He had tried to warn her, but she had insisted that the artists be close to the venue. He would have housed them down the coast a ways, in one of the more exclusive resorts tucked off the highway.

It was, he thought, the only area where she hadn't listened to him. And she was right: She had planned more of these than he had. Most artists liked to have privacy and be close to the venue. That way they could stumble into their rooms when the concert was over.

The parking lot, which extended over two city blocks, was full. A line of cars waited in the entrance to the hotel while guests checked in. The Fourth of July weekend was always one of the biggest on the coast, and it promised to be even bigger this year, what with all of the promotions the casino was putting on. In addition to the large concert, the casino had blackjack, poker, and keno tournaments, plus large bingo pots. It was also having drawings every hours, giving away an escalating prize each time— starting with $250 and ending with a brand-new Mercedes at 5 p.m. on Monday. It was the casino's way of encouraging tourists to stay the entire weekend in Oceanlake, and it looked like the encouragement might work.

People strolled the sidewalks, many heading to the beach and just as many heading to the casino. A lot of families headed toward the casino, something that always shocked him; he believed casinos were for adults and that adults should encourage children to spend their weekends outdoors instead of inside casino childcare or in an arcade.

But he wasn't a parent. He hadn't yet had the opportunity to make that choice for himself.

He slipped inside the hotel lobby. The line to register was ten people deep. Clerks behind the counter had plastic smiles pasted to their faces, and their tones held a trace of strain.

Emily wasn't among them. He had probably missed her. Sometimes it made him feel as if he wasn't working hard enough. Then he smiled. He would feel like that anyway these days; after the years of physical labor, of working difficult and sometimes unrewarding jobs, he had learned the real meaning of working hard. Music, which was exhausting work, was not hard. It was rewarding and fun. He'd had so many jobs that weren't.

He'd never appreciated that in his youth. He had been spoiled and difficult, believing that his suffering was greater than anyone else's.

He'd learned in the intervening years that he had been privileged; he'd been able to do a job he'd liked, and while life was often hard, he'd still had good work and a stable financial base. So many people went through tragedies and other hardships without the work or the base beneath them.

Then he saw Emily come out of the manager's office. Her hair was frizzed and her makeup faded. Her normally well-pressed pants were wrinkled, and she had deep circles beneath her eyes. She wouldn't pass out for a week—she would pass out for a month when this was all over.

"Em," he said softly, and she looked in his direction. When she smiled, her expression was filled with relief.

"Josh."

He approached her, took her arm and headed toward the restaurant. "You need lunch."

"I need to get back," she said. "I haven't had a chance to check the progress of the outdoor stage."

"I can do that," he said.

"No," she said. "You need to work with the band. Are they ready for tomorrow night?"

He shrugged. "If they aren't, it's too late now."

"Josh," she said in shock.

"Well, it's true," he said. "Twenty-four hours isn't going to make much of a difference."

He led her to a table. After a few moments, a waitress found them and gave them menus, then disappeared.

"You're going to need some rest, Em."

"When it's over," she said. The waitress returned with water. Emily ordered a chef's salad, and Josh ordered piece of pie.

"You're not going to eat?" Emily asked.

"I had lunch when normal people do," he said. "At noon."

"I don't know when I ate last," she said.

"I figured as much." He was beginning to get used to Emily's methods of operation. She absorbed herself totally in a project, and if she felt she wasn't busy enough, she added another one. He suspected he had started out as a stop-gap project and had, over time, become something larger.

"It's going well," she said, taking a sip of her water. "All the suites are full."

"All of them?" he asked. The casino had agreed to pay for the block if Emily put together a promotional packet. The user had to agree to eat all meals in the casino and join two of the tournaments. In return, the user got free concert tickets and, if the user spent a certain amount of money in the casino, a free hotel room. It was an expansion of the Vegas "high roller" concept, and Emily had sent the invitation to a number of people in the music industry.

"All," she said with a smile. "We have studio execs coming with their families, several producers, and some scouts. One called me to say he'd been planning to come to the Northwest anyway because he'd been hearing about new talent and he wanted the opportunity to find it."

"What do you make of that?" he asked.

"Everything and nothing," she said. "You've played enough gigs throughout the valley that he could be talking about you. But he could easily be talking about Seattle or Boise. You know the Los Angeles' view of the world."

"There's Southern California, and then there's the rest of the country," he said.

"Exactly." She was wired. Hyper. Talking fast, moving fast, thinking fast. He could barely keep up with her.

He put a hand on hers. "Em, if you don't slow down, you won't be around for the concert tomorrow."

"I'll make it," she said. "I just have to get through today."

He smiled at her. He'd been thinking something similar. It was as if there were only two days left in his life. Today and tomorrow. After that was a great unknown, something he wasn't going to worry about until he woke up the day after the concert. If he did think about it, he did so with trepidation. He couldn't envision himself returning to carpentry or construction, and he couldn't see himself climbing the ladder to musical success.

He couldn't see anything at all.

And they certainly weren't talking about their future, either.

It would all have to wait until the concert was over.

twenty-nine

The casino wants Kassidy Four to do another performance tomorrow afternoon," Bear said. He had caught Emily as she was hurrying from a crisis with Jennifer Shin's costumes to check on Josh's group backstage. She had made it as far as the box office. There Bear had stopped her.

"We can't," she said, glancing over his shoulder through the open backstage door. Her stomach was in knots. She had just heard that there were no seats left for Josh's concert. Somehow she had expected the whole middle section to remain empty. She had had visions of herself dragging gamblers away from slot machines to make them listen to Josh.

"It was such a success," Bear said. "The council would like them to do it again."

She looked at him incredulously. Sometimes she wondered how these people, who had set up their casino so well, who were conducting business so beautifully, who were managing millions of dollars in revenue as if they had done it all their lives, could be so ignorant about other types of business contracts.

"We can't," she said again. "The outdoor concert was all that they were contracted for. We can't renegotiate at this late date."

Then Bear grinned. "You're gullible today."

"You're not very funny," she said, but she smiled anyway. "I'm still swamped and I have so much to do, and I want to watch the band. The worst thing about planning these concerts is that I don't have any time to enjoy them."

"Isn't that why you work in music?" Bear asked.

She frowned. "Why?"

"So you don't have to listen to any of it."

"You're on a roll, Bear."

He shrugged. "The mood at this place is very up today. The concerts are bringing in more people than expected. Security estimates we had five thousand people at the beach concert this afternoon."

"And they all paid, right?" Emily said.

Bear shook his head. "No," he said, "but a bunch of them were in the box office later for tickets to tonight's shows."

"That's good," she said. Then took a deep breath. She had been moving so fast all day that this was the first moment she'd had to slow down. The afternoon concert, which did go well, had been filled with security problems: drunks, a fight near the ocean, a near-drowning, and faulty sound systems. But people seemed satisfied.

Things were going well. With all these sold-out concerts, she'd even have enough clout to take on the canceled band's lawyer. That little problem even seemed smoothed over. The people holding S7 tickets didn't mind seeing Kassidy Four.

Then she heard a voice over the PA, which was filtered into the box office. The voice belonged to Joe Escobal, the nominal head of the casino board. He was the only real music fan on the board, and he had reserved the right to introduce each group. That way, he got to meet them.

"Rolling Waves Casino is proud to introduce one of the bright new lights of this concert season—"

Emily cursed and hurried toward the door. She'd missed talking to the band. She used the side door that led from the box office into the bingo/audience area.

"—a band you've never heard of. What are we doing with unknowns, you might ask—"

The seats were full. They were side by side, the way that the casino put them when it was trying to fill the space to capacity. The house lights were down, except in the back where ticket takers were still working, the side corner where the CDs—including Josh's demo—were being sold, and in the front where the curtains were drawn across the stage.

"—we're creating a memory. You can say you were here when the world met the *Josh Candless Band!*"

She had written that script and it played well, better than she expected. The audience erupted into applause and the curtains slid back. Josh stood up front in a white shirt that reflected the lights and a pair of tight jeans. The rest of the members were scattered around the stage. Bobby was staring into the audience, his face frozen in fear.

Josh turned to Bobby to give the count, and the boy looked at him, breaking the ice. They started energetically like they had with every concert, only Josh picked a different song each time. This time, it was folksy hard-rock tune particularly suited to Josh's voice. She loved this song. She had once told him it was welcoming.

And he had heard her. He used it as a welcome.

A hand touched her arm. She turned. It was one of the ticket takers. Not, fortunately, one of the young people hired specifically for the event, but one of the casino employees, a man who had worked previous concerts.

"Ms. Lukovich?" he shouted over the band. "Can you help us out? We have a problem."

Wonderful. That snippet of song was probably all she'd get to see of one of the most important concerts for the Josh Candless Band. But that had been her choice. She wanted to do this on her own.

"Sure," she said, and followed him to the back of the theater.

A party of people stood there, and her heart sank when she recognized five executives and two producers among the group.

"Their seats seem to be taken," the ticket taker said.

"Do the people in those seats have tickets?"

He nodded.

"Great," Emily said. "These folks are here on my invitation."

"I know that, Ms. Lukovich. Otherwise I would have set up seats in the back."

She bit her lower lip, then made a snap decision. She glanced at the stage. Josh had moved to a jazz piece that shared a thematic sensibility with the first song.

"Move the casino board and their guests. If they have a problem, tell them to talk to me. But when you do so, warn them that they're being moved for package guests. Got that? Package guests."

"Package guests," he repeated.

"You do that," she said, "and I'll keep these folks calm here."

"Fine." He moved swiftly down the aisle. She watched him go, hoping that the numbers would be roughly similar. Casino staff would move for package guests, she knew that. She only hoped that they would move enough of their friends as well.

Then she ran a hand through her hair, adjusted her suit jacket, glad she had dressed in "official" clothes for the night. She approached the group.

"I'm Emily Lukovich," she said. "I'm sorry for the inconvenience. We're clearing your seats now."

One of the producers grinned at her. "It's our fault. We had dinner upstairs and thought we had time. We knew you were giving seats away."

"We weren't certain if we were coming to this one," a female producer said, "until the waitress told us about this Candless fellow. He's not half bad."

She nodded toward the stage, but Emily didn't know if she meant Josh's looks or his music.

"We have high hopes for him," Emily said, amazed that they could even converse with the amplified sound in the room. She wanted to turn and tap her feet to the music. But she didn't.

A tall, broad-shouldered man in a silk suit approached her. His features were half hidden in the darkness but his beautiful silver hair reflected the dim lighting. He looked vaguely familiar.

"You are Ms. Lukovich?"

She nodded, then glanced over her shoulder. The band was now doing a musical interlude as it moved to a big band piece—another one of her favorites. It felt as if Josh were doing the show for her tonight.

"What do you know of this Candless fellow?" the man asked.

She turned her attention back to him. "I'll be pleased to talk with you about him after the show. It'd be easier than shouting over the performance."

"I suppose." He sounded wistful—if a shouting man could sound wistful—and then he looked at the stage. His features were square and rugged, but his skin had that soft, pampered look that wealthy men somehow achieved without losing their masculinity.

Just then, the ticket taker returned. "I have your seats," he said. "Sorry for the delay."

Emily smiled at him and got out of the party's way. They went down the center aisle and as they did, the crowd shifted in its seat, angry that its view of the stage was interrupted.

Josh had been playing for more than ten minutes and no one had left. Everyone had remained in their seats. That had been her other nightmare—that the audience would walk out one by one, tempted by the restaurants and the gaming tables, the tournaments and the slot machines.

No one had left. Not even the displaced casino board. They stood—against fire code—against the walls, watching. She decided against yelling at them. She didn't want to distract from the concert, anyway.

She crossed her arms and leaned against the closed sales booth for bingo. Josh set down his guitar and the band disappeared off the side of the stage. A hand brought out a stool and Josh grabbed the cordless mike. He was going to sing a cappella, as he had on every concert since the first.

He scanned the audience, and she felt as if he were looking for her. She wondered what he could see from the stage. Probably not much. The lights were bright up there, and they were hot. She had been there earlier in the evening when Shaul did their concert, and she'd been amazed at the heat.

Josh apparently couldn't find her, and it didn't really seem to throw him. He smiled at the audience. "We're going to slow things down a bit. It's time for a love song."

Behind him, Debbie played a C chord, and he nodded. Then she left her keyboard. He clutched the microphone tightly and then started to sing.

She was expecting "A Kiss to Build a Dream On"—the only cover he had performed at all his concerts. She had felt as if it were their song, even though he had never said that. This time, he started lower, with a song she had never heard before.

She's always beautiful,

Like a sunset over the ocean—

Always beautiful and always different—

A chill ran up her spine. The song had an intimacy the others lacked. It went on like that, singing about a woman, using ocean imagery, yet done fondly, with love.

She felt as if he were singing about her.

She didn't move as he sang, and neither did the audience. A single spot fell on him, illuminating him, making him seem younger and vulnerable—that look he had when he was exposing a hidden part of himself.

The song was based on little things, yet universal things. He could be singing about one woman and every woman.

It was destined to be a classic, and it had Josh Candless written all over it. Choosing to perform it a cappella was brilliant: It made the song wholly his. The listener had to concentrate on Josh's voice, had to hear his inflections, his emphasis on both the words and the music. The song was his, not just because he wrote it, not just because he performed it, but because no one else could make it this personal and meaningful at the same time.

When he finished singing, he said, "That one's yours, Em."

And then, as if he hadn't spoken, he set the mike down, clapped his hands, and the band came running back. This time, Lisa was carrying a sax. They were going to go from a sweet love song to the blues.

How like Josh.

Innocent and cynical at the same time. As if he couldn't believe that something good would last.

But she hadn't given him any reason to believe this would last. And after that night, the night he revealed himself to her, he hadn't, either. No promises, just as she had asked for.

She clasped her hands together.

She wanted promises now.

But that wasn't the kind of relationship they had.

She stared at the stage. Josh was absorbed in the next piece. But she hadn't gotten over the song he had written for her.

A sunset over the ocean.

Fleeting, beautiful, and memorable.

Just like she'd asked for.

And nothing more.

thirty

osh was hot, covered with sweat, and filled with a nervous energy that he knew would dissipate the moment he sat down. He came off the stage after the third and final encore, carrying his guitar in his slick hand, wanting to shout in triumph but knowing he didn't dare.

He'd seen the casino board get up for that party of newcomers, and even though the lights were bright and he couldn't really see faces, he knew that they were some of Emily's VIPs. And they didn't leave. They stayed for the whole thing. He'd known enough studio executives and promoters to know that they wouldn't suffer through a bad concert if they didn't have to. They would have been out the door before he finished his first song.

"Oh, God, oh, God," Debbie said. "Now I'm shaking. Who'd have thought that?"

"I am, too," Lisa said, and grinned. Her face was sweat-streaked, too, her hair damp. They all looked as if they had just finished a marathon.

Except Bobby, whose eyes were wide and skin was pale. He looked as if he would pass out at that slightest provocation.

"Come on," Josh said. "Let's go to our assigned room."

"And hope Emily thought of champagne!" Luther came forward, twirling his drumsticks, a huge grin on his face.

"Well," said a voice from beside Josh. He turned. It was Jennifer Shin in full makeup, a suede coat with fringe, and boots that cost more than all his musical equipment combined. "I don't care if you are sleeping with your manager. You're good. And I wouldn't mind having a taste of you myself."

Josh almost responded directly—a defense of Emily and himself rising on his lips—but that was what Jennifer wanted, a scene in the back, and he wasn't going to do that. Not at this moment.

"Knock 'em dead, sweetheart," he said.

She gave a half laugh. "I have to wait until they clear the room and come back. And hope that they haven't wasted all their energy on you."

Then she went onto the stage, behind the closed curtain, to supervise the setup for her concert.

"Wow," Bobby said, looking after her. "If I ever get that way, will someone shoot me?"

"You wouldn't look as good in suede," Peter said.

"Or big hair and make-up," Lisa added, and then giggled. Josh hurried them toward the dressing room before they all said something they would regret.

The door was open. Emily had not only remembered the champagne, she had managed to fill the place with flowers. Roses, carnations, lilies—the heady aroma made him dizzy. She was standing in the middle of all the flowers, pouring champagne into fluted glasses.

"Em!" he said.

When she saw him, she set the bottle down, nearly knocking over full glasses, and somehow ended up in his arms. He kissed her deep and full, tasting her and knowing he would never forget that moment, even if he lived to be a hundred.

"I heard the song," she whispered. "It's beautiful."

"It's for you," he said, then cupped her head toward him, holding her. The other band members grabbed their champagne flutes and shouted as they lifted them high, toasting the casino, the concert, everything.

People poured through the door until it seemed as if the room couldn't accommodate them. It was all faces he recognized: men from his crew, the casino board, some of the locals around town. Kevin and Lucy were there, looking as radiant as they had at their wedding, and so were the guys from his construction crew. A few members of the casino board were near the door.

"Hey, man, you're good!" Nick—whose temper had started this whole thing—yelled at him from the hallway. "Just don't sing no one else's material!"

"Don't worry." Josh still had his arm around Emily, and he pulled her close. He wasn't going to let her go, not tonight.

People were toasting and drinking and shouting. Debbie was crying and laughing at the same time. Bobby's face had grown flushed with champagne, and Lisa was trying to take his glass away. He grabbed a rose and stuck it in her hair. Luther was shaking the hand of anyone who would walk into the room.

Emily, too, was smiling, but she gripped Josh tighter. "We only have an hour until the next show."

The noise. The last thing he needed to do was spoil Jenny Shin's concert. She'd never let him forget it.

"We'll have to move this somewhere else," he said.

"The main restaurant's closing in fifteen minutes," Bear said. "I'll see if I can get it for a special party."

Emily grinned at him. "You're sweet."

"He's more than sweet," Josh said as Bear left. "He's handling something so you don't have to."

Peter sidled up to him. "None of the suits are here. Were they in the audience?"

"They were," Emily said. "They arrived late."

"They should be here, shouldn't they?" Peter asked. "I mean—"

"Maybe we weren't as good as we thought." Bobby still had his champagne flute, but it was empty.

"You were great," Josh said. "Just don't expect instant rewards."

"Right," Luther said. "If they're interested, we'll find out. But who wants to talk to a group of tired, sweaty musicians? Emily trapped these folks here for the weekend. They'll—"

"...Candless." A deep voice penetrated the room from the hallway. A shiver ran down Josh's spine. Luther stopped talking and looked in that direction.

"Oh, shit," he said.

The shiver moved the full-blown shudder, and it settled around Josh's heart. Luther turned to him, and Josh thought he saw fear in Luther's eyes.

"What is it?" Emily asked.

Josh swallowed. He had to think. "Why don't you see if Bear got the restaurant?"

She shook her head. "I'm staying with you."

He didn't have time to explain. "Em—"

A shadow filled the doorway.

"Joshua Candless." The name was said with a mixture of sarcasm and contempt.

The power behind the voice shut down the party. The laughing stopped. People set their flutes down and then didn't move.

Josh looked up and saw what he had never expected to see—not on this night, anyway. Not when he imagined it. Not once. He had expected executives. He had expected triumph—and he had expected failure.

But he had never expected to see Jeremiah Kahn standing in the doorway, looking as powerful as ever. He had aged. His hair had turned completely silver, and he had the suggestion of jowls. His acne scars seemed less pronounced. His suit was exquisitely tailored and his hands were manicured, but even with all those changes, he managed to look the same.

As if Josh had never left him.

"Who is that?" Emily whispered. "He came in with the execs—"

Josh squeezed her side, and she went suddenly silent.

"I'm Joshua Candless." His was the only voice in the room. The silence felt heavy, as if the weight of all the laughter still remained in the air.

"Are you?" The sarcasm was Kahn's cover. It had always been his best and only tool to hide and make use of a vicious temper.

Josh didn't know how to handle this. Kahn knew. Kahn clearly knew. If Josh lied—

"Yes," he said. "I am."

"And I'm Colonel Tom Parker," Kahn said. "Now, do we have this conversation in private or do we let everyone in on this stunt you're trying to pull?"

Emily glanced at Josh and then at Luther, who had gone gray. She clearly didn't understand what was going on, only that it was bad. She slipped from under Josh's arm and approached Kahn.

"Excuse me, sir," she said. "I'm the group's manager. Any problems you may have, you can discuss with me."

"Do you have a contract with them, Miss Lukovich?"

"I don't see what concern that is of yours." She put her hand on his arm and tried to lead him from the room. "Now why don't we go somewhere private and see what we can do for you?"

"You can't do anything for me. My business is with Joshua Candless." Kahn tilted his head back. "You made a contract with this woman? Ours supersedes it."

Josh swallowed. This was moving too quickly for him.

"I think—" His voice broke. The nightmare, the one he'd had since he fled, had come to life. Kahn had found him. And Kahn was angry. "I think we'd better be alone, to see what it is that's bothering you."

"That's not necessary, Mr. Candless," Joe Escobal said. "We can use security to get him out of here."

It was so tempting.

"You may as well, Josh," Luther said.

"And you," Kahn said, turning to him. "You could have contacted me."

"Why, Kahn? Do I have to inform you every time I join a new band?"

"Kahn?" Emily breathed. And in that single syllable, Josh knew he'd lost any options he may have had. She probably hadn't even known she spoke. But she had said the word with such trepidation, such knowledge, that almost everyone in the room had known she had history with this person. Or a worry about him.

"Warned her about me, did you, Joshua?" The emphasis on *Joshua* was painful. Kahn used the word like a weapon, mocking Josh with each pronunciation.

"Let us alone," Josh said, and realized how much like Davy Moss he suddenly sounded. "I mean, please. Let me talk to this man. Alone."

"I'm staying," Emily said. "I'm your manager. I have the right—"

"I'm staying too," Luther said.

Josh shook his head. All their good intentions were ruining his only opportunity of blustering his way through this. As if he could.

"Me, too," Bobby said, slightly drunkenly.

"We all will," Lisa said. And in their voices was recovery. The opportunity to lie remained.

Only Josh wasn't sure he had the stomach for it.

"Please," he said. "Let me speak to him alone."

Maybe he could buy Kahn off. Maybe he could make Kahn understand. Bluster wasn't going to work. Nothing would work.

One public performance and Kahn had found him. What were the odds on that?

"Josh," Emily said. "You need representation with you. You need us."

He shook his head. "Em, would you please get everyone to leave the room?"

She opened her mouth, then closed it. "Come on," she said, and helped the band out of the room.

The spectators went as well, with a cautious glance at Josh. He didn't meet any of their gazes. He continued to watch Kahn. Kahn looked at the group leaving with something like bemusement.

"Josh," Luther said, "we'll be right outside."

"Go to the restaurant," Josh said. "I'll join you there."

Then he closed the door behind them. His hands were shaking and his mouth was dry. The energy he had felt since the concert was long gone. His limbs were heavy and he had that old feeling, that trapped feeling, deep in the pit of his stomach.

"Joshua Candless," Kahn said again, the sarcasm like a whip. "You could have thought of something less revealing if you didn't want to get caught."

Josh closed his eyes. "It took you fifteen years."

"It took me five," Kahn said.

Josh blinked his eyes open, put a hand on the plywood door, and turned. Kahn was watching him, his mouth thin. He tilted his head slightly.

"You made a mistake, Davy," Kahn said. "You left a trail. Did you think I wouldn't find that account in the name of a certain dead childhood friend? Did you think I was that dumb?"

Josh didn't move. He couldn't, really. He had thought, if even if Kahn discovered the account, he wouldn't find Josh.

"And then you made a second mistake," Kahn said. "An impromptu stage appearance in Waverly, Iowa, in a bar near Wartburg College. When you left town, a private detective followed you."

Josh felt a flush warm his cheeks.

"I figured it was only a matter of time before you returned to music. And when you did, we'd have this discussion. What I never expected was that you'd hire someone else to manage you. I never expected you to try to rebuild a career under a different name. How foolish, Davy."

"My name is Josh." The words barely made it out of his throat.

"Your name is Davy Moss, and if you want to perform, then you will do so as Davy Moss." Kahn smiled, but the look didn't reach his eyes. "I *own* you, Davy."

"That's right," Josh said. "You own Davy Moss. My name is Josh Candless. You don't own me."

Kahn blinked, and for a moment, Josh saw something flicker across his face. As quickly as it appeared, it was gone. "I made you rich, Davy. I took the five-million-dollar estate you left and turned it into a multimillion-dollar enterprise. I kept Davy Moss's name alive so you could return to it. And I respected your privacy. You could remain in hiding as long as you wanted to, but I kept everything going in case you came back."

"I ran away from Davy Moss," Josh said. "I *hated* Davy Moss. I killed him so I wouldn't have to come back."

"Davy Moss?" Kahn asked, and as he did, his voice broke. "Or me?"

Josh didn't have an answer for that. He didn't know how to answer it. He wasn't sure what the truth was anymore.

Kahn ran a hand through his silver hair, messing its near-perfect neatness. "Davy, you know I can't let you go through with this. You try to make a career with this new name, and I'll leak your identity. I'll make it hell. You let that inexperienced woman manage your career, and you'll see me in court. We signed an exclusive agreement."

"She's not inexperienced," Josh said.

"I checked up on her. She sleeps with her clients and manages their careers into the ground."

The numbness that Josh felt like a shield shattered. "She does *not*. You're as much a victim of someone else's lies as you are of your own."

Kahn didn't move. His lids closed slightly, making his eyes seem small. "So she is sleeping with you. And probably planning to bilk you of all you'll earn."

"Kahn—" Josh said, taking a step toward him.

"It's amazing how you would allow yourself to be taken in like this. Especially when Angela is still waiting for you. She's at least worthy of you—"

"Angela is not worthy of me," Josh snapped. "You let her use me, just like everything else. Angie was a groupie, Kahn. I never proposed to her. I never even liked her. You want me to go back to that?"

"I want you to return to your life. I don't want you to throw it away on a slut with a business degree."

Josh had a hand on Kahn's collar before he'd even realized he'd moved. He shoved Kahn against a wall. Kahn's gaze met his, still calm.

"Honest work has given you muscles, Davy, but no brains. Come home. We'll work this out."

"Emily manages me," Josh said. "She manages the Josh Candless Band. We don't play pop. We don't do Davy Moss's greatest hits. We do what we want."

"Fine." Kahn's voice was slightly strangled. "You can let me go, Davy."

Josh did. Kahn straightened his tie, and then his suit coat.

"I'm going to give you some time to think about this," Kahn said. "But consider this: If you decide to pursue a new career with a new name, I will furnish your history, your name, and your duplicity to any reporter who'll take the story. And it'll be a hot one. Then I'll furnish the history of that little piece who thinks she can manipulate you to the same reporters—and to Angie. The PR tidal wave will be larger than anything you've ever seen. And then you have a choice. You can run away again, or you can ask me to rescue you."

He went to the door, pulled it open, and stopped. "You need me, Davy. You always have, and you always will."

"Get out, Kahn," Josh said.

"I expect to see you in Malibu on Monday," Kahn said, and closed the door.

thirty-one

The fancy dining room in the Rolling Waves casino was on the top floor. It had a spectacular view of the ocean—one entire wall was windows. The windows were salt- and spray-streaked, but the silvery water was still visible through them.

The moon was full, casting a bright light across the ocean. Emily sat at one of the tables near the window, her stomach jumping while she tried to remain outwardly calm. Bear had convinced the kitchen staff to stay late and to provide light snacks to the members of Josh's party.

The band was scattered through the room, talking and laughing, the tense moment in the dressing room seemingly forgotten. Each member had approached Emily individually, asking about Kahn and his mention of the scam. Emily had said that she believed it was nothing serious and that Josh would join them later. That seemed to satisfy the four members, all except Luther. Luther waited for Josh, downstairs.

Someone remembered to bring the champagne up and the four band members were proceeding to get slowly and loudly drunk.

She didn't mind. It was their night of triumph, after all—and it might be their only night. She wished Josh had let her stay below. She could have helped him with Kahn.

But Josh had decided to go it alone. And that only meant one thing: that he had decided to talk to Kahn honestly. Otherwise, why kick everyone out of the room?

She could have helped him bluff. She could have helped him through the difficulty. So could Luther.

"Nice spread."

Emily looked up. One of the studio execs had pulled up a chair near her. He set down a paper plate full of barbecued chicken wings and a glass of champagne.

"People tell me you're the one to talk to," he said.

She made herself smile. Business above all else. She would negotiate until Josh told her otherwise. "That's right. I'm Emily Lukovich. I manage the Josh Candless Band."

"That's some group," the exec said. She was struggling to remember his name. It felt as if her brain had turned to Swiss cheese. "I was planning to listen to Jennifer Shin. I'm up here instead."

"We're glad to have you." She had been in this situation before. She knew how to sound interested and non-committal at the same time.

"Quite an idea you had, giving us free access to this place. I've never been to the Oregon Coast before." He shoved the plate of wings aside and wiped off his fingers with a paper napkin. "It's cold here. Is this normal?"

"That's why people like it in the summer. It's a break from the heat." She tried to keep her gaze on him when what she wanted to do was scan the room for Josh. He hadn't arrived yet. Each additional minute it took wound her stomach tighter.

"Listen," he said. "I've been talking with some of the promoters downstairs. They think your group is highly promotable."

"Do they?" she said.

"They perform well, capture an audience, and that lead singer of yours has what it takes, if he can do that every performance."

She smiled slightly. "He can."

"Since I didn't recognize the material, I take it they write their own."

"Josh does," she said.

"Good stuff. A bit too diverse, though, don't you think? Audiences want to be able to identify their artists."

"Identify?"

"You know, figure out how to find them in a music store. You don't want to confuse them by having one CD under rock and roll, another under jazz, and still another under country."

"I've never noticed Lyle Lovett having a problem," she said.

"Well, Lovett established himself as a country singer, didn't he?" The exec smiled. "Then he snuck in other types of music when his audience wasn't looking."

"I thought you liked the band," she said, sitting up slightly. They were in negotiations, and she wasn't even sure she could be.

Kahn.

A little shiver ran through her.

"I do like the band," the exec said. "But the last thing you'd want, as manager, is a touring show with no CD promotions."

"And you think the only way I can get that is to pin Josh and the group to a category."

The exec shrugged.

Near the impromptu feast, the rest of the band was laughing. A group of locals were standing nearby, smiling with the rest of them. Even the casino board remained, forgetting, apparently, that they had tickets to Jenny Shin's concert.

Another exec came through the door, followed by a promoter. Emily repressed a smile. Josh had done well. He had done better than well. He had done a superb job.

"I tell you what," she said. "This is not the place for negotiations. Give me your card, and I'll call you tomorrow."

"I won't be in the office until Monday. I'm staying for your lovely weekend," the exec said. "I feel like gambling today."

"I hope so," she said. "Give me your card anyway. I don't want to interrupt your vacation anymore than I already have."

"You may not get other offers, Ms. Lukovich." He set his card on the table.

She picked it up and slipped it in her purse. "We'll see. It was a pleasure talking with you."

He left, leaving his buffalo wings behind. As he turned around, he saw the other exec. They avoided each other as if they were afraid of getting fleas. She took a deep breath and another sip of champagne. Then she pushed it away. She had to remain clear-headed.

The second exec, Barry Boyer, reached the table. He was a slender man who seemed to get even skinnier as the years progressed. She hadn't seen him since she had gone to his office all those years ago, since he gave her the idea—and the sideways help—to start her consulting/promotion business.

He hovered near the chair the previous exec had just vacated.

"Emily," he said smoothly, "I thought you weren't going to manage anymore."

She shook her head. "I was just waiting for the right band."

"Wow, and did you. I'm quite impressed. May I sit?"

"Certainly." She shoved the buffalo wings to the other side of the table.

"I saw you talking to Stan."

She shrugged. "I'm pleased so many people could come."

Barry grinned. "Back to your old self, I see. I'm glad. I'm glad it all worked out for you."

"It's worked so far." She took a deep breath. "Listen, I never thanked you—"

He waved a hand, stopping her. "That conversation never happened. I'm just glad we're both still in the business."

Now she smiled at him. It was unusual, with all the hirings and firings at the studio, that Barry was still around. He was good and he was political, and he tried hard to be a decent guy in an amoral business.

"To be honest," he said, leaning forward, "I didn't have a lot of hope for your group. I don't think any of the execs did. I think we were all hoping to steal some of the other performers this weekend. I know Marbles' contract is almost up, and I've heard rumors about Jenny Shin's as well. And when a man can get a free vacation for his family in the same deal, well, who's to argue?"

"I thought you'd enjoy it here." She shifted her chair so that she could better see the door. Another exec walked in, and one more promoter. Oh, Josh. Show up. See your triumph. They're all interested.

"I won't b.s. you, Em," Barry said. "We've worked together before. I really like this group of yours."

She smiled. "They're something, aren't they?"

"They are okay. The bass player and keyboardist could use a bit of stage presence. The second guitarist blew up in L.A. about twenty years ago, not that anyone but me remembers, and Luther is Luther. He's got a reputation for being outspoken, but his years with Davy Moss protect him from too much trouble."

She folded her hands in her lap. She hadn't known that Peter tried to make it before, but that didn't surprise her. It surprised her that Barry remembered him. Either Peter had blown up ugly or he had been considered a hot new talent at one time.

"But it's your lead," Barry said. "He's got charisma. You can't buy that, Em. And too few performers these days have it. John Mayer, maybe. Maybe. But not to this extent. This is early Sinatra. This is Elvis. This is early Beatles. Michael Jackson before the charges. I take it he writes the songs?"

"Yes," she said.

"In collaboration with Luther?"

"The band hasn't been together that long. Josh has been writing songs for fifteen years."

"Wow," Barry said. "What an inventory. All categories, I suppose."

She nodded.

He let out his breath. "You know the risks of that, Em. We can launch them small in several categories and hope that his charisma smooths it. Or we can launch them large, and then hope the audience goes with the change."

"You sound like you have a deal sewn up, Barry," she said.

"We're old friends, Emily."

"So you don't blame me for Ricky's disaster?"

"Ricky." Barry waved his hand. "Who remembers Ricky Fink anymore? You were long gone before that disaster hit."

"But I'm the one who sold him to you," she said. As she watched, another promoter came in the door. Most of them were talking to the locals, apparently trying to gauge the mood of the crowd. Only one had tried to talk with the band. Lisa had headed him off, thank goodness. Lisa had a head on her shoulders.

"And I'm the one who kept him," Barry said. "I'm just sorry I couldn't have helped you more. But he was the name in those days. The money machine. I just never realized it was your management that kept him in line. It was a disaster after you left. He self-destructed and still hasn't fulfilled a two-point-three-million-dollar contract. Confidentially, we're probably going to have to sue to get our money back."

That wasn't confidential. The news had already hit the trades. But she let that slide. He was trying to woo her.

And he was succeeding. They did have history. And Barry tried.

Emily stood. "Give me your card, Barry. I'm in no mood to discuss offers tonight."

"I can outbid Stan," Barry said as he took out his card. She didn't need it. She already had his number, but it was nice to play the game.

"I'm sure you can," she said. "But tonight, with all the champagne flowing, is not the time to talk terms."

"You're as hardheaded as ever, Emily," Barry said.

"I'm a little more hardheaded now, Barry," she said. Then she touched his shoulder. His suit was silk. "I'm sure we'll have a profitable discussion in the next few days."

"I'm here 'til tomorrow night," he said. "I feel like gambling this weekend."

What was it with these guys? she wondered. Did they work from the same script? Then she put it out of her mind as she worked her way to the beverage table.

Promoters stopped her, pressing cards into her hand. Another exec wanted a moment to talk. She took his card and promised to call. It took nearly five minutes to reach the table. She was opening a bottled water when Lisa appeared at her side.

"Josh isn't here yet," Lisa said softly.

Emily nodded.

"That man, he has something on Josh, doesn't he?"

Emily looked at her. "We've discussed this."

"Yes, and you lied." Lisa shrugged. "It's okay. But I'm worried. He'll be all right, won't he?"

"Josh can handle himself," Emily said. "I'm sure it's nothing."

"If it were nothing," Lisa said, "you wouldn't keep watching the door."

At that moment, a promoter tapped Emily on the shoulder. She excused herself and followed him to a more private section of the room. But she glanced back at Lisa as she did. Lisa was talking to Bobby.

The band was worried.

She was worried.

And Josh still hadn't shown up.

thirty-two

Josh remained standing. The cloying scent of all the flowers threatened to overpower him. His stomach was churning and his head ached.

Kahn.

Kahn had been here. Kahn had known.

For ten years.

And done nothing.

Until now.

Now, when Josh finally had a chance to do something on his own. When the concert had gone so well. No one had left. The promoters, the audience, the *fans* had all liked him.

He had thought, for a brief moment, that he could have it again.

I expect to see you in Malibu on Monday, Kahn had said. As if nothing had changed. As if nothing could change. As if they could pick up where they had left off.

Malibu.

Josh's old home.

The door to the dressing room opened and Luther stepped in. He had a towel wrapped around his neck and he had changed shirts.

"What do you want?" Josh asked.

"To see if you're okay," Luther said.

Josh nodded. "You want to see if I'm okay."

Luther stepped inside and closed the door. "Yes," he said cautiously. "I waited until Kahn left."

"You could have left with him."

"What?" Luther asked.

Josh clenched a fist. "You heard me."

"Why would I want to go with Kahn?"

"Because you told him where I was."

Luther's mouth opened slightly, and then he closed it. "You heard him. He yelled at me for not telling him."

"Nice setup," Josh snapped. "It wasn't enough though. It's too much of a coincidence, you showing up, then him."

"I didn't call him, Josh."

"No?" Josh said. "Then how did he find me?"

"I don't know," Luther said. "I haven't talked to Kahn in ten years."

"Ten years," Josh said. "I'm to believe you just found me and joined up, no questions asked. Hell, man, you weren't even angry. You acted like nothing had changed."

Luther's back straightened. He looked taller, and powerful, the muscles in his shoulders rippling. "I was angry. I was furious. After Emily left, I tore up my place. You were my friend, man, and you lied to me. You disappeared on me and you made me think you were dead."

His voice rose on the last word. The anger that hadn't been present before was there now.

"But I didn't think it was you, at first. I thought it was going to be some punk kid who stole Davy's music. Then I saw you standing with the group like you used to, same position, and you turned and you got that closed-off look that I remembered, and I knew. I knew." He swallowed hard. "I hated you at that moment, Josh."

Josh froze. He felt like he was wrapped in a shell.

"And you told me to leave. So I did. I got to the van, and realized that Davy Moss was still alive. The man who taught me to write music. The man who could woo a crowd like no one I'd ever performed with. Davy Moss. And I could perform with him again, maybe write with him again. So I swallowed that anger, and I found you, man. I found you."

Luther's voice lowered to a whisper. His face, normally so genial, was contorted. "I still hate you sometimes, man. What you did to me, no one had the right to do. No one."

This was what Josh had expected. From everyone. Not just Kahn. Not just Luther. But everyone who knew him. Who had known him.

"But I knew who you were, Josh," Luther said. "You were lost and lonely, and I knew at the time that you'd be gone one day. I was that way after my wife died. I just blew off the world. You did it more spectacular than me, but you do everything more spectacular than me. It was about you, Josh, not about me. And I had the sense to realize it."

"You didn't tell Kahn?"

Luther shook his head. "Why would I? The guy was part of the reason you left. I just want to make music with you. I don't want to destroy it."

Josh let out a breath. He was shaking. Luther was the only real friend he'd ever had—the only friend to span two lifetimes—and he'd tried to push him away.

"I'm scared, Luther," Josh said.

"You and me both, buddy," Luther replied. "You and me both."

Thirty-Three

*E*mily was talking with a promoter when Josh came into the restaurant. He was pale, and his features seemed sunken into his face. Luther followed so closely it looked as if he were protecting Josh's flank.

Emily excused herself and crossed the room. She had to stop and talk to another exec, shake the hand of one of the board members, and pat Lisa on the shoulder. Josh couldn't get past the door. Luther was standing beside him, talking politely to a member of Josh's construction crew. Josh was smiling mechanically at that young couple whose wedding he had been in, nodding as if he wasn't hearing any of the conversation.

When she reached him, Luther, not Josh, gave her a smile of relief. "He won't tell me what happened," Luther said to her under his breath. "He wanted to wait for you."

"I need to talk to him alone," she said to Luther.

He nodded. "I figured that."

He stepped out of the way, as if relinquishing his guard of Josh to her. Then she took Josh's arm and steered him out of the dining area, into the shut-down buffet down the hall.

They climbed over the rope in front of the entrance and went to one of the booths in the back. The space, which seemed small during the day, was actually quite large. It held hundreds of people with ease. She had done business here late at night before, and discovered that the size and the silence were conducive to talk.

She sat across from Josh in the booth and felt, oddly, like a teenager sneaking time with her boyfriend in the local hangout. The buffet still carried the odors of the night's dinner, and through the floorboards she could feel the vibrations from the bass in Jenny Shin's band.

Josh put his hands over his face. "I never thought my mood could swing so dramatically."

"I didn't hear yelling as I left," Emily said. "That's good, isn't it?"

He brought his hands down slowly. He let them rest on the tabletop, but they didn't look relaxed. The muscles stood out on the back of his arms. "He's too angry to yell. He wants to destroy me."

"Destroy you?" Whatever picture Emily had had of Kahn, it wasn't of a vengeful man.

"Either I go back to his management as the Davy Moss he knew, or he'll expose me through the press." He spoke with a calm tone, and his face was expressionless. Only the nervous tapping of his left leg revealed that he felt anything at all.

"How did he find you?" she asked. "How did he know it was you?"

"He found me ten years ago," Josh said.

Emily frowned. This was making less sense than before. "Why didn't he expose you then?"

"He figured I couldn't stay away from music. He figured I'd come back."

"He was right about that," she said.

"He's angry that you're managing me. He—" Josh glanced sideways at her. "He—says we have an exclusive contract."

Something about that statement felt wrong to her. She would explore that thought later. "Do you?"

"He and Davy Moss do. I wasn't trying to be Davy Moss."

She closed her eyes for a moment, then opened them and said, "You may need a lawyer, Josh."

"If I choose to fight him," Josh said.

"Why wouldn't you?" Emily's stomach was in knots. She had been approached by so many people tonight. The concert had gone better than she expected, and she actually had her choice of deals. And Josh had seemed so happy.

That look again. That sideways look. There was something he wasn't telling her.

"Josh," she said. "I need to know."

"He'll take you down with me. He'll ruin your reputation."

"He can't," she said, even though the knot in her stomach grew tighter. "It's already bad."

"He'll paint you as a vindictive, unethical manager who'll sleep with clients to get what she wants," Josh said softly.

"Son of a bitch," she snapped. "That's not how it is."

"But that's how it'll look. Kahn's good at making things look the way he wants them to."

She took a deep breath. Kahn was trying to neutralize her, to take her skills out of the picture. She knew how that went. And as angry as it made her, she couldn't let this become about her. It was about Josh—Josh and Kahn. She had to focus on Josh. Not on the threat to herself.

"How's he going to deal with all those years of hiding?" she asked. "How's he going to deal with your disappearance? It's going to seem like he was a collaborator in it."

"You forget," Josh said. "He's had ten years to prepare. All those Davy Moss is Alive rumors had to come from somewhere, didn't they?"

"You think they came from Kahn?"

"He never denied them. He always ignored them. He kept the estate alive. He kept the Davy Moss mythos alive, too."

Emily closed her eyes. Viewed coldly, it was simple. The return of Davy Moss was an even bigger story than his death. Especially if Davy Moss came back older, seasoned, his music enriched by the experience.

Article after article would be written about him. He would be profiled on entertainment shows all over the country, and the major talk shows would want to interview him. His concerts would be sold out.

"Wow." Emily opened her eyes. "He could make you the most famous man in the world. Hell, I could do it, and I haven't prepared as long as he has. The question is, can he make you do what he wants? You're not twenty anymore, Josh."

"He can do anything he wants," Josh said. "He does own Davy Moss, in a way, maybe even more than I do."

"That's not a reason to go back," she said.

"Yeah, I know." Josh shook his head in wonder. "You know, I got the music back. I had a feeling tonight unlike any I'd ever had before. I felt free. I felt joy. And then Kahn comes and he builds the same walls around me. I don't want to leave the music—it would kill me to do it twice—but I can't go back to him. I can't live that way anymore."

"So don't," Emily said. "We can take him on."

"We can't take him on," Josh said. "If we do, he won't just ruin me. He'll ruin you."

She swallowed, then she put her hand over his. Time to make a commitment. Time to stop taking things one day at a time. "Maybe some things are worth that risk."

"Em, it's your future at stake."

"No," she said. "It's *our* future. Imagine how we'll feel if we don't stand up for it. Now all we have to do is figure out how."

Part Five

…Yet another **Davy Moss** sighting, this one in New York City. Moss, according to the report, has lost most of his beautiful black hair and has put on fifty pounds. He works as a sound technician in Madison Square Garden. You be the judge of this one, guys.…

—Sightings page of the
Official Davy Moss website

thirty-four

It had been fifteen years since Josh had been in Malibu, yet he drove Highway 1 as if he'd been on it just days before. The rental car, a red Grand Prix, moved with an easy grace. It had a leather interior and smelled new.

Just like his cars had when he lived here.

Emily sat in the passenger seat. She wore a business suit, a stylish red that matched the car. The suit had a designer label that he didn't recognize, but it and her understated gold jewelry spoke of money. She also wore matching open-toe pumps and more makeup than she'd ever worn in Oceanlake. Her hair was swept back by combs. She looked expensive and businesslike and marvelous.

He couldn't be here without her.

He was amazed at the way she had rallied. She had been exhausted from planning the concert, but as soon as she had seen Kahn, the exhaustion appeared to be forgotten. He suspected she had merely put it off until she had time for it.

In their late-night planning session on Saturday, they had decided to come to Malibu to see Kahn. Emily had insisted on making the trip worthwhile. She had called Kahn and scheduled an appointment for Thursday, making him wait. Then she had meetings all over Los Angeles. Emily had set them up with the execs before they left Oceanlake. It was clear she could have held a bidding war then, but she claimed she wanted to give the companies time to solidify their bids. Instead, she had used that time to pull favors, to make plans with Josh, and to hire one of Los Angeles's best attorneys. Josh had balked at this last, but she had insisted.

We need someone good on retainer, she said, *just in case.*

Then he met the attorney and he was somewhat reassured. The attorney was a woman, LaTisha Morgan, who had a reputation for being tough and successful. She was also an old friend of Emily's.

He had met a lot of Emily's friends this week. They had looked at him with a measuring gaze, as if they expected him to grow horns and spit fire at them. Ricky Fink had left a legacy, not just with Emily, but also with her friends.

They had calmed her a little, but they hadn't calmed him. He wasn't sure if anything could calm him now. His stomach had been queasy for days. He had gone to all this trouble of making his life simpler, and then he had opted to do music again.

And Kahn had found him.

During that late-night session in the buffet, Josh had talked about leaving music again. He had explored more options than he cared to think about again. He knew what was coming, and it terrified him.

He knew how it felt to be the center of such attention that he couldn't cross a room without people screaming at him. The night before, in a hotel room near LAX, he had watched a segment on CNN about some premiere or another, and as he watched movie star after movie star wave to screaming crowds, a sweat broke out on his face.

He would be returning to that. If he stayed in music, he had no choice.

But first he had to go home.

Kahn had left him no choice on that, either.

"How much farther?" Emily sounded calm, but he knew she was as nervous as he was. She'd had to apply the red nail polish to her right hand three times. The brush kept slipping. He'd watched her routine for months now, and he'd never seen her miss while putting on nail polish. Or make-up. She did it with an expertise that would have made Angela jealous.

Angela. She was still in the picture as well, and he knew it. She'd been playing the widow for fifteen years. She had used that status to obtain a place in the estate. She dated, inconspicuously, but never married or had children, making sad pronouncements about her lost romance.

Instead, all she'd done was protect her found money.

"Josh?" Emily asked again. "How much farther?"

"Just up the hill."

Malibu had grown since he'd last been there. And the hillsides were scarred by several bad fire seasons. The ocean looked the same, though. Flat and blue and friendly. It was hard to believe it was the same ocean he saw in Oceanlake. Here, in some ways, it symbolized California: Pretty on the surface and deadly underneath.

"I wish you'd let me close the deal with Barry," she said, not for the first time.

He hadn't answered her before. He'd been quiet about everything, and for the most part, she had let him. But she had completed negotiations with one of the studio execs, one she had known for a long time. He had come in that morning with a pre-emptive offer that was excellent for an unknown band.

She had argued that if they took it, they would hold the moral high ground. When Kahn made announcements that Josh was really Davy Moss, Josh would be able to hold up the contract and say he wasn't trying to capitalize on his old name.

And that had felt wrong.

He had refused to take the offer, and continued on the first plan, the only one he could really live with.

"I'm not ready to sign anything," he said.

She made an odd sound, as if she were trying to stifle a disagreement. Ever since Saturday night, they had been distant from each other even though they had been together. It was as if Kahn's appearance had placed a ghost between them.

The ghost of Davy Moss.

"Josh," she said as they approached the hill he had mentioned, "I'm not sure we should do this."

"I can drop you off," he said and winced inwardly at how cold his words sounded.

Her lips thinned, but she didn't turn on him in anger. He realized, dimly, that he'd been trying to anger her for days, to arouse some kind of passion from her, even an angry one. She felt so far away.

How odd that, at this point in his life, he would find a woman who wanted Josh Candless, not Davy Moss.

"I still think it would be better to go about our business and let Kahn release your identity if he so chooses. His proof may not be very good."

"Then we spend the next few years worrying about what Kahn is going to do." Josh shook his head. "Kahn has controlled my life for too long, Em. I've got to do it my own way now. If you want, you can leave now. He threatened to ruin you too. I can live through anything, but you don't have to."

She turned her head toward the window. "Don't you want me beside you, Josh?" Her voice sounded small.

He reached across the car and took her hand. Her skin was soft, but clammy. She was as terrified as he was.

"I do. I do want you beside me." But he didn't say the rest. *I need you beside me, Em. Stay with me always.* He didn't say it because he felt she needed the chance to escape. She needed to get away from him, to save herself. She had no real idea of the circus that faced them.

He turned the car onto the wide street leading up the hill. Dozens of mansions dotted the hillside where, only fifteen years ago, a handful of houses stood. His place, barely visible on the hill's crest, was one of the smaller mansions now. When he lived there, it had been the largest building on the hillside.

"The only reason I keep speaking up," she said, talking rapidly as if she were going to try to get all the words in before they reached his former house, "is because I don't know what you want from this meeting. Kahn already said his piece. He already made his threats. You can't expect him to change his mind in a few days."

"He caught me by surprise," Josh said. "I want to talk to him, equal to equal. That night, he made me feel like Davy again. Davy's been dead fifteen years. Somehow I have to make Kahn realize that."

"He won't, Josh." She sounded sad. "You're just wasting your time."

Josh pulled onto the familiar side street. The changes here were minor: a flower garden where a yard used to be, different cars lining the road, a curling white drive leading to a hidden house. He pulled up to the gate that led to his house, the house he still owned, if he were only to claim it. His heart was pounding in his chest.

With a press of the button, he brought his window down. The guard at the gate was young—too young to have worked for Josh. For Davy.

Even he was getting confused.

"Joshua Candless and Emily Lukovich to see Jeremiah Kahn," Josh said. "He's expecting us."

The guard checked his list, then waved the car through. Somehow, the ease with which Josh entered the compound made his heart pound harder.

The drive hadn't changed. Flowers he'd ordered still grew beside the road. The outbuildings still stood: the large guest house, done in the same style as the main house; the cabana beside the pool; and the studio tucked behind a natural stone formation. He felt a wave of nostalgia. He had loved this place, and he had forgotten it. He had put it out of his mind. He knew, if he glanced in his rearview mirror, he would see the ocean, blue and powerful and there: an inspiration to all he had done.

He had come back to the ocean when he had come back to his music. He hadn't put that together before.

He drove the car to the main house. It was done in South American colonial, painted white, allowing the glare of the bright sun and the stunning diversity of Southern California flowers to stand out. He had bought the place from an actor who had decided to move somewhere bigger. The actor had disappeared as well, probably not purposely. Careers had their ups and their downs. Josh had just forced the down on himself.

"This is quite a place," Emily said.

"Yeah," Josh said, not wanting to let anything more into his voice. He could barely admit to himself that he missed this estate. If he admitted it to Emily, she might take it wrong. She might think he wanted to come back.

Did he want to go back? He had forgotten so much. He had forgotten how the hot California sunshine felt real in Malibu. He had forgotten how the sea smelled almost sweet-salty here, and rarely turned on its faithful. He had forgotten how easy it had been to make music in the studio he had built especially for himself.

A studio, not the back room of a cheap apartment.

He stopped the car by the large garage that had been built to house the actor's collection of antique automobiles. Josh had never owned a lot of cars, so the garage had been used by the staff and by friends. It still looked half empty.

He squeezed Emily's hand. She looked at him, raising her eyebrows in a small question. He didn't give her a chance to speak.

"We're going through with this, Em."

"All right." She was the one to break the grip. She opened her door and got out carefully, maintaining that uneasy balance between disaster and grace that high-heel-wearing women managed. She stood and stretched surreptitiously, then adjusted the jacket of her suit.

Josh couldn't move quite as quickly. This was it, more than Saturday night. This was the moment where his life would change. And he didn't know how.

He wiped his damp palms on his khaki pants. He hadn't worn a suit—he wouldn't give Kahn the satisfaction—but he'd settled for upper-class casual: khaki pants and a white linen shirt. He wore dark brown deck shoes and he had his hair combed back, away from his face. He knew he looked better than he ever had in Oceanlake.

He stretched, too. Even though he had had the air on, the back of his shirt was damp. He rolled up the sleeves, and then held out his hand for Emily. She grabbed her briefcase from the back of the car, then slammed her door shut.

"Here goes," she whispered.

He smiled at her, then tucked her hand in the crook of his arm. Yes. Here they went. For better or worse.

The path to the door was made of fake cobblestone. He had never realized how difficult it was to walk on until he felt Emily struggle in her heels. If she hadn't had him to lean on, she would have tottered horribly.

They went up the narrow steps to the long porch. The white wicker furniture looked new, but it still matched his old vision for the place. It was covered with green and red pillows, which accented the vegetation that crept around the columns.

He had put a lot of time into the design of this house.

He had forgotten that, too.

Then he paused in front of the door. He was going to knock on his own front door. He hesitated, and in that hesitation, Emily seemed to understand what was bothering him. She set down her briefcase, then reached up and grabbed treble clef knocker, rapping it smartly twice.

He put his hand over the one she had on his arm. She smiled at him.

Then the door opened. A woman stood there. A slender, dark-haired woman whom Josh did not recognize.

He had expected Kahn to answer, although, now that he thought about, Kahn never answered the door, not for anyone.

"Joshua Candless and Emily Lukovich to see Jeremiah Kahn," Emily said before Josh could speak. Her clipped business tones echoed his from earlier.

The woman invited them into the entry. It smelled of lemon polish and lilies, just as it always had. A large vase of lilies rested on top of one of the antique tables he'd inherited when his parents died, beneath a tasteful wooden mirror he had purchased at some art show. The deacon's bench still ran along one wall, and the artwork from his first two album covers decorated the dark wall.

"Mr. Kahn will be with you shortly," the woman said, and disappeared down the hall.

She went the direction Josh expected, to Kahn's old office. He apparently hadn't appropriated any of Davy's space for his own.

Emily had picked up her briefcase and brought it inside. She had let go of his arm, and now went over to admire the paintings. They were large and garish by modern standards, but he had always liked them.

He had always liked what they symbolized.

Success.

The success he had once walked away from.

Suddenly he wondered who was smarter—him or Kahn. By bringing him home, Kahn had an advantage. He had the advantage of the past, the good things.

The things that Josh had once renounced.

The woman came back down the hall. "Mr. Kahn would like you to join him in his office."

She waited until Emily and Josh caught up with her, then she led them down the wide hallway, decorated with large leafy plants and photographs from all aspects of Davy's career: concerts, award ceremonies, and private photos. Someone had added a number of shots, most of them simple shots of Davy playing music. One, tucked in a grouping around a large palm, was the *People* magazine cover blaring the story of Davy's death.

Emily slowed a bit to look at them.

The door to Kahn's office was open. The woman pointed to it, then stepped aside. As Emily and Josh went through, the woman closed the door.

Kahn's office smelled of leather and pipe tobacco. It was dark—done in heavy wood paneling and deep forest greens. A specially made wooden desk the size of some dining room tables was the focal point of the room.

Kahn was not sitting in it. He was standing beside the window. The green velvet curtains were open slightly, revealing sunlight filtering through the vegetation.

He turned, and his gaze met Josh's. "Welcome home, Davy."

A lump rose in Josh's throat. He swallowed hard.

Kahn's hard face had a softness to it. In the softer light of a California day, he did look older. And more vulnerable.

"We missed you here," he said.

"Things don't seem to have changed much."

Kahn shrugged. "Most of the staff never worked with you, Davy. Much of the house is closed off."

Josh nodded. He wished Kahn would call him Josh, but he decided not to insist on it.

Kahn's gaze slid toward Emily, then back to Josh. "I'm not quite sure why you're here. If you've come to accept my offer, then why is Ms. Lukovich with you?"

Emily started to answer but Josh put a hand on her arm. "You caught me by surprise on Saturday night."

"Did you think I wouldn't find you?" Kahn asked.

"I thought we'd have a little time to enjoy our anonymity," Josh said.

Kahn shook his head and crossed to his desk. He sank into the leather chair, then templed his fingers. "I don't understand it, Davy. This need to climb a ladder you've already climbed. Why do the work twice?"

Josh wandered to the bookcase, saw books on business management, copyrights and royalties, and estate administration. "I'm too old to be Davy Moss," he said with his back to Kahn.

Through a small mirror beside the bookshelf, he could see Emily, still standing, her briefcase clutched before her. She realized that she wasn't really a part of this drama yet, and she managed to recede into the background while they talked.

"You are Davy Moss—" Kahn started.

"No," Josh said. "Davy Moss is dead."

He turned. Kahn's face had hardened, the softness gone, the familiar edges and ridges back under the slowly wrinkling skin.

"Davy Moss died at the age of twenty-two. He was a pop star who appealed to teenyboppers, like Donny Osmond, or the young Michael Jackson."

"Michael Jackson made the transition," Kahn said.

"For a time," Josh said. "But that faked suicide of mine destroyed any chance for a transition, and we both know it."

"If you come back, there will be a great deal of hype."

Josh nodded. "A great deal. And it will all be focused on Davy Moss. The return of Davy Moss. Teenyboppers who are now in their thirties will come to reunion concerts and bring their children who'll moan and wonder what the appeal was of this old guy."

Kahn didn't move. He was staring at Josh.

"My way is better, Kahn. Let me establish myself as Josh Candless. Let me play my kind of music, stuff that appeals to adults. Let them find me on their own. And then, if I'm successful, then tell them I'm Davy Moss."

Kahn shook his head. "No one will want your music. It's too undefined. You play in too many categories. They won't be able to market you."

"We have a deal," Emily said, "with Barry Boyer. I have offers on the table for deals with several other companies as well. They're all willing to work with Josh."

"They'll pay him a pittance because they don't know who he is," Kahn said.

"That's right." Emily set her briefcase down. She took a step toward Kahn's desk, and Josh suddenly understood the brilliance of high heels. They made her seem taller, more powerful. She rested her hands on the wood and leaned forward. "Imagine this, Jeremiah."

Josh started. No one called Kahn "Jeremiah." No one.

"Imagine if Josh has the kind of success the suits believe he will have. Right now they're bidding over an unknown. They believe they can create him. Then the news breaks that he's Davy Moss."

"They'll be angry that you didn't tell them," Kahn said.

"And thrilled they got him so cheap. They'll have free promotion for a year or more, and Josh will have had an opportunity to establish his new identity. It won't get usurped by Davy Moss."

Kahn's eyes narrowed. He peered around Emily to Josh.

"You see why you need me? She doesn't know what you're worth." Kahn pushed his chair away from his desk. "Listen to me, Ms. Lukovich." He exaggerated his courtesy to make her lack of courtesy sound unprofessional. "Davy Moss is a multimillion dollar property."

"And Davy Moss will continue to earn his multimillions," she said, "while Josh Candless is establishing himself."

"It's fraud," Kahn said.

"Is it?" she asked. "Anymore than taking money from insurance companies for a man you knew wasn't dead?"

Kahn flushed. Josh's heart was suddenly in his throat. He hadn't thought of that. He hadn't thought of any of it.

"I thought he was dead at the time," Kahn said.

"But you didn't return the money, did you?" she asked. "Nor did you, once you found Josh, offer to relinquish your control over his estate—control which you've been exerting illegally."

The flush still darkened Kahn's cheeks. He glanced at Josh. "I underestimated this woman of yours."

"She's my manager," Josh said, his throat tightening. "She's managing."

Kahn nodded.

Emily straightened. "You claim to have a contract with Davy Moss, a contract that only exists if Davy Moss is alive. Yet you have managed his estate as if he were dead for fifteen years. You can't have it both ways, Jeremiah."

Kahn closed his eyes. He suddenly looked old. The patrician features that had gotten him so far, the pride that had always made him seem strong, were gone.

Josh hadn't moved. He looked at Kahn and then at Emily. She was breathing hard, her cheeks flushed as well, and a strand of hair had fallen from her combs. She was beautiful, and tough, and without asking Josh's permission, she had just backed down Jeremiah Kahn.

Kahn opened his eyes. "Let me speak to Davy alone," he said wearily.

Emily smiled. "Nice game, Jeremiah, but it doesn't do any good to separate us."

Kahn turned toward Josh. "Please. Let's take business out of this for once. I can't talk with her here."

Josh swallowed. "Em says she has to stay."

"Davy," Kahn said, "I haven't seen you for fifteen years."

Josh moved away from the bookshelf. He went to Emily's side, touched her arm. Her skin was clammy and covered with gooseflesh.

She had been terrified beneath that veneer of calm, and he hadn't realized it.

He hadn't realized it at all.

"Let me talk to him," Josh said. "I promise not to agree to anything, not without you."

Her eyes met his, and they were hurt.

"As you wish," she said. Then she grabbed her briefcase and went out the door.

As it closed behind her, Josh felt more alone than he had in years.

Alone with Jeremiah Kahn.

thirty-five

As the door closed behind her, Emily began to shake. She had taken on the mighty Kahn, the man who had terrified promoters and deal makers for nearly two generations.

She had taken him on, and won.

Then Josh had kicked her out of the room.

She held her briefcase so tightly her fingers hurt. Her feet were bent at an uncomfortable angle, and her toes were falling asleep. She hadn't worn heels like this in months and it showed. She wasn't used to it anymore.

Any of it.

She wasn't quite sure where she should go. There were no chairs outside Kahn's office, only the deacon's bench down the hall. The plants loomed beside her, person-sized and healthy, their green leaves brushing at her new suit.

But that didn't bother her. Nothing really bothered her about the house.

Except that it existed. It was a tangible reminder of Josh's former life.

She sighed, feeling more tired than she had in weeks. Reminder, hell. Acknowledgment. Somehow she had convinced herself that Josh was still Josh, even though he had been famous in his past. This house blew that illusion away.

The pictures were the final straw. They plastered the wall: Davy Moss singing; Davy Moss shaking the hand of the president of MCA, the president of Sony, the president of every major record company in the nation. She used to study Kahn's deals: He had been so ballsy in those days, taking Davy from one company to another if the first company didn't fulfill its promises—or, in the case of one, if Davy's sales weren't as high as expected. Most labels blamed the artist for low sales. Kahn had blamed the record company.

Scattered among the photos were pictures of Davy Moss accepting a Grammy—she had never realized that he had received one—and pictures of him receiving each and every one of his gold records. The platinums came later, after he had...died.

They looked so different. It was hard to tell Davy and Josh were the same person. They had similar features and those eyes, but beyond that, there was nothing the same. Josh's face looked lived in. Davy's belonged to a boy. Josh's face was tanned and lined and slender. Davy's was pale and smooth and round.

She wouldn't have known they were the same man by their looks. But Davy Moss and Josh Candless were one person, even though she had still thought of them as two. It wasn't until she walked into this house, until Josh had looked so young and vulnerable when Kahn had welcomed him home, that she realized they were one and the same.

And then it was too late.

Her stand against Kahn had been a last-ditch effort, a way to save face more than anything else. Because Kahn was right. Why should Josh climb a ladder he'd already climbed? Why shouldn't Kahn, the most famous deal maker of the last twenty years, continue to handle Josh's career? Why go with someone young and inexperienced and full of idealistic notions?

Because of love?

That would make her as bad as Ricky Fink. Ricky had used her, used her love, used her strengths because she loved him, not because he believed in her. If he had wanted the best for both of them, he would have looked beyond the emotion. He would have seen her, and known that she was good. Not dismissed her when he decided he didn't love her anymore.

She couldn't expect Josh to keep her on because he loved her. It would mean she was making the same mistake twice, mixing emotion and business and hoping she wouldn't get hurt.

And this time, unlike the first time, she was the wrong person for the job. Jeremiah Kahn was better.

When they called her back in—if they called her back in—she would advise Josh—Davy—to let Kahn manage his career. After her statements, Kahn would understand the need to go slow, the need to reintegrate Davy back differently than he originally planned.

Although she wasn't sure what his original plans had been.

She had never asked.

And neither had Josh.

The woman who had let them in crossed the hall. She stopped, peered at Emily as if she wasn't sure what she was seeing, then came toward her.

"They asked me to wait outside," Emily said.

"You shouldn't have to stand," the woman said. There was understanding in her voice. Every woman knew what it was like to stand too long in heels. "We have a sitting area."

"Actually," Emily said, "I would love a cup of coffee. Is that possible?"

"Sure," the woman said. "Let's go to the kitchen."

Emily had hoped she would say that. She knew she would feel more at home in a kitchen than in a sitting area designed for strangers. She followed the woman down a long corridor. On each side were paintings, framed album covers, more plants. She hadn't expected the place to look lived in. She had expected more of a museum, like Graceland, a tacky monument to the dead.

Instead, she had found a home that was still being used, a place that had light and air and warmth.

And a sense of Josh to it.

Or Davy.

It wasn't just the photos, or the framed artwork, or the reminders of his past. It was a sense of layout, a feeling the decor gave off, a feeling similar to the ones in Josh's songs. She couldn't describe it any better—it was a sense, a way of equating one with the other—but it existed.

It made his past live.

She knew a lot of famous people, but they had remained famous, or they had at least followed the trajectory of their careers. They had been on a path, and that path had shown on their face. They hadn't appeared and disappeared and tried to reinvent themselves, like Josh had.

Like Davy had.

God, she wasn't even sure what to call him anymore.

Josh. Davy. Josh.

Maybe he didn't even know.

Several doors opened off the left side of the corridor. As she walked, the right side became a wall of windows opening onto a beautiful enclosed garden. There were chairs scattered invitingly about, and flowers the size of her fist throughout.

And then, suddenly, the woman led her through two double doors into a room the size of the main floor of her house in Oceanlake. This wasn't a kitchen. It was a working space. It had stainless-steel appliances, a stove the size of most counters, and a refrigerator that belonged in a restaurant. It was a catering kitchen, designed for parties and main events. A man worked in the corner, cutting vegetables and putting them in a pot. The room smelled of beef broth and tomatoes.

Her stomach rumbled. She had been too nervous to eat breakfast. And now she was going to pay for it.

The woman stopped in front of an expensive cappuccino machine. "Do you want real coffee or something special?"

"Have you got a pot made?" Emily asked, looking at the man.

"If I did not make coffee when I arrived," he said, his deep voice rumbling in the small space, "I would be fired within the space of an hour. Mr. Kahn, he likes coffee and he likes it real, not with any sprinkles or foaming milk."

Emily smiled. Somehow she had expected that. "Real coffee is fine."

The woman led her through the working area and into another section of the room. Four booths had been built into the wall, facing the garden. It felt as if they were actually in the garden. She slid into one, and so did Emily. The man brought them coffee on a silver tray, along with a small pitcher of real cream and tiny lumps of sugar of a kind Emily hadn't seen since she was a little girl.

"Thanks," she said.

The coffee was in a silver pot, but instead of small fragile cups, as she would have expected, large black mugs sat beside it. The woman took the pot and poured.

"I didn't introduce myself," she said. "I'm Mr. Kahn's assistant, Louise."

"Emily," she said.

"He wouldn't tell me anything about you," she said. "I hope you don't mind my prying a bit."

Emily smiled thinly, wishing she didn't have to respond. She was beginning to like the easy familiarity that had arisen between them. It eased the nerves raised by the meeting.

"I'm Mr. Candless's manager," she said.

"I gathered that much." Louise handed her a mug. "But Mr. Kahn won't say any more about you, except that Mr. Candless is quite a musician."

"He is," Emily said.

Louise settled back in the booth. "I can't imagine Mr. Kahn taking on another musician. The death of Mr. Moss hit him so hard."

Emily raised her head. "That was fifteen years ago."

Louise nodded. "Before I came here. But I once heard him shouting at some old friend who wanted him to take on a new client, wanted him to get past Mr. Moss. He said there was no getting past Mr. Moss. If someone didn't handle Mr. Moss's career, Mr. Moss would be dead for sure."

Emily poured a bit of cream into her coffee. Then she spooned in two lumps of sugar. "He's right. You can tell which musicians had good executors for their estates, and which ones didn't."

And she didn't say any more, since she had just accused Kahn of fraud by using his executorship when he had known that Davy was alive.

"I don't normally talk about Mr. Kahn like this," Louise said. "It's just that he's been so worried about this meeting. And I've been worried about him. He's not a young man anymore."

Emily nodded and cupped her hands around the warm mug. The cook came over with some muffins and a small container of whipped butter. Emily thanked him, and prepared one for herself. She was so hungry suddenly. Hungry and nervous.

She hoped Josh was doing all right.

Then she looked up at Louise, who was watching her. Louise hadn't really been talking out of turn. She'd been trying to get Emily to do so. She'd tried that warm girl-buddy thing that often got so many women to open up. But Emily had been in the male business world too long. She had learned that girl-talk had no place in business, not even over coffee in a comfortable kitchen.

Then one of the garden doors opened, and a slender woman with long, blond hair entered. She wore a white sundress that accented her tan. Her arms and legs were toned. With an expertise born of many years in the entertainment business, Emily quickly noted all the expensive accents: the hair was well colored, the tan was too even to be from the outdoors, the toning was the result of hours spent with a personal trainer. The woman's features were familiar, but Emily couldn't place them.

Louise stood. "Miss Angela."

Emily went cold. She had forgotten about Angela Caputo, Davy's former fiancée, said to be so grief stricken she could never marry, never have another man. Emily hadn't realized that she lived in the house too.

Angela's eyes were the clear blue of the ocean, and her movements were practiced, as if she knew she had an audience.

"Are you Kahn's mystery guest?" she asked.

Emily didn't know how to answer. So she slid out of the booth and extended her hand. "I'm Emily Lukovich."

"Angela Caputo." She smiled. "If you're the mystery guest, Kahn will kill me for talking to you."

So Kahn had banished Angela from the area. He didn't want to chance her recognizing Josh. Was it protection for Josh? Or was it protection for Kahn and his plan?

Or was it both?

"There are two guests," Louise said, with more finesse than Emily would have expected. She probably did know more than she was letting on. "The other is still with Mr. Kahn."

Angela pouted attractively. "And I wanted to come out of my exile."

"I thought you had a lunch in Century City this afternoon."

"A late lunch," Angela said. Her voice was smooth, like honey. She smiled at Emily. "What's your business here?"

Emily smiled back. It was hard to judge what the attraction had been. Josh, her Josh, would not have been interested in this brittle woman. But Davy had.

Fifteen years ago.

When they were both young.

People changed a lot in fifteen years.

"I'm afraid I'm not at liberty to discuss my business," Emily said.

Angela shook her head and looked at Louise. "You know, you'd think that once women got into business, they'd be more open than men. Instead, they turn into men." She flounced out of the room without saying goodbye.

Louise bit her lip, then looked apologetically at Emily. "I'm afraid I really should go with her. Mr. Kahn was explicit about not having her near his office today."

Emily waved a hand. "Go. I can find my way back." Then she shrugged. "Or wait until I get an escort."

"You don't need one," Louise said, "if you stay to the corridors."

"I will," Emily said, and sank back into the booth. Louise followed Angela out of the kitchen. The cook banged some pots, but remained unavailable.

Emily stared at the flowers through the tinted window. This place was comfortable and uncomfortable at the same time. The problem was that she was unsettled. Josh had become more inexplicable than ever. He had left somewhere this beautiful for a life on the road. He had money, but he never spent it. He hadn't even balked when she set the budget for the band. He lived in that tiny apartment, and he dressed like every other contractor in Oceanlake, and yet he knew how to cross into this world, how to please an expensive woman like Angela.

Would he remember all that now that he was here? Was he, despite what he had promised, cutting a deal with Kahn right now? She could almost imagine it: the conversation about how to buy off Emily.

Almost.

He wouldn't do that to her, would he?

Ricky would have.

But Josh kept saying he wasn't Ricky.

She would have to trust that.

She sighed and made herself take a sip of the now lukewarm coffee. It was hard to trust him. She had thought she knew him, but walking into this place made her realize she didn't know him at all.

And that was as much her fault as his.

She hadn't believed him, not really. Hadn't realized what being Davy Moss meant.

She believed him now.

thirty-six

Kahn remained behind his desk long after Emily had left. He said nothing, but looked at Josh, just looked at him, as if he hadn't quite seen anything like him for a long, long time.

Josh continued to stand. He felt he had no choice. If he sat, he would turn into Davy Moss. Not the superstar entertainer Davy Moss, but the sixteen-year-old Davy Moss, the kid who had grabbed onto Kahn to make a career.

"Fifteen years ago," Kahn said, his voice loud as it broke the silence of the room, "I was roused from bed at 3 a.m. to find the police at my door. They had found your Porsche, with your jacket inside. They wanted to see you. You were gone. No note, no nothing. Three people had seen you leave, including Luther, who said you were looking wild. They said you had taken the Porsche."

Josh felt his shoulders tighten.

"The police assumed you were dead. The news reported it that way from the beginning. But fans lined that river. They searched for you. Idaho Search and Rescue risked their lives looking for you."

A flush built under Josh's skin. He could feel its warmth. Kahn could make him feel young and out of control without even trying.

"But I kept thinking you weren't that dumb. You drove fast—every kid did—but you were the best driver I'd ever seen. It wasn't raining. There was a full moon that night. The river is hard to miss. And yet you went off on a corner well-marked as dangerous, and there weren't even skid marks."

Kahn leaned back in his chair. He was watching Josh as he spoke.

"Everyone said I was in denial. They said I was wrong. And I believed them. I did. I never married, Davy. I never had kids. You were the closest thing to a child I ever had, and I didn't want to believe you were dead."

"So you didn't," Josh said, knowing Kahn's stubbornness.

"Oh, I believed," Kahn said. "In the middle of the night when I was alone, I believed. I would sit in that garden—." He stopped himself, shook his head, and took a deep breath. "But in the daytime, I'd search. It was pretty easy. I was executor now. I tracked all the money. I found the Candlesses, heard the story about their poor son Josh, and how you'd been such good friends, how you'd sent them money for years because you were so kind."

"And you figured I wasn't that kind," Josh said.

"No," Kahn said. "You've always been kind, Davy. But not without reason. And I figured you had to feel guilty about Joshua Candless's death. Only you couldn't. The kid died of leukemia. You didn't throw rocks at him; you hadn't called him names. You'd been good friends. No. I figured you were paying them for something else."

Josh swallowed. "I was paying them for the use of the name."

"It took me years to figure that out," Kahn said. "The name, and the birth certificate. A birth certificate can get you a long way in this culture, can't it, Davy?"

Josh didn't answer.

"A birth certificate, a name, and half a million dollars."

Josh started.

"Did you think we wouldn't catch that? That's a lot of money to funnel outside the organization. But you assumed that we'd investigate the payments to the Candless family and leave it at that, didn't you?"

Josh nodded.

"I would have," Kahn said. "If I had been able to stand in front of your dead body at the funeral and mourn you. Instead, I had this doubt. I was like a man whose kid had disappeared off the face of the earth. I was clutching at anything. And I found that there were two Candless accounts. You hid the second one well. No one would have found it if they weren't looking for something unusual. The checks were a brilliant idea. Made out to 'Candless,' all the same. They were even cashed by the same bank. Brilliant, to do all that research, Davy. Brilliant."

Josh didn't move.

"But not enough. I studied those check stubs, and I finally noticed that the bank had stamped a different account number on some of them. And that's when I located the second account. The one that was emptied two days before Davy Moss died."

Josh closed his eyes. He'd had the money wired to a different bank—this one in Vegas—then closed that one and wired the money to several accounts, splitting the money among banks. He'd used the account in Denver first, then decided that he would try not to live off his savings; he would try to earn money. And he did, waiting tables, washing dishes, even collecting garbage in one town. He learned how to be self-sufficient, and in a few years, he didn't touch the money at all.

But he managed it. He always managed it, investing, making the interest work for him. He had played with the money as if it were merely numbers on a screen, making it grow until he was, for all intents and purposes, rich again.

The chair squeaked as Kahn leaned forward. Josh opened his eyes. Kahn was staring at him, the hawklike expression back.

"I think you wanted me to find you," Kahn said. "I think you're smart enough to cover your tracks better. I think, if you really wanted to disappear, you would have. You would have stayed out of bars, you would never have sung again, and you would have used a fake name that had no connection to you at all."

The flush had grown deeper. Josh actually felt as if his face were on fire.

"And that gave me hope," Kahn said. "I waited. I figured you'd come back. And I'd keep everything here for you until you did."

It all felt true. In fact, Josh knew it to be true, right down to the accusation. Kahn had told him on Saturday that he had known where Josh was for the past ten years. If Kahn had known that, he could have come after Josh at any point. Instead, he allowed Josh to live his own life.

"Why didn't you bring me back?" Josh asked.

Kahn ran a hand through his thick silver hair. A strand fell from his head onto the shoulder of his tailored suit. "You wouldn't have stayed. You made it abundantly clear that you didn't want to be here. I was hoping you'd eventually realize you did. But you're ready to come back now, aren't you?"

Josh shook his head. "I can't. I'm not ready to be Davy Moss again."

"You don't have to do the work. We'll promote you differently," Kahn said. "We'll handle the P.R., give you the kind of shows you want—"

"And I'll be a laughingstock. Everyone will expect one thing and get another. No, Kahn." Josh took a deep breath, then sat in the chair across from Kahn. He no longer felt sixteen. He felt every one of his thirty-seven years. "Davy Moss is a celebrity. If I come back now, my every move will be watched. If I have a drink in a bar in Billings, Montana, my picture will be in *People* the following week. I wouldn't have to do anything and I'll get press coverage."

"Exactly," Kahn said.

Josh shook his head. "Davy Moss is a celebrity. Josh Candless is a musician. Do you see the difference, Kahn? Josh Candless will rise or fall based on his music. If it gives him celebrity, fine. If it doesn't, that's fine too. But he'll be judged as a musician."

"Davy Moss made his reputation as a musician."

"Yes," Josh said, "and I was wrong to leave it."

Kahn blinked, a sign of surprise.

"But when I faked the death," Josh said, "then I made Davy Moss into a celebrity. He'll always be a curiosity, a subject of speculation, like James Dean. What would he have done if he had lived? Whatever it is, if fans discover he does live, they'll be disappointed. How does a man compete with fifteen years of imagination? He doesn't."

Josh sighed and repeated softly, "He doesn't."

Kahn was frowning. He folded his hands together and placed them on the desk.

"So, if I tell the world you're Davy Moss," he said slowly, "I'll take your music away from you."

Josh blinked and looked up, surprised. He hadn't thought of it in quite those terms.

"Yeah," he said quietly. "I guess you will."

thirty-seven

Emily had been alone for nearly fifteen minutes when Josh found her. She had had a second muffin and a fourth cup of coffee while she watched the birds in the garden. It was an active place, filled with flowers and greenery and creatures of all types. It seemed both soothing and demanding, a place that took all of a person's attention and refused to give it back.

She couldn't think about Josh and Kahn while she watched, and yet, somehow, she couldn't think of anything else.

"Em?" he said softly.

She hadn't even heard him come into the kitchen. He was standing uncomfortably beside the booth, his skin pale, the shadows under his blue eyes deeper than they had been when he went into the house. He glanced over his shoulder at the cook, then held out his hand to her. "Ready?"

His voice sounded funny, strangled, and she wondered if he were making it sound that way so no one would recognize it.

"Yes." She took his hand and felt the familiar warmth run through her. She loved touching him. She always would.

"So you're the mystery guest."

For the second time in a week, Emily watched Josh freeze at the sound of a voice. He turned, and so did Emily, to see Angela standing behind them.

She had changed from her white sundress into a pair of jeans and a white T-shirt. The gold chain around her neck and the diamond earrings made the look expensive.

Emily took a breath. "This is my partner, Josh Candless."

Angela was staring at him. "Aren't you stunning?" she said. Then she held out her left hand. "I'm Angela Caputo."

He took it and stared at the ringless fingers. "I thought you were engaged to Davy Moss," he said in that strangled voice.

Emily's heart pounded. He had been in love with this woman once. She had loved him. They had planned on marriage.

And she didn't recognize him.

"Fifteen years ago, darling," she said, her smile warm.

Josh still held her hand. "I read the trades for years. I never saw the announcement. You don't wear your ring."

She snatched her hand away. "You're mean."

"Just curious." He was watching her. Emily was trying not to watch him.

"Everyone knows that we hadn't publicized the engagement. Everyone knows Davy had the ring on him when he died." Her voice hitched. She sounded distraught.

"Everyone, it seems," Josh said softly, "except me."

Emily stiffened. He had never been engaged to her? And he was using this as a way to tell Emily? Or to test Angela?

"Stunning but cruel," Angela said, backing away from him. "I don't know what you're doing here in Davy's house, but you really should get out."

"I think we will," Josh said, nodding at her once, a movement that looked courtly but felt rude, at least to Emily.

They left the kitchen and he steered her through a different hallway. He had his hand on her elbow, and he said nothing as they walked. The pace he set was rapid, as if he wanted to get out of the house as quickly as possible.

He opened a door that led to the front porch. They crossed the wood, past the wicker furniture, and took the stairs that led to the cobblestone walkway. Still he said nothing.

She didn't push him. She wasn't really willing to talk here, either. She thought of this as an enemy camp, which was funny, considering it had once belonged to Josh.

Actually, it had never belonged to Josh. It had belonged to Davy, and now to Kahn.

When they reached the car, she walked to her side, pulled open the door, and stood back as a wave of heat hit her. In a few short months in Oceanlake she had forgotten about too-hot cars and baking interiors. She set her briefcase on the backseat, then slid inside. Josh did the same.

He started the car, turned on the air, and rolled the windows down. Then, without waiting for her to put on her seatbelt, he backed up, turned around, and drove down the driveway like a maniac.

Like she had imagined Davy Moss had driven on the night he died.

When they left the estate, she finally felt like she could attempt conversation. They turned on the side street, and she glanced at Josh. His mouth was pinched, his eyes narrow. He looked like a man who had confronted his past and lost.

"Angela didn't recognize you," Emily said.

"She never saw me in the first place." Josh's hands were tight on the wheel. He said nothing more.

Emily didn't want silence. She needed to know what had happened in that house.

"What did Kahn say?" she asked.

"Nothing," Josh said.

"That's a lot of talking for nothing," she said.

He glanced at her, and as he did, his face softened. "He told me how it felt, thinking I was dead. He told me how much I hurt him."

An ache grew in her heart. She had never thought of that, of the way the others had felt when Davy disappeared. Luther had bit back his anger, had dealt with it, he once told her, in the privacy of his home after she had left. But she remembered the look on his face when he saw the musical scores: the stark, stunned, pain-filled look, so full of shock, as if he had seen a ghost.

"I'm sorry," she said.

Josh shook his head. "I deserved it. I deserve more, really. I made a mess of it, Em. Maybe I am being selfish, trying to come back."

"Or maybe," she said softly, "you were selfish going away."

He turned on another street, and they were facing the ocean—a different Pacific than the one she had lived near these last few months. This one was blue and friendly and calm, like the face a beautiful woman wore only in public.

She put a hand on his knee. It was now or never. "Josh, I don't want you to take this wrong, but I was doing a lot of thinking in that house."

"You and me both," he said.

She glanced at him. He was staring determinedly at the road, his jaw set. When she said nothing after his comment, he smiled without warmth. "You first."

She nodded. It was better for her to go first. That let him off the hook.

"I love you, Josh," she said, and she felt a jolt go through his entire body. She suddenly knew how it looked. She had been in the house, she had seen the wealth, she had real confirmation that he was Davy Moss, and then she said she loved him.

"You needed to know that first," she said. "Because after seeing Kahn, after seeing the house, I realized something."

"What?" Josh's voice had the strangled quality again, as if he couldn't quite keep the emotion from it.

"I used to study Kahn's deals. I used to admire him so. And he's the same man, just as difficult, just as harsh."

"You got the better of him in there," Josh said.

"Once." She kept her hand on Josh's knee, but with the other hand, she gripped the side of the car seat. "But I read about him too. I read that if someone got the better of him, he figured out how they did it, made a note, and then memorized it. That way no one could take advantage of him in the same way again."

"I know," Josh said, and in the blandness of the comment was a lot of history, a huge, untold story.

"I admire that. He's the shark, Josh, not me. I'm just learning. He knows it. He has the connections. He kept Davy Moss alive and kept the estate growing and making money. He is still the manager to beat. He is one of the most powerful men in the music industry. And he could handle you."

"He already handled me," Josh said.

"He should again," Emily said.

Josh's leg tensed beneath her hand. "Don't you want to work with me anymore, Em?"

"What I want doesn't matter," she said. "Except that I want what's best for you. And I'm not. Kahn is. He can rebuild you. He can take you to places I can't even imagine."

Josh turned on another street, one they hadn't been on before. It was a real street, but it would be called an access road in most towns. It went past shops and restaurants and a small, discreet, hotel. Josh pulled into a parking lot, put the car in park, and left the air on.

Then he turned to her, and that strange, expressionless look he got when he was the most startled, the most hurt, had returned. "Em, I want to work with you."

She shook her head. "I was lying to you. I was lying to both of us. I hadn't realized it until we reached that house. I guess I didn't really know, deep in my heart, what it meant to have you be Davy Moss."

She cleared her throat and leaned her head back. This was the most difficult thing she had ever said in her life.

"I'm not capable of managing a superstar, Josh. And that's what you'll be. The day the news breaks, whether it's tonight or five years from now, you'll be a superstar, and I'll be out of my depth."

"And you're afraid you can't handle it," he said.

She nodded. Then she crossed her arms, hugging herself. "I'm not afraid for me. I'm afraid for you. I may have already made some mistakes,

Josh. You were right. Kahn was right. You can't sign contracts for such a small amount of money, no matter what the royalty rate. You are Davy Moss. You're worth more. Kahn knows that. He can manipulate it. He can put his force behind it, and the force of the Davy Moss empire. I can't."

She looked miserably out the window. A couple pulled up beside them, glanced at the car, and then glanced away.

"You don't have to manage a superstar," Josh said softly.

"Yes, I do." She leaned her head against the glass. It was warm from the day's heat. "At some point, Kahn will reveal your identity or someone else will figure it out, and then you'll be Davy Moss again. I won't be able to handle it."

"You thought you could create a star."

"A star, Josh," she said. "I've done that before. But a superstar? A celebrity who had fame simply because of who he is and not because of what he does, well, that's something different. That's something that requires business skills I have yet to learn, negotiation tactics I've never even heard of, and a constitution of iron. I might be able to gain these things with time, but the day you're discovered, the day the world realizes you're Davy Moss, you'll remain Davy Moss. I won't have the time. You'll go from zero to sixty in five seconds flat. And you'll leave me in the dust. Or wish you had."

The air from the vents made her cold. Her forehead was warm. And the silk blouse stuck to her back. She was uncomfortable and tense, and Josh wasn't saying anything.

He wasn't saying anything at all.

She couldn't bear to look at him. He would think she was abandoning him. And maybe she was. Maybe she had looked at the future and panicked.

"Emily," Josh's voice was soft, musical—the voice she had fallen in love with. "Can you listen to me for a moment? Just listen?"

It was the same request Kahn had made of Josh, the request that had sent her from the room unwillingly. It had a personal ring, a feeling of import to it, as if she would not leave this conversation the same as when she entered it.

"Yeah." She did not turn and face him. She couldn't move. "Go ahead."

He sighed softly. She could feel the brush of his hand on her sleeve, and then, just as quickly, the touch went away. "Em, when you met me, I was running."

She knew that. He'd told her that before.

"I hadn't stopped. I was running away from Kahn, from my parents, from everyone. I had achieved a success at twenty-two that most people never achieved, and I ran from it. I hated it. You were worried, when we started, that I'd hate it again."

She sat up, turned toward him. He was leaning against the seat, his hands on the wheel as if he were still driving. Stopped, the car felt small.

"You were right," he said. "I would have hated it, if it happened in the same way as it did before. You see, I remembered something today."

And now he faced her. The expressionless face was gone, replaced by Josh, the Josh she had met in January, the man full of doubts and fears and beliefs. The man who knew who he was, and wasn't sure he wanted to change that.

"I remembered why I left."

She frowned. "Why?"

He glanced at the hill. His house wasn't visible up there, but it remained, a presence, looming above them.

"I had everything up there. I had money. I had my own studio. I had people who believed in me. I had fans. I had everything, and I'd lost the one thing that made it worthwhile. I'd lost my music. If—" and then he smiled "—if I ever had it. I'm not sure I ever had it."

"What do you mean?" she blurted.

He took her hand, traced the red polish on her fingernails with his thumb. "I wrote music for me. I always had. I never showed it to anyone until my first band, and we played it. Then Kahn came, and he told me which songs to play and which ones to throw out. But I kept writing what I wanted. Because the composing was for me. The performing never was. I was on stage from the age of four, Em, and I was there because I was really talented, my parents' little Mozart, kind of like a trained monkey. So when I finished my music, I did the only thing I knew. I performed it."

He stopped moving his thumb, then cupped her hand, and covered it with his other one. She didn't move. Somehow, having his hands around hers like that made her feel protected.

"I wasn't ready for the success because I hadn't really figured out what I wanted. And when I did, I rebelled. I pissed on Kahn, on my fans, on Luther, on everyone. And then I left. I left it all behind. No music, no nothing."

"But your instruments—"

"I acquired them one at a time. I started writing again somewhere in Montana, when I saw the most spectacular sunset of my life. Then I got a guitar. And then I acquired more and more until I had my own little band in the comfort of my own place. And I kept thinking I didn't need to perform. I didn't need music anymore."

He took his hand off hers and traced the line of her jaw. His touch was gentle, his calluses rough and familiar against her skin. "Then I met you. I wanted to share it all with you, Em. All of me. And that meant my music. The composing—and the performing. It had nothing to do with audience or Kahn or my parents. It had to do with me. And with you."

"You're just replacing those other people with me," she whispered.

He shook his head. "I thought of that. But no. I'm not. If fifteen years alone can't teach you who you are, nothing can. I'm a man who makes music. My music. And if I'm successful at it, fine. I'll be successful at it on my terms, and no one else's."

"But Kahn," she said, "and Davy Moss. You can't escape them."

"No," he said. "I can't. They're part of my past. But I don't want Kahn in my music. There's too much history. And I don't want Davy Moss either. He was too early, a success I wasn't prepared for. Imagine how betrayed all those fans will feel when they learn I'm still alive. They'll be fascinated, yes, but underneath, they'll be as angry as Kahn was. As Kahn *is*."

He was right. She hadn't thought about that She'd thought about most of it, but not that.

"I don't need a recording contract, Em," he said. "I'm a musician with or without one. I don't need national success. I don't need international success. I can play high school dances and be happy."

"But you're better than that," she said.

"Yes, I am." Then he smiled. "You know, it's funny. Most artists start out climbing a ladder. They go from playing in their basement to playing for their buddies to playing at school. I didn't. I had violin lessons before I could walk. I played recitals before I could read. I played with the St. Paul Chamber Orchestra when I was ten. When Kahn asked why I wanted to climb a ladder I already climbed, it bothered me, and I didn't know why until I came here today."

He tucked a loose strand of hair behind her ear.

"I never climbed a ladder, Em. I got a platform and I was a dancing bear. And I danced until I couldn't anymore. When I dropped, I dropped all the way. The ladder's necessary, Em, and I want to climb it. With you."

She swallowed. His touch was wonderful, but it was distracting. "What about Kahn?"

"I treated him badly, Em. I treated so many people badly. If you don't want to stay with me because of that, I'll understand—"

"No," she said. "What about the fact that he knows? What if he exposes you as Davy Moss?"

"We do what you said in the first place," Josh said. "We make the contracts. We do the gigs. We climb that ladder. And if Kahn wants to reveal my secret identity, fine. If he does it now, I'll do interviews. I'll be a fifty-second sensation, and then I'll sell my songs. I'll compose, I won't perform. If he waits, then let's hope that Josh Candless is established enough that we can ignore the rumor, wait for proof, laugh it off if we have to."

"That's still leaving the control in someone else's hands," Emily said. "Kahn can make you or break you."

"No," Josh said. "He can't."

He sounded so sure. He hadn't sounded that certain since Kahn reappeared in his life.

"But you gave him the choice. He can decide when to reveal the information and you'll react," she said.

Josh shook his head. "I've already acted, Em. It was subtle, and I didn't realize it until today. I have chosen to return to music for good or ill. I have chosen the career myself. Before, it was chosen for me. But no one can predict the trajectory of a career, of a life. No one. It's a risk that everyone takes. Mine is just a bit more dramatic, that's all, and more obvious."

She frowned at him, uncertain.

"Kahn doesn't control me. No one does. He can throw me a curve, but you showed me today that I can throw one right back at him. Or I can chose to go a different direction." He grinned. "For the first time in my life, the road is clear. My choices are *mine*. They're not reactions, they're not induced by circumstances, and they're not created because I'm hiding. I can stand out in the light because I choose to."

He ran his fingers lightly on her cheek. "You gave me that, Em. With your belief in me."

"You were just ready for it," she said. "Or you wouldn't have been performing in that bar."

"I had performed in bars before as Josh Candless, and I never made that choice." He smiled. "The difference, this time, was you."

She had nothing to say to that. There was nothing she could say.

Josh's smile faded. He put his roving hand on her shoulder. "I have one more question. Did you mean what you said earlier?"

"Which thing?" she asked, even though she had meant it all.

"The thing you said first, in the car here." His face had flushed, and it wasn't heat. The car was an iceberg. "About love?"

"I meant it all, Josh," she said. "I'll get out of the way if I have to. But I'd do it for you. Because I love you. I want the best for you."

He brought his head down, and rested it against hers. It was almost as if, by touching her, he could absorb her thoughts. Then he sat up.

"Em," he said. "I don't know where I'm going. I might be a construction worker for the rest of my life. I might be Davy Moss tomorrow. I may live in obscurity in Oceanlake or I may have to hide here in Malibu. And I want to ask you, right now, with everything unknown—ah, hell, Em."

He took her face in his hands. His eyes were as blue as they had been on stage in that first performance in Eugene. It was as if his whole soul were open to her.

"I love you, Em. I have since that first night. I told you once, and I didn't say anything again because of me and my past, and then because of yours, and then because I didn't know where everything was going. And I still don't know, but I will soon. This moment won't come again, Em, this moment when we're just us. And I don't want to lose the chance. Because this is the moment, Em, when we can best make a decision."

She was motionless in his hands. It felt as if time had stopped. She wasn't quite sure where he was going with this, but she was willing to wait until he expressed it.

"Marry me, Em," he said.

Whatever she had expected, it wasn't this. She had expected him to leave her, to go back with Kahn, to declare himself Davy Moss and to deal with the world.

She hadn't expected a proposal.

Marriage. It was a negotiation. A contract. She knew that much. She had learned business so well that she understood negotiation. Since she was a little girl, she had planned to treat this moment with the serious-ness it deserved, to hash out details before she entered into a lifelong compact. She opened her mouth, and instead of the calm, rational response she had prepared years before there was even a man in her life, instead of saying that, she said, "Of course I'll marry you, Josh."

And then she kissed him.

Part Six

...**Joshua Candless**, lead singer of **The Josh Candless Band** whose first album, *Songs on the Run*, is nominated for six Grammy awards, married his manager **Emily Lukovich** on February 14. Entertainment lawyer **LaTisha Morgan** was maid of honor, and band member **Luther Tigoro** was best man. The private ceremony was held near the couple's new home on the Oregon Coast....

—*People Magazine*

thirty-eight

The house overlooked the ocean. Josh liked that part best. Every morning when he got up, he walked to the beach, using it as a route to the post office. That was his excuse to go out every day, to see the world as he used to see it, before he regained a small measure of fame.

To be fair, the people in Oceanlake, his old friends and his acquaintances, protected his privacy. They never told anyone where Josh Candless lived, and after they got used to his musical talent, they treated him the way they always had. It was the tourists he had an occasional problem with, and it wasn't a problem he worried about.

Not like he would have if the world knew he was Davy Moss.

Josh Candless had his own small measure of fame, but it was nothing compared with Davy Moss's.

So far, no one in the music industry had mentioned on similarities between Davy Moss and Josh Candless. There were several websites dedicated to proving both men were one and the same, and two tabloids had published speculative articles. But they had nothing more than supposition: Davy's missing body; Josh's looks, age, and guitar style; and Luther's presence in the band. No one had given interviews, and no one had proof.

It was, all in all, less than he had expected.

When he got back from the post office, he would bring the mail in, set it on the kitchen table, and fetch Emily from her office. She got up at five so that she could be on the phone by six. She kept East Coast hours on the West Coast, and she usually spent the three hours before he brought in the mail negotiating, talking, planning. They had breakfast together because he insisted—he insisted on all their meals or Emily would simply forget to eat.

They would have breakfast, then Josh would go to his makeshift studio in the back of the house for a few hours alone, to compose, before the band arrived.

This morning, he brought the mail in, set it on the table, and called Emily. Then he stopped.

He never looked at the mail when he picked it up. Reading it was, along with the morning paper, a breakfast ritual. But this morning, he couldn't wait for Em.

The envelope on top was cream. The return address, embossed in gold, read *Davy Moss Enterprises*. The letter was marked *private* and sealed with wax.

The handwriting looked familiar.

The letter was from Kahn.

Josh swallowed, wondering if he would ever get over the case of nerves that Kahn gave him.

Emily came in. She was wearing a tight pair of jeans and a Josh Candless Band T-shirt that showed her figure to great advantage. When she saw him, she stopped.

"What is it?" she asked.

He handed the envelope to her and she turned it over in her hands. Then she looked at him.

"Wax?" she asked. "Kahn must like dramatic gestures."

"Wax is great and old-fashioned. It is impossible to reseal without marring the stamp." His finger traced the pattern. It came from a signet ring Davy had owned. "He knew I'd recognize it."

Emily's grin was reluctant. "He's always smarter than I give him credit for. He wanted to send the letter without attracting attention like a Federal Express package might do, and yet he had to guarantee that no one else saw it."

Josh nodded. Then he thrust the envelope at her. "You open it."

"No, Davy," she said softly, using a name she almost never spoke. "It's your past."

He took the letter back from her. His empty stomach had suddenly gone queasy. It was notification from Kahn that he was going to reveal Josh's past.

It had to be.

He slid a finger underneath the wax, breaking the seal. Then he opened the envelope. His own wedding photo fell out, the one that had gone to the press. This copy was grainy black-and-white, obviously from a newspaper. Emily caught it and frowned at it.

He pulled out the card. It was also embossed in gold, with *Davy Moss Enterprises* stamped lightly in the corner.

Kahn's handwriting filled the interior.

In the twenty-two years I have known you, it read, *I have never seen you smile with such joy. All men should have such an opportunity to achieve their dreams.*

I cannot give Josh Candless a material wedding gift without raising questions, but I can do this: I can make sure you keep your music.

If anyone—a reporter, a gossip columnist, a fan—asks whether I believe there is a connection between Josh Candless and Davy Moss, I will say no. As far as I'm concerned, Davy Moss died in a car accident sixteen years ago.

I wish only the best for you and Emily.
—Jeremiah Kahn

Josh sank into a chair. As he did, he handed Emily the note. His hands were shaking.

"So it's official," Emily said. "Davy Moss is dead."

There was relief in her voice. Josh felt it, too, and a bit of regret. He wouldn't miss Davy Moss. But he would miss the danger of it. The living on the edge.

As if his new career didn't provide enough excitement. Kahn was right. Josh was happy here. Happier than he'd ever been.

"Did you expect this?" Emily asked.

"No," Josh said. "But maybe I should have. I underestimated him all the way along."

She ran a hand through his hair. "We know the future's path, then."

Josh smiled. "Maybe. There will always be rumors."

"But they remain rumors without confirmation."

"Yeah," Josh said, then he captured her hand and kissed it. "Now that you know the path, are you willing to stay?"

"Always," she said. Then she clutched the letter to her heart. "Are you?"

"My running days are over," he said. "I'm facing whatever comes."

She smiled and wrapped her arms around him. "With me beside you."

He leaned his head against hers. "I wouldn't have it any other way."

about the author

Bestselling science fiction, fantasy, and mystery writer Kristine Kathryn Rusch also writes romance under three pen names—Kristine Grayson, Kristine Dexter and Kris DeLake. Her mysteries (written as Kris Nelscott) have been nominated for the Edgar Award, the Shamus Award, and the Oregon Book Award. Her short fiction has appeared in many prestigious markets, including *The North American Review* and the Best American series as well as 18 other year's best volumes. Her novels have been published in 14 countries. For more information about her writing, go to www.kristinekathrynrusch.com.